The Fatal Entanglement and Other Stories

Espionage Missions

VASANT K. SARAF

Rupa & Co

Published 2003 by

Rupa & Co

7/16, Ansari Road, Daryaganj,
New Delhi 110 002

Sales Centres:

Allahabad Bangalore Chandigarh Chennai
Dehradun Hyderabad Jaipur Kathmandu
Kolkata Ludhiana Mumbai Pune

ISBN 81-291-0126-2

Typeset in 11 pts Aldine by
Nikita Overseas Pvt Ltd.
1410 Chiranjiv Tower,
43 Nehru Place
New Delhi 110 019

Printed in India by
Gopsons Papers Ltd.
A-14 Sector 60
Noida 201 301

Dedicated to my granddaughters Samyukta and
Akanksha who made me a storyteller

Contents

Contents

Colonel's Canine Pet

"I SUGGEST YOU IMMEDIATELY PROCEED TO RAMPUR, and take your inseparable assistant, I mean Khot, with you." Joint Director Bankar who headed the Mumbai outfit of the Intelligence Bureau, advised Mundkur. Gurudas Mundkur was in charge of the Counter Intelligence Unit in the Mumbai office of the Bureau. He was a man of proven track record. He had many a trophy by way of catching foreign spies in Mumbai and elsewhere to his credit and was highly rated by his superiors. Before coming over to the Intelligence Bureau he had served with distinction for several years in the Crime Branch of the Mumbai police where he had acquired a deep knowledge of the Mumbai underworld. This became a great asset when Pakistan's infamous Inter-Services Intelligence outfit linked up with Daud Ibrahim gang and took the gang leaders under its wings that enabled it to use the latter's operational capabilities in Mumbai, in fact the whole country, for its own purpose. Mundkur's services were, therefore, often requisitioned whenever a spy ring with possible underworld connections came to light anywhere in the country.

That morning Bankar had received a fax message from the Bureau's Delhi headquarters asking him to dispatch Mundkur to associate himself with the collateral enquiries that IB officials in Uttar Pradesh, Saxena and Pandey, were making in the killing of Lt.Col. Pravin Kumar. The Colonel was killed, in fact blasted a couple of days ago with the help of explosives right in front of his bungalow. The Intelligence Bureau perked up its ears because of the peculiar manner in which the execution was carried out. It was not only horrendous but also ingenious. No one was sure how exactly it was carried out. What made it more intriguing was the discovery by the Uttar Pradesh CID that had taken up the investigation immediately because of the anxiety it had caused in the army headquarters and the publicity it was receiving in the media, that no social feud or family discord appeared to be behind the gruesome killing.

The circumstance that now prompted the IB to step in squarely was the report of the Forensic Science Laboratory scientists that RDX was the explosive used to blow up the Colonel. Obviously it was not the job of mere criminals, not even professional criminals commonly encountered in Uttar Pradesh. There had to be a highly sophisticated hand and a wily brain behind it. Hence the call for Mundkur's services.

Within twenty-four hours Mundkur accompanied by his equally versatile assistant Ramakant Khot arrived where the hub of the frenzied investigative activities lay. He thoroughly examined the scene of the macabre crime and held consultations with his IB colleagues as well as the CID officers who were in charge of the investigation. So far they had discovered no worthwhile clue. The crime had taken place in the front garden of the Colonel's bungalow. There were in fact four casualties. The Colonel and his dog were completely shattered with pieces of their bones and flesh flung all over the garden. The gardener who was perhaps tending to the plants was seriously wounded in the head and shoulders. Mangeram the dutiful batman of the Colonel was the other person who suffered serious shrapnel injuries all over the front part of his body. The gardener died the next day without gaining consciousness and, therefore, could offer no clue. Batman Mangeram had gained consciousness but was in a state of intense shock and, therefore, the doctors attending upon him at the army hospital where he was receiving treatment, had not till then permitted the police to question him. The police were unsuccessful in locating any other eyewitness, therefore, till then their investigation was a wild goose chase.

Mundkur decided to make a bid and persuade the doctors. He was clear in his mind that batman Mangeram was the one who would give them the much required breakthrough for, not only that he was present on the spot when the blast occurred but by all other accounts, he was also in charge of the Colonel's dog. Somehow Mundkur thought that the dog's was not an incidental casualty. It had to have a more intimate connection with the incident. He, therefore, immediately proceeded to the army hospital and met the chief surgeon. He was able to convince the surgeon with his persuasive language stressing that he had come all the way from Mumbai to look into the case, and that asking at least a few questions to Mangeram was of vital importance for giving direction to the otherwise stalled investigation. The chief surgeon permitted him to put a few questions to Mangeram without in any way agitating him. Mundkur offered to keep one of the army doctors present so that he would stop the moment the doctor thought that the patient was getting stressed or excited.

When Mundkur reached Mangeram's bed in the General Ward he found him bandaged all over the body. He was restlessly tossing his head and muttering faintly to himself. Mundkur introduced himself gently and engaged Mangeram in seemingly casual conversation.

"Did you like the Colonel's dog very much, Mangeram?" Mundkur asked.

"Yes very much. The dog was also fond of me. His name was Zulfie. Every evening we went out together. You won't believe *Sahib*, he used to get impatient and bark at me if I delayed taking him out any day."

"That day also you took out Zulfie?" Mundkur continued his questions.

"Yes, indeed."

"Do you recollect where all you went during the course of your stroll?" Mundkur persisted. Mangeram paused for a brief while and said faintly, "Nowhere in particular except that I went to the panshop of Ramlakhan Yadao that is round the corner. I occasionally purchase *gutkha* from him."

"I am sure, you returned to the bungalow thereafter," Mundkur asked suggestively.

"Yes, I did." Mangeram admitted.

"What happened when you two reached the bungalow, Mangeram?"

"Colonel *Sahib* was out in the garden talking to the *Mali*. As soon as I opened the gate, Zulfie saw Colonel *Sahib*. He jerked himself free from my hold and rushed to him. Colonel *Sahib* loved Zulfie like his son."

"I imagine so. What happened next?"

"As I closed the gate and turned, I saw Zulfie jumping up at Colonel *Sahib* and Colonel *Sahib* also stepping forward to hug him."

"Yes, go on Mangeram, I am listening," nudged Mundkur, as Mangeram paused. His face contorted with grief as he recollected the gruesome event. After an obviously tormenting break he began faintly, "As they came together there was a deafening sound and a flash as if a lightening had struck them. I don't know what happened next. When I regained consciousness I was here lying on this bed." He was now crying, looking pityingly at Mundkur. "I don't know how it happened, I really don't know," he added between sobs.

This was lead enough for Mundkur. He patted Mangeram lightly on the shoulder and thanking the doctor profusely for the consideration shown, left the hospital.

His next target was Ramlakhan Yadao, the *pan* shop owner. After initial reticence and evasive replies, Yadao confirmed that it was Mangeram's daily routine to visit his shop in the evening. He invariably brought along the Colonel's dog. In fact it was his duty to walk the dog in the evening, and he came to Yadao's shop to obtain his daily fill of *gutkha*. Talking of that fateful evening's happenings, he said, "Mangeram was accompanied by a guest of his. After they had *gutkha* and *pan* at my shop, Mangeram left with the guest leaving the dog in the care of his friend Rambux, who was also a frequent visitor to my shop. He came back after some time and took away the dog."

"Who is this Rambux? You say, he visits your shop frequently. How much do you know about him? Is he very friendly with Mangeram?" It was an interesting disclosure, Mundkur interjected.

"*Sahib*, this Rambux started visiting my shop only a few months ago. He became very friendly with Mangeram after they met at my shop. Mangeram is fond of telling tales of his war exploits. Earlier he used to inflict them on me going over the same stories again and again. I used to get bored. Besides I had customers to attend to. Rambux was a willing listener, therefore, Mangeram would single him out to tell his narratives. One more thing, *Sahib*. The dog also became very fond of Rambux because he used to unfailingly bring biscuits for him."

"I see, that's interesting," Mundkur remarked. "Do you know where Rambux lives?"

"No, I have no idea, but I recall his having told me once that he worked in a factory down the road," Yadao replied.

"Do you think he will come to your shop this evening?"

"I am not sure. He has not come to my shop since the day of the blast."

"Are you sure of that?" Mundkur asked, thinking that the coincidence might not be incidental.

"Quite sure, *Sahib*. Whenever he comes he asks for a special type of *pan* which I have to prepare for him. How can I miss noticing him?" Yadao reasoned.

A quick check with Mangeram's wife revealed that her brother had indeed come on a visit to them from Uttarkashi and had left that afternoon in the company of her husband.

Mundkur decided to focus his enquiries on Rambux. His professional sense told him that all was not well with this elusive character. Ramlakhan Yadao obviously held the key as, he had observed him from near. He asked Yadao to close the shop for the day and accompany him for a chat. For good measure he promised Yadao to amply make good the loss of revenue that the latter might thus suffer. That put Yadao in a good mood. He quickly closed his *pan*shop and got ready to accompany Mundkur.

Taking Yadao to the government rest house where the officers were lodged Mundkur ordered a cup of tea for him. While they were having tea Mundkur collected information about Yadao's background just to gauge for himself as to how much he could be trusted, and to rule out the possibility of his involvement. When the *Khansama* removed the empty tea cups Mundkur got down to a serious session of questioning. He took Yadao back to the day Rambux first visited his *pan*shop and then systematically brought him forward till the day of the tragedy. Yadao's disclosures undoubtedly established that Rambux had ingratiated himself with Mangeram as well as the Colonel's dog. Yadao insisted that while giving biscuits to the dog had become a routine every time they met, he had once or twice seen Rambux handing out small presents to Mangeram as well. It was evident to Mundkur that that was not merely out of fondness for them but part of a design.

Mundkur was convinced in his mind that he had got the right lead and decided to pursue it further. He obtained a detailed description of Rambux from Yadao and also learned from him that Rambux did not speak the local lingo. "His accent is different," Yadao insisted. "Lot of Urdu words he uses in his speech. One thing more, *Sahib*, he uses certain words that were not intelligible to me. Those are not Urdu words, I am sure of that. Sometimes we hear them in Hindi films."

"I see. Any other thing you noticed about him that you thought was peculiar?" Mundkur egged him on.

"He also blinks involuntarily especially while talking," Yadao answered after pondering a while, and for good measure mimicked the action.

Mundkur sent for the CID portrait artist and made him draw Rambux's portrait with Yadao's help. While this exercise was going on he obtained names of other regular customers of Yadao's and sent for them. There was a fair chance that they also knew Rambux by face if nothing else. They were asked to have a good look at the pen-sketch of Rambux that the CID artist drew up after about an hour's labour, and make inputs. Finally a sketch was drawn that met with everyone's approval.

Armed with the portrait Mundkur sent Khot and the local police officers to the industrial establishments down the road, but they drew a blank. None recognised the name or the portrait. Obviously Rambux had bluffed to Yadao. This was a great impediment but Mundkur was not the one to be easily discouraged. He again questioned all the persons who claimed they had occasions to talk to Rambux, in the hope of obtaining a hint if nothing else from the conversations they had had with him. Mundkur firmly believed that perseverance pays, and it did pay him in this case too. Ramdulare Sharma, who lived in a neighbouring locality and was a frequent visitor to Yadao's panshop, had on many an occasion exchanged pleasantries with Rambux. During the course of renewed questioning he disclosed a very interesting incident. About a month ago, one afternoon Rambux had boarded the same city-bus in which he was travelling, when the bus stopped at the Moulaganj bus stop. Both subsequently alighted at the bus stop that was close to Yadao's *pan*shop. During the bus ride Sharma asked Rambux out of curiosity if he lived in Moulaganj, which was a predominantly Muslim locality. Rambux, strangely, became so evasive that he did not speak to him during the rest of the journey.

Mundkur decided to scan Moulaganj till he came across someone who knew Rambux. He drafted a CID officer as well as the local Thanedar to assist him. Of course his alter ego assistant, Ramakant Khot, was also with him. Armed with Rambux's sketch, and knowledge about his peculiarities of speech and appearance, Mundkur and his team started with the bus stop where Ramdulare Sharma had told them the suspect had boarded his bus. After an hour's painstaking enquiries they came across a petty grocer who hesitatingly acknowledged having often seen a man answering to that description. "He comes to my shop occasionally to purchase odd bits like tea and sugar," the shopkeeper told Mundkur. "I am not very sure but I have a feeling he lives nearby, perhaps in the block across the street or thereabouts, because he often emerges from the by-lane."

It did not take Mundkur and his companions much time thereafter to locate the room where Rambux lived. An old man from the building told them that Allahbux—that was the name by which he was known in the neighbourhood—had hired the room some three months ago and lived there with his wife. He was a salesman for a Mumbai-based manufacturing company of machinery parts. Last week he suddenly left with his wife for Mumbai. "I was standing outside the building. It was dinnertime. I saw Allahbux locking the room and leaving with his wife and baggage. He seemed to be in a hurry," the old man narrated. "I asked him as to where he was going at that odd hour and in such haste. He wasn't in a mood to talk. Briefly said, my mother is very ill at Mumbai. When I asked him further, when would you come back? He said, he wasn't sure how long he would be required to stay. He then quickly dashed away with his wife in tow."

Mundkur could not have asked for more. It was a tremendous achievement given the fact that he had landed there less than twenty-four hours earlier. He was now very sure that Rambux alias Allahbux had a hand in the assassination of the Colonel and that he was a plant, meaning thereby that the schemers were a different set of people. His companions agreed with him. Moreover, all the pointers suggested Allahbux's connection with Mumbai, his home turf.

The landlord of the building, who was then summoned, was frank and forthright in answering Mundkur's pointed questions. "I don't know much about Allahbux. He was introduced to me by Imtiaz, the owner of Bismillah Cyber Café that is situated some distance away in the same locality," he said unhesitatingly. "I had no complaints about Allahbux, essentially because he paid rent punctually every month in advance. I have no idea about his whereabouts because he did not inform me before going away."

"Allahbux seems to have locked the room while leaving. How will you open it?" asked Mundkur.

"The lock on the door is mine. I had given a set of two keys to Allahbux when he occupied the room. A spare key is with me," he said without showing concern. Mundkur asked him to bring the key and open the room. The room was empty except for some trash lying here and there. Mundkur knew by experience the importance of discarded material one often found in the trashcans and elsewhere. Sometimes it threw up important leads, even provided valuable evidence. He, therefore, asked Khot to collect all the bits and pieces carefully for detailed examination. While he was looking for some tell-tale evidence that would point to Allahbux or his wife's identity, Khot spotted a cash voucher of a shop in central Mumbai. That was indication enough that Allahbux had visited Mumbai some months ago and reinforced his view that Allahbux had a Mumbai connection. But that was all.

Mundkur also visited Bismilla Cyber Café and questioned Imtiaz who said very much the same things. "I know very little about Allahbux and took no interest in his activities," he said. "I fixed up a room for him at the behest of a mutual friend of ours from Rampur." It was obvious to Mundkur that both Imtiaz and his professed friend from Rampur were significant cogs in the conspiracy, that had culminated in the murder of the army officer. He was sure that he would be able to fix the identity and possibly also trace Allahbux or whatever was his real name, by working at the Mumbai end. Once he was located it would not be difficult to get at the people who ordered the killing. He asked the I.B. officials, Saxena and Pandey, who were assisting him as well as the CID officers to pursue the Imtiaz lead by tracing his Rampur friend and interrogating both thoroughly for, in his opinion Imtiaz knew much more than he had so far admitted. Maybe he had also played an active role, but it was more urgent to uncover the

Rampur connection. He decided to rush to Mumbai where his sixth sense told him, Allahbux would be in all probability hiding. All criminals who operated in a wide range cooled their heels in Mumbai when things got hot for them elsewhere. Allahbux, he was sure, would do the same. He asked the officers to inform him of all the things they would unearth during the course of their enquiries, so that the two ends could be neatly tied together.

On arriving at Mumbai his immediate move was to visit the Crime Branch office of the Mumbai police—his workplace for several years. He was always happy to go there and meet his old colleagues; exchange notes and pick up the latest gossip. At the Crime Branch, he checked photo albums of criminals of all hues and varieties but none tallied with the sketch of Allahbux. This did not discourage him the least. "If Dame Luck smiled so easily we would become lazy and lose our professional acumen." He reassured Khot who was accompanying him.

He then had a confabulation with his one- time colleagues and good friends, Inspectors Sawant and Joshi. Of course, he took care to include Havaldar Tukaram Tawde, who was a moving encyclopedia on Mumbai's underworld. Now about to retire, Tawde Havaldar—as he was referred to by his colleagues—had joined the Crime Branch more than two decades ago and had known Daud Ibrahim and his siblings since the time they roamed about as street urchins in the Musafarkhana area, occasionally indulging in petty crimes. They were the neglected children of his senior in the Crime Branch, Havaldar Ibrahim Parkar. He had felt sorry for them but had never ever thought—in fact none in his officers did—

that on growing up they would become such a pain in the neck for the police, more so the Crime Branch.

Mundkur showed the trio the pen-sketch he had with him, briefly narrating the case in which he was suspected to be involved. He however, drew a blank. Even Havaldar Tawde could not place him. The inference he drew from this disappointing event was that Allahbux was positively not active for quite some time in Mumbai city, and that if he ever operated in the city it must have been for a short while. None talked of giving up. It was a challenge to their professional expertise to trace him out. They agreed with his surmise that Allahbux had a Mumbai connection, and if so then they should be able to lay their hands on him, in fact they must. Even if it meant sweeping the whole city.

True to his reputation, Tawde Havaldar got an idea while the other two were still lamenting their failure to tag the offender. "You know, Sir," he addressed Inspector Sawant under whom he worked, "We have Kanya Karim in our custody. He is Shakeel's man. Inspector Pradhan hauled him up in an extortion case. I hear that he is 'singing' a bit. If that is indeed so, he may be able to throw some light on this elusive Allahbux. Otherwise I will show the picture to my sources in other gangs."

"That will be fine," Mundkur interjected, brightened by the prospect of getting a lead.

"I will talk to Pradhan just now and fix up a meeting with Kanya Karim. We have worked together. I am sure Pradhan would not decline, though I am aware, how investigating officers are reluctant these days to let some one else handle the accused in their custody, what with the Human Rights

Commission going for their jugular vein on the slightest complaint." The other two nodded their assent.

"Pradhan has a mobile phone. I'll get him on the line," Inspector Joshi volunteered.

"That would be excellent," said Mundkur.

In a couple of minutes Mundkur was talking to Pradhan. Inspector Pradhan readily acceded to Mundkur's request. He knew that Mundkur relied more on skillful interrogation than the third degree, therefore, the possibility of the prisoner in his custody getting assaulted, something he would have to answer for, was indeed remote. It was arranged that Mundkur would meet Pradhan in his room at ten the next morning when Kanya Karim would be made available to him for questioning. Mundkur requested Sawant to let Tawde Havaldar also remain present to give him a helping hand, and took leave of his friends.

"Do you recognise this man?" Mundkur put a straight question to Kanya Karim after showing him the portrait of Allahbux. He had first taken care to put Kanya Karim at ease by asking a few innocuous questions of personal nature and then enquiring after his welfare. Kanya peered at the picture for a while and pondered.

"What's is his name?" he asked, fixing his gaze on Mundkur.

"Don't know. You tell us if you do."

"Do you have a photograph of this man? It is difficult to be certain about the identity from a drawing like this." Kanya tried to wriggle out. Mundkur was not the one to give up so soon, especially when he could discern from the expression on Kanya's face that he had made a fair guess if not definitely fixed the identity.

"No, we haven't got a photograph of his but the drawing is quite faithful. If I knew the person I would easily recognise him from this picture. Have a careful look. I am sure, you will have no difficulty in placing him." Mundkur egged him on.

"Is he my height, rather thin and dark complexioned?" Kanya asked, to seek reinforcement to the guess he had made in his mind.

"Yes, yes. You are right," Mundkur said enthusiastically. That brightened Kanya's face but he still wanted further confirmation to be sure.

"Does he flutter his eyelids when he speaks?"

"Yes very much so. Kanya you are on the mark! You have placed him correctly. Now be good and tell us, who is he?" Mundkur asked eagerly.

"He was known as Fadfadya Siddiqui. Fadfadya because he used to blink rapidly, that attracted attention." Kanya clarified triumphantly, but the next moment he became gloomy with apprehension.

"Why did you want me to identify him? Where did you get this sketch? I haven't seen him for years now, and have no connection with him." Kanya went on the defensive.

"Don't worry. We are not connecting you in any way with him. Just wanted to get his identity confirmed from you because we were sure, you knew him," Mundkur assured him, and further asked, "Where can we find him? What are his favourite haunts?"

Kanya did not reply. He was now repenting having identified Siddiqui, fearful of the consequences that might befall him if his boss, Shakeel, got wind of what he had disclosed to the police. When Mundkur coaxed him further he asked reproachfully,

"Why don't you kill me yourself rather than let them pull my guts out when I go out from here? Wasn't identifying him for you bad enough that you now ask me to tell you where to find him? You know what is the punishment for this crime in our fraternity?"

"I know, I know, but Kanya you must trust us. We take care of our friends and allies, people who help us. We are not novices in this business either. No one besides the few now present in this room shall ever come to know what you told us about Fadfadya Siddiqui. We will cover you well. Now be good and tell us where we can find him. I can guarantee you that none will ever suspect that you tipped us about it." Mundkur was at his pleading best.

Kanya pondered for a while. He was tired working for the gang, and slightly despairing too. It was getting increasingly difficult for him to cope with the demands being made by his bosses. He wanted to be away from it all, at least for a while so that he could ponder over his future. He had been in this business for over a decade now, and was lucky not to get a bullet in the head yet. He knew that he could not escape it for long if he continued to be active. He wanted to ruminate over his prospects, to work out a way to escape this unenviable fate if he could. That's why he had decided to discreetly co-operate with the police so that he could be convicted for the crime he had committed. That would give him a year or two in prison—long enough time to mull over, he thought. The police might even help him to settle down to a peaceful life. He had enough of money safely tucked away at his native place. He finally decided to co-operate with Mundkur. Somehow he felt confident about Mundkur. He was the officer he could trust to cover him up properly. He looked up and peered searchingly in Mundkur's eyes.

"Do you assure me that you would not involve me any further in this Siddiqui affair whatever may be the crime he had committed, if I tell you what little I know about him, and that you would securely cover my tacks?" he asked plaintively.

"Yes, yes. It's my word, and I keep my word even when I give it to a scoundrel. You are a thousand times better, as I can easily see." Mundkur assured him again, placing his hand on Kanya's shoulder to enhance the effect.

Kanya braced himself up and began, "Sir, I met him for the first time some five years ago in the wedding reception of Barkya Bashir's sister. He had come along with Rajpalsingh. Both belong to UP. They are perhaps from the same place, I am not sure. These UP chaps call every one from their State gaonwalla. Anyway, they seemed to be on friendly terms. It appeared to me that Siddiqui was a recent addition to our gang."

"Was that the only time you met him?" Mundkur interposed.

"No. I am coming to that. Thereafter, I met him on several occasions. Actually once we were part of the same team that was detailed to bump off a restaurateur but before we got a chance he squared it up with Shakeel, and we were asked to drop the plan."

"So, that's how you came to know him well." Mundkur wanted to gently lead him into disclosing more about Siddiqui.

"Yes, that's so. But soon thereafter he went missing. Once I asked Rajpalsingh about him. Usually if a gang member is caught or liquidated we come to know about it on the gang grapevine even if his name has not appeared in newspapers. I was, therefore, curious. Rajpalsingh was a bit evasive in the beginning but later confided that he had been sent to U.P. by the boss to take care of jobs there. I accepted it as our business activities had indeed expanded multifold in the north."

"You mean to say, you never met him or heard about him anytime thereafter?"

"That's true. In our business one can't be too inquisitive either. That's calling for trouble," Kanya replied.

"Now tell me, if Siddiqui was in Mumbai where could we find him?" Mundkur led him to the original question.

"Why? Is he in Mumbai?" Kanya was slightly jolted. There was anxiety in his voice.

"Now don't get nervous. Just make your guess. We don't need him. Some one else does," Mundkur lied. "As you know, he is not active here. So you don't have to be so fearful." he further assured him.

"No, that's not the case," Kanya also bluffed.

"Then why don't you tell us where can one find him?"

"I really have no idea. Never met him recently."

"Will he take shelter with Rajpalsingh?" Mundkur asked a leading question and fixed his gaze on Kanya to seek confirmation.

"Well, yes. That is a possibility. They are chums. Earlier also he stayed with the Thakur. That's the surest way of getting a twenty-four hour protection. But remember that all these things are done on the direction of the boss. If he is required to go in hiding that is the way it would probably be organised." Kanya elaborated inspite of himself.

"Okay, where's Rajpalsigh holed up these days?"

"Why do you ask me? Your people would know better. I never went to his den. But I know that he prefers to be in the suburbs, more particularly in Andheri," Kanya added.

Mundkur did not press him further. He knew that the Crime Branch people would already have that information, and if they didn't it would not take them long to find out. He looked meaningfully at Tawde Havaldar who faintly nodded in affirmation. Mundkur, therefore, decided to call off the interview.

"Okay. Thank you, Kanya, for the help. We will see you again if we need more information."

"Sa'ab, be mindful about me," Kanya pleaded.

"Sure, sure. That's my promise to you," Mundkur assured him again and left the room.

It did not take Tawde Havaldar long to find out where Rajpalsingh had pitched himself these days. He had arrested Ralpalsingh a year or so ago and since then knew his contacts and the joints he frequented. Though Rajpalsingh lived for a while in Andheri, of late he had shifted to Saki Naka where he had secured a room in a nondescript chawl of considerable vintage. It provided him better cover and hence protection.

"Why do not we surround the building after nightfall and lie in wait for Rajpalsingh to arrive?" suggested Mundkur to Inspector Sawant, who had been on his request, designated by the Crime Branch Chief to assist him in this case. Tawde Havaldar had found out by making discreet enquiries in the neighbourhood that Rajpalsingh was away most of the time during the day and returned only at night often in the wee hours of the morning.

"Yes, that's the only way of getting him but he is a desperado and a very violent person. In all probability he would be carrying a weapon on his person," replied Inspector Sawant.

"We will have to fortify ourselves well in that case," remarked Mundkur.

"Yes of course. Only our having arms won't suffice. I will requisition the assistance of sharp shooters from the Special Operations Squad. It's their job to provide armed assistance to policemen investigating organised crime," said Inspector Sawant, and got busy putting together the raiding party. Thus a motley team comprising Mundkur, Khot, Inspector Sawant, Tawde Havaldar and his assistant, who also knew Rajpalsingh well and hence would be useful in spotting him, and three SOS gunmen, was formed to lay siege and accost Rajpalsingh. A vehicle-borne armed party headed by Police Sub-Inspector Bagul was to be on call at a discreet distance. Its assignment was to rush to assist the team or to give chase if the need arose.

Around ten o'clock when inmates of the rooms in the vicinity shut their doors the team members took positions. Earlier, Tawde Havaldar had guardedly ascertained that Rajpalsingh's room was indeed locked from outside and there was none within. The police party waited and waited patiently but Rajpalsingh did not turn up. One by one lights from the neighbouring rooms and buildings went out. Finally, there was hardly any light left except the distant street lamps and a dim bulb pathetically hanging from the roof above the staircase. The rats and bandicoots came out in strength, to promulgate their reign over the territory. They scurried about, making it difficult for the policemen to keep their positions without making sound.

It was past 2 o'clock when a taxi stopped at a distance from Rajpalsingh's chawl. Every one got on the alert and watched with bated breath wondering if their quarry had indeed arrived. Two persons emerged from the taxi and proceeded towards the staircase in a leisurely manner. From their gait, it was obvious that they were heavily drunk but in spite of their inebriation they were quiet. As they approached the stairway they moved under the only light that was hanging from the roof. Tawde Havaldar was quick to spot Rajpalsingh as the one in the lead and signalled to Inspector Sawant who was close by. Sawant raised his hand, the pre-arranged signal for the remainder to come forward and surround the target. In a flash everyone sprang into positions that left no room for the duo to flee. Inspector Sawant called in a loud and clear voice,

"Rajpalsingh, raise your hands and stand where you are. This is the police."

Rajpalsingh and his companion froze in their tracks. As the police party started closing in on them, Rajpalsingh suddenly turned and fired. He missed hitting anyone but that was provocation enough for the SOS sharp shooters to get into action. Two of them fired at Rajpalsingh while the third remained in the ready. There was no need for him to fire for, Rajpalsingh collapsed. The bullets fired by the two marksmen had obviously found their mark. Inspector Sawant rushed forward and picked up the revolver that had slipped from Rajpalsingh's hand.

While everyone's attention was momentarily rivetted on the sprawling body of Rajpalsingh who apparently was mortally wounded, his associate vanished. Mundkur was the first to notice his absence.

"Where's the other fellow?" he shouted. It was Tawde Havaldar, the veteran of many encounters who responded, "He ran towards the staircase; must be hiding underneath. There's no way out. I was watching him. He cannot escape but we will have to be careful. He may also have a weapon."

Everyone now aimed his weapon at the staircase. Again Inspector Sawant commanded, "Come out with your hands up otherwise we will all shoot and make mincemeat of you there itself." As if to make his point he fired a round from his revolver aiming at a high point on the staircase.

"Stop, stop. I am coming out. I have no weapon," came an anguished cry. A moment later a young man emerged from behind the staircase, his hands raised high. Tawde Havaldar caught him by the hair from behind and his assistant locked handcuffs on his wrists. When he was brought under the light Mundkur and Sawant stared at him as if in disbelief, and then knowingly grinned at each other.

They had no doubt in their minds that he was indeed Fadfadya Siddiqui, their most wanted man. They had least expected to find him so readily. What they were looking for was a reliable clue about his whereabouts from Rajpalsingh. This was a bonanza.

While Inspector Sawant and others stayed behind to take Rajpalsingh who was profusely bleeding to the hospital and complete the legal formalities, Mundkur, accompanied by Khot and Tawde Havaldar, whisked away Siddiqui to the interrogation room in the Crime Branch office. Mundkur believed in striking when the iron was hot. He wanted to interrogate Siddiqui immediately when he was psychologically disturbed and had had no time to think of a strategy.

"So, how are you Mr. Siddiqui alias Allahbux alias Rambux? And where is your young wife? Have you already given her *talaq* now that the purpose was served?" Mundkur fired his first salvo straight from the shoulder that he knew would incapacitate him.

Siddiqui was completely unnerved. The message was loud and clear. Till then he had been under the impression that the police had come solely for Rajpalsingh. He had intended to bluff his way through by posing as an old friend of Rajpalsingh's, who had come to Mumbai in search of a job.

It was impossible for Siddiqui to withstand for long Mundkur's intensive grilling, especially when it was clear to him that the later knew about his involvement in the Colonel's murder and had searched his room and questioned many of his acquaintances. As a measure of tactics, Khot occasionally sympathised with him, while Tawde Havaldar as a true policeman became aggressive and threatening every now and then. Within a short period Siddiqui literally broke down. The emotional strain of first seeing his friend and patron gunned down before his eyes immediately followed by an interrogation where the die was heavily loaded against him, was too much for even a hardened gangster like him.

Mundkur offered him a glass of water and also some tea. When Siddiqui regained composure, he quietly asked him to come clean and not beat about the bush that would only make things worse for him. Siddiqui nodded in acknowledgement and began his narration. As soon as Mundkur got an outline of the whole story especially the roles of Imtiaz and Anwar, the Rampur man, who was indeed the kingpin of the operation, he called off the interrogation asking Siddiqui to take some rest.

It was obvious to him that the venue of the investigation must shift expeditiously to Rampur, for, Anwar must be nabbed quickly lest he escaped for good. Though Siddiqui could not give him any authentic information it was clear to him that he was now working for the masters across the border. He rang up Saxena. "I and Khot would be reaching Delhi by the morning flight and would be bringing along Siddiqui alias Allahbux with us. Please arrange transport and police escort for us from Delhi to Rampur," he instructed, and further asked, "What's the progress at your end?"

"Unfortunately Sir, we could not so far locate Anwar because Imtiaz was not able to give any clue. It seems that Anwar always took the initiative in contacting Imtiaz and never talked about anything personal."

"That only brings home the need to rush Siddiqui to Rampur," Mundkur remarked, unhappy that Anwar was still at large.

When confronted with Siddiqui, Imtiaz came clean about his role as a facilitator for which he was paid regularly by Anwar. He still maintained, however, that he had no notion about where Anwar lived in Rampur or for whom he actually worked. Mundkur had reason to believe that he was telling the truth knowing by experience how networks are usually operated. Only a lapse on a crucial operative's part could give them the much-needed lead. Siddiqui was the best bet as, he had an important role to play and, had come in prolonged contact with Anwar. He decided to have another exclusive session with Siddiqui.

Mundkur grilled Siddiqui for hours on, taking him over again and again all the occasions he could remember of having talked to Anwar in person or on phone. There was no reason to believe that Siddiqui was not co-operating, but the problem was that Anwar had never given him an inkling of where he lived. Every time they met—and it was always in a public place like a restaurant or park—Anwar fixed up the day, time and location of the next meeting. Of course, the latter had worked out a facility by which he could establish contact with Siddiqui in an emergency. He had asked Siddiqui to befriend the owner of a nearby shop and arrange with him to summon him whenever there was a telephone call for him. This facility was not to be extended to any other friend or relative.

When Mundkur persisted, Siddiqui finally said "A small incident comes to my mind, see if it would help you. Last year when we were having drinks and dinner at the Shafi Kabob Corner where he had called me to brief me about a new job that I had to do, he asked me after he had had a couple of drinks, if I was married. He appeared to be rather relaxed and in an expansive mood. In reply I started narrating the virtues of bachelorhood but he cut me short saying that it was all very well when one was young and did not want any encumbrances, but a time comes when one wants to live a peaceful settled life. Before I could say anything he said that for his part he had made a provision. He had married a primary school teacher. That would ensure financial stability and social respectability."

"Did he tell you where she was employed? Was it here in Rampur?" Mundkur asked impatiently, elated at the prospect of finding a foothold.

"I asked him precisely the same question. He said, no, she was serving in a small village close to Mirzapur in eastern U.P. He also gave the name of the village. Let me see if I can recall." After pondering a while he said, "Oh yes. I remember now. The name of the village is Himayatpur. It's about three kilometers from Mirzapur. That's what Anwar told me."

"Did he tell you any other particulars, say the name of his wife and so on?"

"No, he didn't. He changed the subject, perhaps realising that he was getting too personal with me. A little later we broke off."

This was something worthwhile to work upon. Mundkur convinced his associates that a place like the wife's house in a remote village would be a very attractive proposition to Anwar who had obviously found out from Imtiaz that the police had reached his café and had made himself scarce. They decided to check up there immediately. Instead of Siddiqui whom Mundkur did not want to expose much, he took Imtiaz with him to identify Anwar. Travelling overnight they reached Mizapur in the morning and took assistance from the city police station to go to Himayatpur. Mundkur decided against going directly to that village as, it would create commotion, thus affording a chance to Anwar to flee. They went to a nearby village that was hardly a kilometer away and sent the Mirzapur police station constable accompanying them to fetch the Sarpanch of Himayatpur.

On learning that the police officers in strength were from the CID the Sarpanch took a co-operative stance from the beginning. "Yes, a Muslim lady teacher Jaitunbi by name, teaches in our village primary school. She joined a couple of years ago," he said in reply to Mundkur's query.

"Is she married?" asked Mundkur.

"Yes, she got married last year to someone from a distant place."

"Does her husband live with her?"

"No, normally she lives alone. She has rented a house in the village itself. But for the past few days her husband who is said to have come on leave is staying with her. He does not come out much and keeps to himself. Most likely he would be in the house now." He readily agreed to lead the police party to Jaitunbi's house.

Taking care to cover the house from the rear as well, Mundkur asked the Sarpanch to knock on the door. A moment later a young man opened the door. When the Sarpanch pointed to him as the husband of Jaitunbi two policemen caught him by the arms and giving him no chance even to ask a question, whisked him away to one of the police vehicles. Mundkur asked Imtiaz who was sitting in the other car if he was the right man, and to his great relief Imtiaz nodded in affirmation. Asking the Sarpanch to appropriately explain the situation to Jaitunbi, and thanking him for his help Mundkur and party immediately left the village. Mundkur was keen to reach Rampur at the earliest. Interrogating Anwar and nabbing his other associates in the network was uppermost in his mind.

Anwar, his real name being Meer Mohmmad Khan, was the hardest nut to crack. He was a trained ISI agent who had been taught during training how to cope with hostile interrogation. He also was given a 'cover story' to sell to his interrogators. It was a real test of Mundkur's interrogative acumen, ably assisted by Khot and other IB as well as CID officers. The latter were rearing to 'soften' him up a bit when he gave tailored replies but Mundkur dissuaded them. He believed that the real truth could be elicited only by clever interrogation. Ultimately he did manage to get Anwar 'singing'. He hastened to dispatch the CID officers to nab the remainder operatives whom Anwar controlled. They were lucky to get them all within a matter of days. Meanwhile Mundkur concentrated on the two prize catches he had, namely Anwar and Siddiqui. He questioned them at length together and separately till he was sure that he had the whole story and all the network operatives in his bag.

Piecing together the versions of all the persons who were arrested he prepared a detailed report for his bosses that read:

Major Pravin Kumar, lately a Lt. Colonel of the Indian Army, was deemed responsible by the Pakistan army for killing several of their soldiers masquerading as Mujahideens in the Kargil offensive. The Pakistani Army brass was very upset and propositioned to the ISI to settle scores since the Pakistani Army couldn't do anything about it. The chief wanted Pravin Kumar killed in the most brutal manner. The ISI code-named it as "Operation Ku-Kheema,' the objective being to make mince meat of Pravin Kumar. After the Kargil conflict subsided, Major Pravin Kumar was promoted and posted at a peace station in Uttar Pradesh.

The ISI decided to get the 'action operation' executed through its UP-based spy network that had the requisite capability. The choice naturally fell on Anwar—Meer Mohammad Khan in real life—their resident agent stationed at Rampur. He was a third generation Muhajir, his grandfather having migrated from UP when partition took place. Trained and sent to India in 1995, he had acquitted himself well as the nodal agent handling a network that had four other agents positioned at strategic places in western UP.

Going by the delicate nature of the mission it was necessary to assign its actual execution to a trustworthy and competent person who was crafty and at the same time ruthless. Luckily, this network had such a man in Aamir Siddiqui. The ISI had obtained Siddiqui's services from the 'D' Company. When ISI wanted an executioner who could operate in that region they asked Shakeel, a trusted lieutenant of Daud Ibrahim who conducted 'business' on his behalf in Uttar Pradesh as well. Shakeel had highly recommended this man who had at his behest liquidated two *supari* targets with the finesse of a seasoned butcher. He was a college dropout from Moradabad and had been working for the 'D' Company for the past five years and more, first in Mumbai where he had obtained his spurs and later in UP itself. When the ISI took over Siddiqui it increased his retainer that was credited to his bank account every month without a lapse. The ISI had but one occasion so far to test his mettle and skill. And he had given a good account of himself. Now was the second opportunity.

Considering the intricate nature of the operation that was not without substantial risk, Major Omar Qureshi, the ISI officer who was in charge of action operations in northern India, decided to personally brief Anwar about the mechanics of operation, that is, how the operation would be carried out. One morning Anwar received a letter at his 'accommodation address' that is, the address of a shop keeper who had agreed to lend his address to Anwar to receive his mail, that asked him to meet 'Abbajan' at Shafiq's house on the following Friday. This meant to Anwar that he had to be at the 'Safe House' in Delhi whose location he knew, at 4 o'clock in the afternoon on Thursday, and that his operational boss from Islamabad would himself be there to brief him about some important job. Accordingly Anwar went to Delhi and met Major Omar Qureshi at the appointed place. Qureshi explained to him the purpose and the nature of the operation and instructed him to assign the actual job to Siddiqui. Anwar was to keep the headquarters informed through the usual channel, and receive instructions that would help him guide Siddiqui.

On instructions from Anwar, Siddiqui reached Lt. Col. Pravin Kumar's station along with his newly acquired young wife who provided him the cover of a family man. On arrival he contacted Imtiaz, the owner of Bismilla Cyber Café, and with his assistance rented a room that was to serve as his abode till the mission was accomplished. It was in a locality that was rarely visited by police. He was not to disclose his true assignment to Imtiaz though the latter being himself on the pay roll of Anwar would provide him all the help required of him. Siddiqui was to give his name as Allahbux to Imtiaz and others in the neighbourhood who were mostly Muslim weavers, and as Rambux when moving around in the military establishment. He was also to tell his neighbours that he was a salesman for a Mumbai-based company that manufactured industrial filters. That would inhibit inquisitive people from asking many questions, and at the same time explain his irregular hours of work.

True to his character, Siddiqui soon commenced his reconnaissance trips to the camp area where the army officers' bungalows were situated. It took him just three days of discreet enquiries to locate Lt. Col. Pravin Kumar's bungalow. Hereafter Bungalow No: 29/A was going to become his prime target. Not far from the bungalow but in civilian area was a *pan*shop owned by a Ramlakhan Yadao. Siddiqui decided to make the panshop his observation post. Under the pretext of purchasing pan and *gutkha* he introduced himself to Yadao as Rambux who had recently taken up a job in a manufacturing unit down the road. The contact grew as days passed and so did the frequency of his visits to the *pan*shop.

During a casual conversation about military officers and their servants that surrounded them Ramlakhan Yadao gave out that Mangeram, Lt. Col. Pravin Kumar's batman, often visited his *pan*shop late in the evening to purchase *gutkha* sachets. That was the time when he took out the Colonel's dog for a walk. This was a gem of information. However, Siddiqui showed no particular interest in it although his heart was gladdened beyond measure, and drifted to other subjects and persons.

Siddiqui let a week pass before he quietly delayed his visit to the *pan*shop to coincide with the time that Mangeram visited it for his daily fill of *gutkha*. Luck favoured him the next time he made the trip. A young man who looked every inch a *Garhwalee* was sitting on the bench that Yadao had lain in front of the shop for the benefit of the regulars. He had a middle-sized long-haired dog sitting in front of him, wearing a bored look. There was no mistaking him. The way he was narrating his *fauzi* adventures to Yadao he would only be Mangeram. Slowly Siddiqui introduced himself into the conversation, which was mostly a monologue, and when Yadao got busy with a customer, took on the burden of listening to Mangeram's exploits. That day onwards the evening gossip sessions were essentially between Mangeram and Siddiqui, much to the relief of Ramlakhan Yadao. In Siddiqui, Mangeram had discovered the most patient listener he ever had. Soon he started anxiously waiting for Siddiqui to arrive if he was not already there.

Everything that Mangeram had with him had a tale hanging from it. Even the dog and his name had a juicy antecedent. "Do you know how this dog came to be with Colonel *Sahib*?" he asked Siddiqui one evening. Without waiting for a reply Mangeram launched a marathon narrative, the long and short of it was that at a forward post in the Kargil sector where Pravin Kumar was stationed some two years ago he found one cold evening this dog—it was a pup then— whining outside his bunker. Out of pity, Pravin Kumar took him inside and fed him a few biscuits. Since then the dog tagged himself on to Pravin Kumar so much so that—if one is to believe Mangeram—he accompanied him even on nightly assaults on enemy positions during the conflict. The dog was given the name Zulfie, because of the long hair that hung all around his body in unkempt locks.

Siddiqui dutifully reported every development by e-mail— courtesy Bismilla Cyber café—to the given address. In response, he was asked to ingratiate himself with both Mangeram and his dog and obtain a duplicate of the collar the dog may be wearing. Siddiqui made it a practice to occasionally take small gifts of articles of every day use for Mangeram and biscuits every time for Zulfie, which seem to please either. One day while patting the dog in a visible display of fondness Siddiqui noticed that the dog had a new collar. When he casually remarked to Mangeram about the outfit he perked up.

"Oh, that collar? Colonel *Sahib* purchased it for him as a birthday gift," Mangeram clarified.

"Whose birthday? The dog's?" Siddiqui asked in disbelief. "I remember you told me the other day that he just walked into Colonel *Sahib's* bunker one day."

"That is true, but that is the day Colonel *Sahib* celebrates as his birthday. He thinks, Zulfie brought him good luck and all the honours he received in the war. He is, therefore, very fond of him and celebrates the day Zulfie came to him." Mangeram explained.

"Looks attractive. Must be very expensive. Did Colonel *Sahib* bring it from Delhi?" Siddiqui probed gently.

"Oh no, purchased here itself. From a shop in Bohra Bazaar that sells everything you need for a dog, even medicines. I went with Colonel *Sahib,* because he wanted to take Zulfie along," Mangeram added authenticity to his earlier assertion.

This was enough of a clue to Siddiqui. He evinced no further interest in Zulfie's collar, and took leave after casual chat on other topics. Siddiqui went straight to Bohra Bazar. He had no difficulty in locating the shop, for there was only one shop that specialised in canine stuff. He was lucky to find an identical collar. He purchased it and made for Imtiaz's outfit to report the happy break. He was not sure as to what precise use the collar would be put. He had acquired it only because he had been asked to do so as an imperative task.

Within two days he was asked to meet Anwar who would be waiting for him near the fountain in the municipal park at 4.35 p.m. the following Wednesday. He was also to carry with him the collar duly packed in a plastic carry bag. When they met, Anwar congratulated him on the excellent piece of work he had done, gave him gifts for him and his wife, and fixed the last Friday of the following month for their next meeting—at 11.15 a.m. in front of the newspaper stall at the entrance of the railway station. In the meantime he was to carry on his tete-a-tete with Mangeram and his canine companion, and also discreetly reconnoitre the landscape surrounding Pravin Kumar's bungalow to get familiar with paths that would quickly take him out from the area, and to locate a vantage point close enough but safe, wherefrom he could closely observe the bungalow.

Anwar made a trip to Delhi and met a representative of Major Omar Qureshi's at the safe-house. He handed over the collar to him. Anwar was asked to collect the collar after exactly three weeks from the same place.

Siddiqui met Anwar on the appointed day. He was taken to a lodge nearby where Anwar had obviously booked a room in advance. In the privacy of the room Anwar explained to him the next crucial part of the operation. He had brought with him the collar that he passed on to Siddiqui. Though it looked a little fatter, it still wore the same look, albeit a bit used. Anwar also handed a tiny remote control device to Siddiqui and showed him how to use it. He then wished Siddiqui good luck and asked him to leave.

From that day on the collar and the remote control device became Siddiqui's constant companions whenever he visited Yadao's *pan* shop for a chat with Mangeram. The question that baffled him was how to replace Zulfie's collar, for that meant getting exclusive possession of the dog for a while. A semblance of an opportunity came his way a few days later when a relative of Mangeram's came along with him. After a *pan* and some gossip the relative wanted to leave lest he would miss the last bus. Mangeram very much wanted to accompany him to the bus stop but was a bit hesitant because of the dog. In a flash Siddiqui saw the opening for him, and seized it with both hands, as it were.

"Don't worry about Zulfie, Mangeramji. I will hold him while you see off your guest at the bus stop. He will not misbehave, I am sure. We are friends." For good measure he took out a biscuit from his pocket and tossed it to the dog. While doing so he calmly took hold of the leash, thus giving very little chance to Mangeram to think over the offer. Cautioning him to be careful and promising to come back soon Mangeram left with his guest for the bus stop.

As soon as the duo were out of sight, Siddiqui fed the dog one more biscuit. Stroking him around the neck, at the same time muttering endearing words, he turned his back towards Yadao and placed the dog between his two legs. Yadao who was busy attending to his customers could not now see the dog even if he wished to. Quickly Siddiqui pulled out the collar from his satchel and secured it on Zulfie's neck, fixed the leash hook on it and unfastened the original collar, which he slid into the bag. The whole operation did not take more than a few seconds. When Mangeram returned, he found him scratching Zulfie between the ears, whispering endearments to him. Mangeram was profuse in expressing his gratitude. It was time for him to go. He thanked Siddiqui again and took leave.

It was difficult for Siddiqui to keep his composure. He was exhilarated by the smooth success of the most difficult part of his assignment and excited by the prospects that awaited him. He purchased a *gutkha* sachet from Yadao and followed Mangeram maintaining a discreet distance.

A little while later Siddiqui strayed to the left and took position under a tamarind tree that was some fifty meters ahead of the Colonel's bungalow and offered a clear view of the front courtyard as well as the verandah, despite the fading light of the evening. Good luck had obviously decided to favour him. That's what Siddiqui thought when he actually saw Lt. Col. Pravin Kumar in the garden giving instructions to the *Mali*. His heart started pounding in anticipation. He prayed to Allah to soothe his nerves and pulled out the remote control device from the satchel. He released the safety catch and paused in expectation of the events that would follow. He did not have to wait long. As Mangeram entered the front gate, the dog on seeing his master jerked himself free and rushed to him barking softly. Pravin Kumar turned to face him, calling endearingly, "Zulfie, my pet". Zulfie placed his front paws on the Colonel's midriff who held the dog's face in both his palms and stooped as if to kiss the crown of his head. There was a blinding flash and a deafening blast. The next moment Zulfie and his Master lay in a heap, cut to smithereens.

Siddiqui calmly placed the remote control contraption back into the satchel and hurried away by the path he had already chosen for retreat. His destination now was Bismilla Cyber Café. He nodded to Imtiaz and entered the cubicle that was reserved for him. The e-mail that he sent out read,

'Nikkah performed. All are happy', which as pre-arranged, conveyed that the mission was successfully completed without any mishap.

He handed over the duplicate key of his room to Imtiaz and instructed him to vacate the room at the end of the month, for which rent had already been paid in advance. He briefly thanked him for all the help he had rendered and taking his leave walked up to his room that was not far away. He asked his wife to get ready, packed all their clothes and everything that could be a giveaway if they fell in police hands, in a suitcase and left. To a prying neighbour Siddiqui told that his mother was seriously ill at Mumbai, therefore he had to rush and did not know when he would be able to return. At the bus station he boarded the bus that was the first to leave the town, for which destination he did not bother to ask, nor did he care.

Shabeer Mohammed Sheikh

"SIR, I HAVE AN INTERESTING INFORMATION TO SHARE with you," Ramakant Khot, one of Mundkur's most trusted assistants told him excitedly on entering his office. Gurudas Mundkur, was the head of the counter-intelligence unit in the Mumbai regional office of the Intelligence Bureau.

"What's it?" Mundkur asked briefly.

"Sir, I was on my usual visit to the Air Force Missile Base at Madh Island this morning when my contact—a reliable fellow I would say unhesitatingly—whispered to me that Airman Sukhdev Prasad Yadao seemed to be getting prosperous of late. He is often seen these days in clothes that carry famous brand labels when he is off duty. He also sports a Tissot wristwatch. As it is, he does not live in the Air Force quarters. Nothing unusual about that, though. There is a shortage of quarters so the Air Force authorities permit their personnel to rent flats outside. A number of Air Force employees working at the Missile Base live in Dindoshi, where flats are more easily available and the locality is also not very far from the Base. Sukhdev Prasad Yadao has also been living in a small rented flat in Dindoshi ever since his posting to the Base a year and a half ago," Khot explained.

"That's fine, but what is the source of his affluence? Has your contact anything on that?" Mundkur asked a bit impatiently.

"No Sir. He was not able to tell me anything about it. I propose to find that out now myself," Khot disclosed. "If you approve Sir, we will mount a watch on Sukhdev," he suggested.

"Yes, do it," Mundkur readily agreed. "This newly acquired affluence does not seem to gel well, unless of course he got married recently and received a huge dowry."

"He is still unmarried. I checked that out. In fact my contact told me that Sukhdev has remained unmarried because, he has a family to support back home in Bihar. His father died some years ago leaving a large family behind for him to look after. That's why he lived a very frugal life when he came here on posting. His affluence is a recent phenomenon."

"That makes it more intriguing," Mundkur observed.

"Precisely Sir."

"Go ahead. Mount a total watch when he is off duty. Also ask your contact to keep an eye on him when he is at work. You know what to brief him about. Right now we will not alert his bosses. They would expect us to produce more substantive evidence."

"Very well, Sir," Khot affirmed, and took leave of Mundkur.

A fortnight later Khot appeared in the doorway of Mundkur's cabin the moment Mundkur had settled down to work in the morning.

"Yes Khot. Anything in particular?" Mundkur queried on seeing Khot. "Did not hear anything from you about your Air Force Missile Base target," he added by way of a remark.

"I have come to tell you something about that case only. Nothing happened for nearly two weeks. We had started wondering if we were barking up the wrong tree. Then yesterday suddenly the scenario changed drastically. A very interesting thing came to the notice of our men who were keeping a tab on Airman Sukhdev."

"What was that?" Mundkur asked.

"Yesterday, our quarry left his flat around eight in the evening neatly dressed up as if going to a party. He walked up to the Western Express Highway which is about half a kilometer from his building and then took a taxi. He went straight to Bandra, Linking Road. Paid off the taxi and walked a couple of hundred meters straight ahead before turning right into a lane. A little inside there's a posh restaurant. He entered that restaurant. Peculiarly, another young man was waiting for him at a table for two. Both greeted each other in a low-key manner not usual with young friends, and settled down to a drink. Later they had a lavish meal together with the other man always taking the initiative in ordering dishes. Obviously it wasn't a get-together of two friends. From the expression on their faces they seemed to be discussing some serious matter. When they finished the other man paid the bill. Then they rose to leave. While Sukhdev made straight for the door his companion went to the toilet."

"Interesting. What happened next? Did your men cover the other person as well?" Mundkur asked getting more curious.

"Yes Sir. They covered both. Sukhdev again took a taxi and reached his flat. Soon thereafter he retired for the night. He had an early morning shift," Khot explained.

"And the other man?"

"His going to the toilet was perhaps a ruse to avoid being seen coming out together from the restaurant, but it helped our men. In the meantime they quickly divided themselves into two teams to trail both. After doing a bit of window shopping on the main road he hailed a taxi and got in. Interestingly, the taxi also reached Dindoshi and stopped at a building not very far from Sukhdev's. Very fishy indeed," Khot concluded.

"Well, anything on the new friend?" Mundkur asked.

"Not yet Sir. We are working on that. Maybe by evening I will be able to give you something more on him," Khot said.

"Khot, I think we are into a big game. That's my gut feeling. Your boys are doing a fine job. Ask them to stick to those two like a leech. Do tell me as soon as you get more dope on your new friend," Mundkur instructed Khot.

"Sir," Khot said in acknowledgement, and left Mundkur's cabin.

Khot was back in Mundkur's room the next morning.

"Sir, we were very lucky to get good line on Sukhdev's friend, or shall I say accomplice," he said on entering.

"Is that so? Good. Now tell me what you know about him?" Mundkur queried.

"One of the residents in that building is known to the husband of Gayatri Monappa, who is these days working in my unit. She persuaded her husband to ferret out information about this man, and he obliged. Both paid a social call on her husband's friend and obtained enough of dope for us to come to a conclusion about this mysterious man's probable role in this fishy business," Khot made a longish introduction.

"I see."

"The name of Sukhdev's friend-cum-accomplice is Surendra Mohan Singh. He has taken a one-bedroom flat on rent in that building and has been living there for the past six months or so. He has let it out to the other residents of the building that he is from Varanasi, is an IT professional and teaches in a computer institute in the northern suburb of Dahisar. Goes every morning to the institute but is quite irregular about returning. People attribute it to his being single. He generally keeps to himself, otherwise he is friendly to talk to. No one has seen any friends or relatives visiting him at his flat," Khot concluded.

"Any check on his job claim?" Mundkur asked.

"Yes Sir. We did that. He does teach at the Adelphi Computer Training Institute in the morning, but the salary he gets would be hardly enough to pay for the rent of the flat, let alone taxi rides and expensive dinners for friends," Khot expressed his suspicion.

"It's true that he treats his friends to expensive dinners to friends. That's how you got him."

"Whether it's a friend or business contact whom he entertained so generously that day is yet to be established if I may put a rider, Sir."

"If the latter supposition is true, it would mean that this man has some other business interests too. Have you found out how he came to be friends with Sukhdev?" Mundkur asked.

"No Sir, not yet. My contact at the Missile Base is not aware of any friends of Sukhdev, besides his colleagues at the Base. But we shall persevere with this line of enquiry."

"Keep both under intensive surveillance. What they are doing together right now is far more important to us than how they got together," Mundkur advised Khot before the latter took leave of him.

It was for the umpteenth time that he glanced impatiently at his watch. It was five-twenty. Five more minutes yet to go. He felt silly doing so but did it so time and again nevertheless, as though by the force of habit. This was not his first occasion nor was it past the appointed time. But somehow, rather inexplicably, he felt anxious, a bit nervous to be precise. Maybe because of the vital importance of the occasion, he reasoned to himself when he could not deny that feeling. He looked up in irritation. A noisy crow had perched itself right above him in the tree under which he was sitting. He was worried if it would foul itself and ruin his clothes. He could neither shoo the crow away for, that would attract attention, nor could he change position. He was supposed to sit under that tree. It was the farthest tree in front of the Nana-Nani Park at the Chowpatty. Shifting to some safer place might jeopardise his rendezvous with possible disastrous consequences. This had considerably added to his anxiety.

It was nearly five-twenty five. He looked straight ahead at the western horizon over the heads of the lounging men, women and children in front. Then almost involuntarily he turned his gaze to the right. The man was supposed to approach him from the BandStand side. He could see none approaching him. A nervous chill went down his spine. He quickly ran his eyes all over himself. Yes, he was wearing a red-and-black check shirt over black trousers, an issue of Stardust was on his lap, and of course the black canvas shoulder bag was by his side. What is more, despite the menace of the croaking crow he had stationed himself under the right tree. Every thing was in perfect compliance of the instructions he had received a few days ago, he assured himself. It was Surendra Mohan Singh waiting at the Chowpatty beach for a visitor whom he had never met before.

As he glanced up he saw a young man a few paces away intently looking at him. He had not seen him approach. That was his mistake. He should have been looking out rather than at himself, he brooded. He had thus missed an important pointer. He cursed himself for the momentary lapse. Nevertheless, the clothes of the man standing close by and gazing at him were right, and he had a black canvas bag too, just like his own hanging from his right shoulder. Perfect, he assured himself. There was a pregnant pause. 'Is he the right person?' both seemed to be asking themselves. The visitor took the initiative, and approaching Singh asked gently, "Could you kindly tell me where the public toilets are?"

"Oh, sure. Come along I will guide you. I was also thinking of going there myself," so saying Singh sprang to his feet and started moving to the left. The visitor accompanied him walking closely. "Are you Awasthi from Ghatkopar?" he asked almost in a whisper. "No, I am Sharma from Chembur," Singh replied in a hushed tone. Both smiled at each other in recognition. "Salam Walekum," the visitor greeted him under the breath. "Walekum Salam," Singh responded.

While the two were strolling in a leisurely fashion towards the public toilets, a young couple sitting some twenty paces behind Singh in a sprinkling of similar couples, got up and followed the duo. To an outsider, they looked very much like a couple in love, but they were in fact Ramakant Khot and his assistant Gayatri Monappa. They had followed Singh from his building when he had left his apartment, confident that he was today on an important mission. There was good reason for their belief. Last night Singh watchers had reported to Khot that he had gone in the evening all the way to Chowpatty where he had roamed around Nana-Nani Park and its vicinity for a while and returned; he did not do anything else. Mundkur and Khot had surmised that Singh was on a dry run, and maybe in a day or two he would again visit Chowpatty in the evening for some secret transaction. Therefore, when Singh left his flat again the next day in the evening and proceeded towards Chowpatty, Khot and Gayatri preceded him there as already planned, and casually took up positions behind him without his suspecting in the least.

At the toilet the visitor requested Singh to hold his shoulder bag while he went inside. Singh obliged. When the visitor returned Singh handed him his own similar looking bag and retained the visitor's bag with himself. Both then moved in tandem towards the main road. Khot and Gayatri followed maintaining a discreet distance. On reaching the edge of the road where several taxis were parked, Singh gently waved 'Khuda Hafiz' to the other man and got into a taxi. The latter took to the footpath and proceeded in the direction of the Nariman Point. Khot and Gayatri also separated. Khot followed the stranger on foot while Gayatri took another taxi and followed Singh.

Gayatri did not have anything eventful to report. Singh went straight to his apartment and did not come out. She apprised Mundkur of this and went home. Khot on the other hand had a very exciting experience. His quarry strolled along the Marine Drive and later turned left to enter the lane leading to Charni Road railway station. He boarded a north-bound local train. Khot did likewise. He got down at Santacruz West railway station. Khot followed him. He entered a restaurant outside the railway station and settled down to eat. Khot took advantage of the respite that he thus received and contacted Mundkur on the cell phone to ask for immediate dispatch of a team of watchers to meet him outside the railway station, where he would be waiting at a distance but within the sight of the restaurant.

Within fifteen minutes three men from the counter-intelligence unit arrived. Khot heaved a sigh of relief, as he did not want to lose the man at any cost. Dinner over, the man lit a cigarette and slowly proceeded up north by the footpath. He was apparently in a relaxed mood, probably because he had successfully accomplished the task. Within ten minutes he reached Hotel Asiana—a modest lodge. It was obvious that the man had checked in earlier in that hotel for, he straight away proceeded to his room. Khot waited for a while to see if he would come out again but he did not. Khot instructed the watchers to mount a nightlong vigil and report to him at intervals. He then left to meet Mundkur who was, to be sure, waiting for him in the office.

On reaching the office Khot gave a detailed account of all that happened on the errand. Mundkur told him that Gayatri had rung him. She had 'homed' Singh and left him under the care of their watchers. It was unlikely that he would stir out. Mundkur then straightened up in his seat and looking into the eyes of Khot said in a solemn voice, "Khot, do you know what I feel, and believe you feel likewise?" Khot did not reply but gazed at his chief expectantly.

Mundkur continued, "Some very consequential developments are likely to take place that may call for quick decisions and swift action on our part. I have a feeling that this man, this visitor has brought some technical gadgetry to be eventually handed over to Sukhdev for clandestine use. No spy master will be content with getting only verbal reports especially if they are of technical nature, which if pertaining to the Air Force would surely be. He would ask for documents, photographs and the like by way of authentication. To me it appears that the black shoulder bag contained photographic or communication equipment, if nothing else."

"I quite see your point Sir," Khot nodded in agreement.

"If my hunch is right," Mundkur proceeded, "then Sukhdev must hand over that equipment to Sukhdev at the earliest opportunity. It could be even tomorrow if he has already fixed up a meeting with him. We still haven't found out how they communicate with each other. It could even be on the mobile phone. We could find that out from the phone companies but I don't suppose we should waste time on that right now. We assume that they are going to meet shortly and proceed. Our objective would be to catch them in the act of transferring the equipment so that both can be roped in successfully."

"I get it Sir."

"Now about the other man, I mean the man who has made himself comfortable in Hotel Asiana. Let's call him Q-1 until we know his real name. His is a more urgent case that requires immediate decision as regards the line of action. He is not going to hang around in that lodge any longer unless he is to carry back something bulky on his return journey, and that something could be only from Singh. A good spymaster does not use the same courier in two different operations while on an errand. I doubt very much if Singh would be in a position to give him anything substantial so soon. If he had something like film roll, documents etc. to be handed over those would have been delivered in the same meeting. It stands to reason, therefore, that Q-1 would leave for whatever his destination, latest tomorrow morning," Mundkur reasoned.

"I agree Sir. He may not leave at night because, his demeanour suggested that he was in no hurry to pack up. Lodgers who wish to leave at the dead of night or very early in the morning usually settle their bill at night itself. He did nothing of the sort. He perhaps has the whole night to relax," Khot presented his deduction.

"That's correct. So, he will leave only tomorrow morning—maybe by train or by plane. I don't suppose he would catch a flight. Again no spymaster worth his salt squanders money like that on a courier on a return journey. Besides there is stringent security check at the airport to be reckoned with. Therefore, in all probability he would leave by train. Our watchers are already at the hotel. They will follow him. I am afraid, Khot, they will have to continue because they are the only ones who would recognise him."

"That should be alright, I suppose. Our chaps are used to performing long hours of duty, Besides, those three are a especially dedicated lot," Khot surmounted the difficulty.

"What needs to be decided right now, Khot, is, what we should do with Q-1, should he be discovered leaving by a long distance train which in all probability he would? I suggest, you reach the hotel early morning and take charge. You take one more officer with you. You will require more hands."

"Very well Sir."

"The five of you should pursue him when he checks out from the hotel. If he gets into a long distance train—and now listen carefully—keep three men behind to take care of him and you immediately seek the assistance of the railway police and nab him with their help. See that the action attracts minimum attention. So, use some clever ruse to pull him out from the compartment. Once in our custody he becomes incommunicado, and that is what we want till Singh makes the next move. I will in the meantime speak to the Railway Police Commissioner so that he would instruct his officers to expect a call from you. Is that clear to you?"

"Yes Sir. Quite clear," Khot nodded.

"I do hope Singh does something foolish soon enough so that we nab both of them—I mean he and his protégé the blackguard Airman—so that we don't have to keep this man, Q-1, under wraps for long."

Mundkur's prognosis came true but not before Khot and his men spent several harrowing hours watching their quarry. Q-1 woke up late in the morning and confined himself to his room. Around noon he checked out from the hotel, took a taxi and went to down town. He roamed around in Fort area, mostly window-shopping. Thereafter he had lunch at a restaurant on the Mohammed Ali road and then drifted towards Mumbai Central railway station.

As soon as Rajdhani Express arrived at the platform from the yard he took his seat in a sleeper coach. He evidently had a berth already reserved for him. This was the time for Khot and his men to act. Khot got in touch with Inspector Jadhao of the Mumbai Central railway police station and sought his assistance. With the help of a Ticket Checker whom Jadhao roped in, they called Q-1 out on the pretext that there was some problem regarding his reservation, and leading him a little away from the train, whisked him out of sight.

Nothing much happened the next day at Singh's place. As usual he went to his institute in the morning and returned in the afternoon, thereafter keeping himself confined to the room. Khot was in touch with his contact at the Air Force Base. In the morning of the following day he got a tip off from the contact. Airman Sukhdev Prasad Yadao had not reported for duty in the morning and was not going to turn up that day. He had taken casual leave claiming some urgent personal work that required his immediate attention.

Khot rushed to Mundkur with the information. Both agreed that a meeting between Singh and Sukhdev was to be expected during the course of the day. Mundkur decided to take the reins of the operation in his hands. He sent a message to all the watchers to be on the maximum alert and promptly report all happenings concerning the two. He formed two teams; one led by Khot and another by Bhadang, another competent assistant, and asked them to position themselves in vehicles at a discreet distance from the buildings of Singh and Sukhdev respectively. They were to move on the command go. Simultaneously he asked the special transport arrangement to be put in place. This meant that two taxies fitted with microphones that would record as well as transmit conversation that might take place inside the vehicle, and to be driven by IB drivers dressed in taxi driver's uniform, were to cruise near the buildings of Singh and Sukhdev. They were to trap the quarries into hailing them should they decide to take a taxi.

Mundkur also rang up the Mumbai City Crime Branch chief and requested for the immediate assistance of two officers. They arrived shortly. Mundkur briefed them about the nature of the job to be done and asked them to accompany him when the need arose.

Around 11 o'clock Mundkur's cell phone rang. It was one of the watchers at Singh's building. "The quarry has emerged from the building. Appears ready to go out. He is carrying with him a black canvas shoulder bag," the watcher reported. Mundkur knew that the moment of reckoning had arrived. A moment later Mundkur's phone rang again. This time it was a watcher from Sukhdev's building. "Subject came out of the building and is walking towards the main road, that is, the Western Express Highway," he said briefly. By that time Mundkur was himself on the move along with the two Crime Branch officers. His cell phone rang again as his car was speeding towards the Western Express Highway. It was the first watcher again. "Sir, he has taken the bait. Hired our taxi," he said.

"Good. Damn good. We will soon catch up with them," Mundkur said jubilantly and disconnected. He turned to the driver and asked him to be on the look out for 'Alfa Taxi'. The driver was aware of its registration number and special identification marks. He nodded in affirmation.

Mundkur turned to the two police officers accompanying him and said, "Now listen carefully. We will hear on the speaker in our car all that happens in the taxi. It is bugged." But before they could hear anything on the speaker Mundkur's phone rang again. It was Bhadang. "Sukhdev did not take a taxi but waited by the side of the road. A taxi came—it was

'Alfa Taxi'—and stopped close to Sukhdev who hopped in and it sped away. I am following the taxi," he informed.

"Oh, that's marvellous! They are meeting in the taxi itself. A meeting on the move," Mundkur told his companions. "I thought they might have fixed up a room in a hotel where giving lessons in the use of gadgetry is easier. But this helps us a lot. We will have recorded evidence," he added.

Soon sounds of conversation emanated from the speaker in Mundkur's car. All the three listened intently. After the preliminaries and asking the taxi driver to take them to Ghod Bunder road, Singh began talking seriously to his companion. It appeared to the listeners that he was taking out gadgets one by one from his bag and instructing the other man how to operate them. He was making Sukhdev handle them to gain confidence.

When the instruction session ended Singh packed things back into the bag and handed it to Sukhdev, saying clearly and loudly enough, "These are now yours. We expect you to make full and proper use of them. Rest assured you would be amply rewarded. I will let you know in the usual manner how the results are and on what to concentrate more."

"This is the time to swoop on them," Mundkur told his companions. "Before one of them gets dropped they must be nabbed." He asked his driver to close in and also asked Khot and Bhadang who were following the taxi in their cars, to be ready for action. Mundkur's car sped past Bhadang's and Khot's cars and then the taxi, and then blocked the road asking the taxi driver to stop. The driver readily obliged, despite the duo asking him to go ahead. Before they could open the doors of the taxi to flee it was surrounded by

Mundkur's men on all four sides. The police officers pointed revolvers at Singh and Sukhdev and sternly warned, "Don't make any move. We are the police. You are under arrest." The others pulled them out and handcuffed them. Within minutes all the four vehicles started on the return journey to Mundkur's office.

"I suggest, we take up Q-1 first for the treatment. He is the weakest link among the triad of those culprits and perhaps the least involved. All said and done, a courier is not likely to have been given insight into the operation. Secondly, he has been with us the longest and, therefore, by now quite softened. Our chaps, I am sure, have been brainwashing him in the meanwhile. He will break easily. Thirdly, whatever he spills can be made use of against the others especially Singh," Mundkur made the proposition to Khot. Along with their team of expert interrogators, they were sitting in the IB's interrogation room that provided them unhindered privacy.

"I also feel, that would be the right approach," Khot agreed.

"Then, ask them to bring in Q-1," Mundkur directed.

Within minutes a haggard looking Q-1 was standing before them.

"Sit down," Mundkur pointed to the vacant chair in front of him across the table. The latter took the seat hesitatingly.

"Have you had proper food and tea since you have been our guest?" Mundkur asked him gently. Q-1 simply nodded in confirmation.

"Now tell me, by what name should I call you? What's your name?" Mundkur asked brusquely.

"Rakesh Kumar" Q-1 answered evenly.

"I know, that's the name under which you stayed in Hotel Asiana, and that's the name under which you wanted to travel by train. I am asking you for your real name."

"I am Rakesh Kumar," Q-1 reiterated.

"Where did you learn Urdu?" Mundkur asked suddenly as if changing the subject.

"Urdu?"

"Yes, otherwise what were you doing with that Urdu novel in your bag?"

"Oh, that novel? That's my friend's," Q-1 tried to explain.

"Now don't try to be clever. I have been trying to be gentle with you but if you get too smart then I will hand you over to this gentleman. Then God help you," Mundkur warned him, pointing to the burly man with a big moustache sitting next to him. He was a police officer from the Crime Branch. On getting his cue from Mundkur the police officer leaned forward as if to take charge.

"No Sir. I will tell you, please don't hurt me," Q-1 pleaded.

"Then be quick and tell us what's the name that your parents gave you?" Mundkur asked him again.

"Sir, my real name is Mustaq Mohammed."

"Now, out with it. Where are you from? What were you doing in Mumbai?

"I am from Delhi. I came here to see Mumbai."

"You are again being crooked. Have a look at these photographs and tell us what you were doing with that friend of yours?" Mundkur threw a bunch of photographs on the table. Those were the photographs that Khot had clandestinely taken at the Chowpatty with a mini camera. The expression on the face of Q-1 alias Mustaq Mohammed changed perceptibly, yet he would not give in easily.

"He is some stranger I met casually when I went to see Chowpatty," he lied.

"I see. Then why did you have to give him your bag? Have a good look at the last photograph," Mundkur ordered. While MM was trying to frame an answer Mundkur spoke again, "Don't try to bluff. I want to know what is the name of the person you met at the Chowpatty, and what did you pass on to him in that bag? He is in our custody. Keep that in mind."

"Have you arrested him too?" MM asked apprehensively.

"Yes of course, therefore, you better come clean," the Crime Branch officer said sternly.

MM pondered for a while and then meekly started, "I really do not know the name of that man or what was there in the bag. I met him for the first time. I was given that bag by someone in Delhi to deliver to him, which I did."

"Who was the man who gave you the bag?"

"Sir, I don't know his name either, I swear by Allah. But I know that he works in the Pakistan High Commission in Chanakyapuri."

"How did you come to work for him?"

"My grandfather wanted to visit his brother who had migrated at the time of partition and now lives in Sialkot. For generations we have lived in Daryaganj and none had been to Pakistan. I, therefore, went to Pakistan High Commission to make enquiries about the procedure to obtain a visa. There I met a person who works in the Consular Section. He asked me how much I was educated and what I did for a living. When I told him that I had passed SSC and did odd jobs here and there as, I did not have a permanent job he was helpful in getting a visa for my grandfather. That occasioned my meeting him several times. During one of those meetings he told me that if I wanted he could fix a permanent job for me. I was overjoyed. I immediately assented. He asked me to see him again after a week, which I did. He asked me to see a merchant in old Delhi. He would employ me. But, he added, there was a condition of his own attached to the job. I would have to occasionally run errands outside Delhi for him, for which he would pay me additional money. I readily agreed."

"So, you went to the merchant and got the job?" Khot intervened.

"Yes, I did, I went to him the same day and he employed me straightaway."

"What about your second assignment for the good man from the High Commission?" Mundkur asked eagerly.

"When I rang him up to inform him about my having got the job and to thank him, he asked me to see him the following Friday. When I met him, he took me out for lunch to a restaurant. While we were eating he explained to me the exact nature of my work which was to carry a parcel or packet from him to an indicated place in UP, Punjab, Maharashtra etc. It would have to be delivered to the person who would meet me at a given place. He assured me that the packets would not contain any contraband, when I expressed anxiety. He promised to pay me in advance of each trip a lump sum that would look after my travel expenses and leave a good margin as my commission. The thought of getting extra bucks lured me. I showed readiness to undertake the errands for him. After the lunch he took me to Nehru Park and we practised the drill of meeting a stranger as per the instructions given. On subsequent two Fridays we practised at Connaught Place and

Karol Bagh. It was easy. When he realised that I had gained confidence to handle a transaction on my own, he stopped giving me practice."

"When did he actually put you on the job?"

"A week or so later. He rang me up at the shop and asked me to see him the next day. When we met he told me that I had to go to Jodhpur the following Saturday. He had made all the arrangements for my train journey and stay at Jodhpur. I was to travel under an assumed name. He then took me to Khan market and there we practised the drill that I would have to follow at Jodhpur. When he was satisfied that I would not bungle, he asked me to see him again at the same place in the evening on Saturday. I was to come ready for travel. I was not to worry about my employer. He would take care of that. When we met on Saturday he gave me a bag in which another sealed bag was kept. He also gave me enough money, two-way rail tickets and address of the hotel where I was to stay. He made me repeat the drill for his satisfaction. I performed that task successfully."

"How often have you been going out on these errands?" Khot asked.

"There is nothing regular about it. Once in two months would be the average."

"From your demeanour this does not seem to be your first visit to Mumbai. How often do you come here?" Mundkur asked a very crucial question.

"This is my fourth visit in the last three years that I have been in this business."

The interrogating team exchanged meaningful glances. This remark meant that there were at least three more spies operating under their noses.

"Which were the meeting places?" Mundkur asked.

"First time it was at the Gateway of India because I was new to the place and that is a very prominent landmark. The next time it was in Kamla Nehru Park on Malabar Hill and the third time it was at Worli sea face. Each time it was a different person that I met."

"What do you know about the person you met the other day at the Chowpatty?" Khot asked.

"Nothing whatever. I was told never to ask any personal questions, and to keep the meeting as short as possible. Do the transaction and clear out. That's the rule," MM said, somewhat patronisingly.

"What's your rule about reporting the completion of the task?" Mundkur asked.

"On returning I used to ring up the High Commission man at a telephone number he had given me from a PCO at the railway station."

"Now that you have not rung up on the scheduled day what will he do?"

"I don't know. But I am more concerned about my parents, they would be worried. I had told them that I would return yesterday. Sir, please, can something be done to inform them?" MM pleaded.

"Don't worry. We will inform them. Now that you have co-operated with us we will look after you. We are aware that your role is limited, therefore, we will not unnecessarily harass you, but you must admit before the other man that you handed over the bag to him that was given to you by a man from Pakistan High Commission at Delhi."

MM nodded.

"Now go and have your food. We will call you back if needed. Give your father's name and address as well as telephone number to us. We will contact them," Mundkur assured him, and beckoned the escort to take MM away.

The interrogating team met again after the lunch.

"Let's now work on the flying black sheep," Mundkur proposed.

"You mean Airman Sukhdev Prasad Yadao, Sir?" Khot queried.

"Yes, who else? Ask them to bring him in," Mundkur directed.

A few minutes later Sukhdev was brought in. The moment he was in the middle of the group sitting in the room he started sobbing uncontrollably, covering his face with both hands.

"Now, now, stop that drama, will you? You are supposed to be the pride of the nation, or is it the shame of the nation?" Mundkur thundered. "Because there are traitors like you even in the armed forces, a small country like Pakistan plays eyeball with us. What's your problem? Why are you crying? We haven't even touched you. The real ordeal is yet to begin." Mundkur asked. His voice was harsh and intimidating.

"Sir, I feel very ashamed of myself."

"You should be, but that does not make amends. The best thing for you is to come clean without our having to apply the thumbscrew. You know that you are badly trapped. If you have even an iota of love for the country left in you, you would co-operate with us and help us book that scoundrel, the real villain," Mundkur was his aggressive best.

"I want to tell you everything."

"Then go ahead. We are listening. But remember that we already know a lot about the whole shameful affair and your role in it. So don't ever think of bluffing. You will repent," Mundkur ruthlessly drove home the point.

Sukhdev composed himself and began;

"I was posted at the Base some sixteen months ago. I come from a village in Darbhanga district. My father was a schoolteacher there. He died three years ago. After his death the burden of feeding my mother, three sisters and two brothers fell on me. I had just joined service in the Air Force. That was a saving grace otherwise we all would have starved.

In order to maintain the family I had to send nearly sixty percent of my salary. That left very little for me to even think of marriage.

"On arrival here I hired a small flat in Dindoshi because the Air Force reimburses the rent. I used to cook at home but occasionally whenever I felt tired I would go to a restaurant on the main road. There I got acquainted with Surendra Mohan Singh. He was also alone and often took his meals in the restaurant. We became friendly. By and by I told him about my family circumstances. He said that he was in the same predicament and had therefore, come all the way here to earn a living. Luckily, being a qualified man he got a good salary. He would cheer me up whenever I was depressed. On two or three occasions he even helped me with money when I was not able to send the usual amount to my mother. Last Diwali when I went home on leave he sent gifts for my mother and siblings. I was so grateful to him.

"Our friendship grew. Gradually he started asking me cursorily about my job and the activities at the Base. One day I was particularly gloomy because my mother had written to me asking for more money as, my brother needed medical treatment. He had broken his leg. Surendra Mohan offered to help. I could not refuse. During our conversation he suggested to me an easy way of earning extra money. He said, he was doing the same and I could join him. What I was to do was to give him information about the Missile Base that I already knew and he would make me payment every time I gave him useful information. I found no harm in earning the much-needed extra buck in this manner. I agreed. That's how it all started.

"One day he told me that the people who actually paid for the information were not very happy with what I was giving though they were paying handsomely. He then gave me a list of points on which I should give information. He asked me to memorise the points and then destroy the paper. By now I had become dependent on the money he gave me, therefore, I began to work on those lines though it meant poking my nose in my colleagues' business. A month ago Surendra Mohan again complained. He said the best solution was to photograph the inner precincts and record conversations. He assured me that he would teach me how to do it without any fear of detection, and also give me the required equipment. Instead of going somewhere he said that it was safer to speak in a moving vehicle. We could even practice a bit by going outside the city. He offered to pick me up. That's how we were together when you caught us," Sukhdev stopped.

"Is that the whole truth?" Mundkur asked dryly.

"I have told you everything, Sir. Have mercy on me. The spectacle of my family starving because of my greed haunts me all the time ever since you arrested me," Sukhdev started sobbing again.

"Now don't cry. That's not going to help matters. You must now see to it that the villain who lured you into this treacherous business is properly punished," Mundkur gave him his concluding advice, and asked him to be taken away.

It was past ten at night when the team assembled again. Mundkur wanted it that way. He thought that the best time to interrogate the kingpin, the star performer was the quiet hours of the night. When everyone was seated Surendra Mohan was shepherded in. Mundkur knew that they were now dealing with a trained spy who would be already armed with plausible stories and alibis, and undergone mock interrogations during his training. The better course, therefore, was to surprise him by mounting the attack from a totally unanticipated end and to corner him fast before he regained his composure. Mundkur did not ask Surendra Mohan to sit.

He began in a businesslike manner. "Khot, play the relevant portions of the tape," he asked. Khot complied. For more than fifteen minutes the tape was running with every one intently listening to the conversation that was being replayed. When it ended Mundkur looked straight at Singh and remarked, "I assume you have correctly realised that this was the conversation that took place between you and your friend Sukhdev when you were travelling in a taxi. It would be clear to anyone who listens to the tape that you were instructing your companion on how to use the miniature video camera to map the whole of the interior of the Air Force Missile Base where Sukhdev works, and how to bug the Commander's as well as the Adjutant's tables in the office so that you could record the proceedings sitting in your room." Observing the look of surprise on Surendra Mohan's face he said, "You are perhaps surprised as to how we got your conversation tape recorded. Well, I may tell you, you neatly fell in our trap. The taxi you hailed and later invited Sukhdev in belonged to us. It's fitted with all the gadgetry we need. Further, the taxi was driven by our man. Just look behind and you would recognise the man who chauffeured you that day. He will give evidence against you. That's not all. Sukhdev has made a clean breast of every thing." Singh did not dare look behind. His eyes wore a distant look.

"Now some more facts for your information. Your salary at the computer institute is Rs. 4000 a month and you pay Rs. 5000 as monthly rent for the flat you live in. Besides you have a very comfortable style of living. Sukhdev told us that you helped him with money from time to time, and of course you gave lavish dinners to him in expensive restaurants that even our people who watched you would bear testimony to. One more thing, you gave your employers a Varanasi address as your home address, where your parents are supposed to be living. We checked on that. A Bengali family lives in that house and they have never seen you or heard of you. Now, look at these photographs." Mundkur placed before Singh the photographs Khot had taken at Chowpatty.

"You got a gadget-filled bag from that person, the same bag with which you were caught in the taxi. You would, I am sure, not know the name of the man who gave the bag to you but I know. His name is Mustaq Mohammed. He is from Delhi and now cooling his heels in our lock-up. He has told us his part of the story which is very damaging for you."

Mundkur pushed one more photograph towards Singh. "Have a careful look at this photograph. You would readily recognise that it's your photograph with your pants down. Our hidden camera took this photograph this morning when you were in the toilet. What does it show?" Mundkur asked but without waiting for a reply from Singh answered the question himself. "The photograph clearly shows that you are circumcised. Since when have Hindus living in the holy city of Varanasi started circumcising themselves?"

Mundkur paused for a few moments for his devastating disclosures to sink in, and began, "Lastly, Mr. Surendra Mohan Singh or whatever you are, remember that the cardinal rule in the spy world in which you are so deeply involved is that a spy when caught is on his own. His masters deny any connection with him therefore their coming to his rescue is out of the question. Talking of you, it is in your interest to come clean. You are alone at this distant place and totally at our mercy. Even if we torture you to death none would come to save you. But we have yet another method. If you do not co-operate, we will hand you over to the Crime Branch. They will get every bit of juice out of you and then—I need not tell you all this in such detail—they have 'encounter' specialists who will take care of you. You get my point? Your masters sitting in the ISI headquarters in distant Islamabad would perhaps never come to know about your fate. Your family would be living in an illusion of its own. The punishment for espionage in our law is not that severe. Besides if you do not cause us any headache you can expect us to treat you well. We are not fiends. So make up your mind. Which option you choose is your privilege," Mundkur concluded.

Every one looked expectantly at Singh. He was trembling. Mundkur asked him to sit down. His sixth sense told him that his harangue had the right effect. After a silence of a minute or two Singh asked for a glass of water which was given to him. He drank it in big gulps, placed the glass on the table and began, "Sir, I want to tell you everything," he said looking up at Mundkur.

"Good, that's very sensible. But don't conceal anything otherwise we will get nasty. We are old hands at this game. Keep that in mind."

"No Sir, I will not conceal anything. I know the game is up for me, and none would help me. Only you can show me some mercy."

"Go on then."

"Sir, I come from Karachi. My real name is Shabeer Mohammed Sheikh. I belong to a Muhajir family. My father was killed in Shia-Sunni riots some years ago. We have a small house in Millatabad locality in Karachi. After the death of my father my mother did odd jobs to keep the family going and to educate us. I passed my High School Certificate examination and did a course in Computer Science in the hope that it would fetch me a good job. My mother borrowed heavily to pay for my fees. We were all greatly disappointed when I still could not get a job.

"One day when I returned home after a disappointing job interview, I saw Qureshi uncle sitting in our house talking to my mother. He is a Muhajir like us. He and my father were friends. He had joined the army where he became a Subedar Major. We knew that he later worked for the ISI. On retirement he came back to live in his ancestral house in our locality. Occasionally he used to drop in at our house to enquire after our welfare. That day also he had come on a similar visit.

"When I told my mother as to what had happened, Qureshi uncle told that if she had no objection he would try for a job for me. My mother was only too happy. I was also tired of job hunting. Therefore, when after a week or so Qureshi uncle brought the news that a job was available but it was a bit risky and would entail my remaining away from home for long stretches of time, I was overjoyed. The salary would be good, he assured us. My mother was a bit hesitant but I eagerly lapped it up. A few days later he called me to his house where a soldierly looking man interviewed me. At the end of the interview he asked Qureshi uncle to bring me along to Islamabad. As soon as he left Qureshi uncle congratulated me saying that I had been approved for the job. The following month we went to Islmabad. Qureshi uncle did the running about. Finally I was lodged in a room in a private house in Rawalpindi. The authorities there gave one thousand rupees to Qureshi uncle to be handed over to my mother. That pleased me. That was my first contribution to the family.

"It did not take me long to realize that I was actually recruited by the ISI, the outfit in which Qureshi uncle once worked. It was perhaps his job now to scout for new recruits like me. Anyway, my training started in right earnest from the next day. I was trained alone and in my room itself. Three or four instructors visited me every day. One of them was in charge of me. I was supposed to call him Ustad. None ever told me his name.

"To my great surprise, they started teaching me about India, its geography, its people, its culture and so on. What is more, every day I had two hours of lessons in Hindu religion. I was told the essentials of Hinduism, its symbols and deities, manner of worship and so on. I was also taught stories from Ramayana and Mahabharata. Most importantly, I was asked to live like a Hindu and forget my Islamic upbringing. I had to say Namaste to my teacher rather than Salam Walekum or Adab Arj. I was tested from time to time. After about three months I was taken to a Hindu temple in Lahore to observe the rituals and to actually go inside and worship. It was clear to me that they wanted me to masquerade as a Hindu.

"After a month or so when the basic lessons were over I was taught about army, navy and airforce, how to identify units, weapons, aircraft, ships etc. In about six months I was reasonably ready. My Ustad told me that I would have to go on a short familiarisation trip to India. I was taught my life story. I was supposed to be born in Varanasi. The task before me was to go to Varanasi, stay there in a hotel for a week, visit all places of worship in the neighbourhood and return. I was given enough money to look after myself. A week later we left for an unknown village along the Indo-Pakistan border. At night—it was the dark phase of moon—I was asked to accompany a stranger who would be my guide. I soon realised that he was a smuggler. After midnight we left the village on foot and reached a Ranger outpost. We waited there till the rangers gave us a go-ahead, that is, when the BSF patrol passed by and would not return for another hour or so. We walked in the dark and after quite a few hours of trudging reached a village on the Indian side. We stayed till dawn at the house of a friend of my guide. In the morning he put me on a bus that was bound for Ganga Nagar. From there I was supposed to catch a train. Eventually I reached Varanasi and completed my ordeal. I was extremely nervous but luckily none suspected me. I returned the same way.

"On returning to my room I was thoroughly questioned by every instructor. The next part of my training immediately commenced. After three months I was tested by an ISI Major who certified me to be fit for field duty. I was given a forged birth certificate, a forged SSC examination mark sheet and what is more, a forged Diploma certificate of NIIT. I was told that after going to India I should stay for a fortnight at Varanasi, go round and acquaint myself with customs of the people and social as well as political conditions and then move to Mumbai. I was to then try for a job in a computer-training institute that would afford me enough time to do my real work, that was to penetrate the Air Force Missile Base.

"When the day of departure arrived I was given a Pakistani passport on which the Nepali visa was already stamped, and a one-way ticket to Kathmandu. I was then taken to Lahore and placed in a Kathmandu bound PIA flight. I was asked to go to Crescent Travel Agency office on landing at Kathmandu and hand over my passport. The manager would thereafter make all arrangements for my reaching Varanasi. I thus landed at Varanasi one afternoon and eventually at Mumbai. It was not difficult for me to hire a flat in the locality where Air Force personnel lived. I was given enough money. I get a monthly allowance of Rs.5000, which is credited to my bank account. I also managed to get a job by bribing a job agent.

"In the beginning I sent by e-mail whatever little information I could gather by talking to airmen whom I met in the bazaar or in restaurants. Then I came across Sukhdev Prasad and cultivated him under the guidance of my headquarters. I eventually succeeded in making him a conscious agent, that is to say, he agreed to work to my bidding. That was a great success and I was congratulated by my controller. Yesterday when you caught us I was in the process of handing him a miniaturised video camera that is capable of taking clear pictures even in semi-darkness. I also gave him tiny microphone-cum-transmitters to stick to the underside of the tables of his bosses. They are very sensitive as well as powerful. Their signals would be auto recorded on a machine in my room. I received all this equipment in the bag that you saw the man handing over to me. I was given instructions to meet him but I really do not know him or wherefrom he came. Now it's up to you to show me mercy or hang me," Singh alias Shabeer Mohammed stopped. He looked completely exhausted.

"That's like a good boy. This should be enough for the first session. We will have several more chats. You are going to be our guest for quite few days. You look tired," Mundkur summed up. Turning to the people who had brought Singh in the room Mundkur said, "Take him away, and give him a cup of tea."

When Shabeer Mohammed left, Mundkur glanced around at his companions and said, "Well gentlemen, you heard a very interesting story. We were lucky in nipping a master spy in the bud. He would have done great damage to the Air Force. Thank you, we will meet again. I must now apprise the Air Force authorities."

Scientist in a Snare

MANJU MATHUR WAS A COMPULSIVE PARTY GOER. WHEN invited to a party the temptation to have a binge was so overpowering that she rarely gave a thought to the kind of people who were inviting her, once she was reasonably sure that she would have a great time with lots of people to frolic with and delicious food to savour. Thus it was not rare to see her, with husband in tow, circulating in parties thrown by people who were relative strangers to the Mathurs. She attributed her popularity to her sense of humour and affability. She was now over thirty but neither this circumstance nor the fact that her husband held a responsible position in a sensitive organisation could dampen her reckless enthusiasm in the least. Thus her husband, Dr. Maneesh Mathur found himself rubbing shoulders with businessmen, film producers and people of that ilk on many an evening. He hated it with all his might but nevertheless dutifully followed his wife whenever she announced that they had an invitation to a party. This was partly to keep peace with his volatile spouse and partly to shield her from prowling vulturine freebooters of whom there was no dearth at those jamborees.

Dr. Maneesh Mathur and his wife were studies in contrast. Manju was vivacious from childhood and distinctly inclined to be gregarious, a trend her liberal parents did not try to bridle. Maneesh on the other hand was shy and retiring. Brought up under the tutelage of a scholarly father who taught Mathematics at the Allahabad University, and a devout if somewhat conservative mother he soon established himself as a brilliant student at the university. After obtaining a first class Master's degree in Nuclear Physics Maneesh joined the Tata Institute of Fundamental Research at Mumbai and obtained a Doctorate within a short span of two years. The Bhabha Atomic Research Centre beckoned him and he joined it as a scientific officer to be soon placed in the section that conducted research concerning nuclear reactor fuel. Manju and he were married soon thereafter.

Once the euphoria of the recently solemnised marriage was over and Maneesh became preoccupied with his research work, Manju realised how lonely and out of place she was in the new surroundings, though Mumbai was far more glamorous than Allahabad where she had grown up. She missed her convivial friends and the outings with them that had become an inseparable concomitant of her young life. Disagreements and arguments between the young couple became increasingly acute. Finally, Maneesh decided to let her have her way to buy his peace, which he desperately needed to concentrate on his research job. But this had a wholly unexpected tortuous fallout for him. As Manju widened her friend circle, invitations to parties and dinners increased. Inevitably he had to attend if only to accompany her. He stoically accepted the new realities as part of the peace bargain.

That is how one Friday evening he found himself in the seventh floor spacious apartment of Mr. Hasmukhbhai Shah, that overlooked the Arabian Sea across Warden road. It was not a big party; just four couples besides the hosts, and of course a somewhat paunchy middle-aged man whom Hasmukhbhai introduced as a businessman friend of his from South Africa who was on a brief visit to Mumbai. Maneesh hardly knew Hasmukhbhai. In fact they were strangers to each other until that evening. It was Manju who had become friendly of late with Rashmi, the young and somewhat debonair second wife of Hasmukhbhai. Their getting to know each other had a rather bizarre beginning.

About a month ago Manju had been to Dr. Toddywalla's dental clinic one afternoon for root canal treatment of one of her molars that had been giving her trouble. While waiting for her turn she got talking to the young lady sitting next to her who had also come for a similar treatment. Outgoing by nature, Manju introduced herself and whiled away her time till called in, making small talk with her neighbour whose name she elicited, was Rashmi Shah. It so happened that they got their subsequent appointments on the same days. Their acquaintance thus grew into greater familiarity as they both were effervescent and fun-loving. Rashmi invited Manju to her apartment one afternoon after they had their sittings with Dr. Toddywalla. Manju was thoroughly impressed by the rich interior décor and the several objets d'art that adorned the shelves, and the paintings that ornamented the walls. A week later there was a phone call from Rashmi inviting Manju and her husband to a small party she was throwing the following Friday. Rashmi was very persuasive which she need not have been. Manju was very keen to get to know Rashmi's husband and get introduced in their circle of friends.

Rashmi's husband was a bit of a disappointment. He was far older than she had imagined, pot-bellied and pock-marked. Worse still, his small beady eyes exuded a viciousness that was not easy to ignore. By any reckoning he was not the social bird that Manju had imagined him to be from the look of his house and his charming wife. Except Dr. Toddywalla and his doctor wife, she did not find any one interesting enough to get friendly with. Maneesh suffered them all stoically with the detachment of a saint. Hasmukhbhai's interests were limited to business and politics which neither Manju nor Maneesh found engrossing. The African friend of Hasmukhbhai who appeared to be of Gujarati origin, concentrated on imbibing whisky and soda, only intermittently breaking the ritual to make some brief remarks to his host which no one else comprehended.

Maneesh was greatly relieved when it was time to take leave. The other couples left in quick succession. Maneesh was making every effort to catch the eye of his wife, who was animatedly talking to the hostess, so that he could signal her to rise but did not succeed. Finally, only the Mathurs and the African visitor were left. Getting impatient Maneesh mustered up enough courage to stand up to thank the hostess and seek permission to leave, hoping that his wife would take the hint and quickly join him. But before he could utter the mentally much-rehearsed adieu, the African friend who was snoozing in the couch having snorted several pegs of the brew, stirred to announce his desire to leave for his hotel. Seeing his physical condition Rashmi suggested spontaneously to her husband,

"Why don't you drop him at his hotel instead of sending him by a taxi at this late hour all the way to Juhu?"

"I don't mind," said Hasmukhbhai. "But I don't suppose I could manage the car as well as him on my own. He may not remain steady on the seat." It was now Manju's turn to play the Good Samaritan.

"Why, my husband would accompany you. I am sure you wouldn't take more than an hour to return. I will spend that time chatting with Rashmi," she spontaneously volunteered on behalf of her husband. Before Maneesh could think of a plausible excuse to wriggle out, Rashmi butted in, "That's an excellent idea. Dr. Mathur, don't worry about Manju. We have lots of things to talk about. I was so busy all this time, couldn't even exchange greetings properly."

Maneesh had no choice now but to accompany them. Shah went to his bedroom and returned in a minute. Perhaps to fetch the car keys, Maneesh thought. Both helped the African visitor down to Shah's car. Finding his guest getting a bit garrulous, Shah suggested to Maneesh, "Why don't you drive the car? I would sit on the rear seat along with this gentleman to keep him under control."

"As you wish," Maneesh acquiesced.

The African became animated and wordy. Soon an argument ensued between the two. Maneesh was not able to follow the language they were using and did not care. He wanted to get it over with as quickly as possible and therefore, drove fast occasionally throwing a glance at the rear seat occupants via the rearview mirror. They had hardly crossed Bandra when Maneesh heard a loud report from the rear and a shriek. He looked at the rearview mirror to see what was happening behind. To his horror, he saw the African slumping in the seat and Shah pointing a revolver at him, ready to shoot again. There was blood all over their clothes. Maneesh slammed the brakes involuntarily, nervously asking at the same time, "What's happening?"

"Shut up and continue driving," Shah commanded, pointing the revolver now at him. He was a transformed man, Dr. Jeckyll giving way to Mr. Hyde, as it were. Maneesh complied though he was shaking with fright. A little while later Shah ordered Maneesh to take the car to Ghodbunder Creek. Shah spat directions in short gusts whenever he found Maneesh unsure of the road to Ghodbunder. When they reached a secluded spot where the creek ran close to the road Shah growled, "Stop, stop, take the car to the extreme left and stop under the big tree in front." As the car stopped he came out of the car and said, "Now Mister, help me extricate the body from the car. It's damn limp." Maneesh was taken aback.

"Why not leave me out, Mr. Shah?" he stuttered, hesitatingly.

"Why, do you want to meet the same fate?" Shah snarled menacingly. Maneesh thereafter followed all the instructions that Shah spewed in quick succession, in a daze. They carried the body to the creek. Shah emptied the pockets of the dead man's slacks and bush shirt of all their contents that included his wallet and passport. "Luckily the bugger was travelling on a fake Nigerian passport, that too in a different name. The hotel entries won't help anyone trace him back to his native place. Then, this place is outside Mumbai limits," Shah remarked, softening his voice for the first time. Shah had shot the man through the jaw, which had disfigured his face beyond recognition.

They dumped the body into the waters of the creek. Luckily for them it was low tide. That ensured that the dead body would be sucked into the sea, before it was thrown out much later. Shah took off his blood stained bush shirt, washed it in the creek water, and put it on again. Then started their return journey. There was barely any conversation except to seek or give directions for the correct road to be selected. As the car hit Warden road Shah snarled under his breath, glaring at Maneesh, "Look Mister. Let me make it clear to you. You saw the murder didn't you?" Maneesh did not respond. "You were a witness to it—in fact the only witness. Am I right?" This time Maneesh nodded. "You helped me dump the body into the creek."

"But did I have a choice?" Maneesh protested.

"Shut up," Shah growled angrily, "I am narrating the facts." Maneesh kept quiet, not wanting to annoy the brute any further. "If you sing to the police or anyone else my life would be in jeopardy. Don't harbour the idea that I would let you have that control over me?" Maneesh was frightened. Fearing that it was now his turn to receive a bullet in his skull, he pleaded for mercy.

"Mr. Shah, believe me, I will never utter a word to any one, not even to my wife. It's a nightmare I would like to forget at once," he bleated. Shah was unrelenting in his offensive.

"You have seen what happens to a man who argues with me. My men are all over the place. They are equally ruthless. On the slightest hint of your having betrayed me I will see to it that you don't live to breathe another day," he threatened.

"Believe me Mr. Shah, I will not open my mouth," Maneesh folded his hands in submission, not caring if the car swerved to the side. Shah did not reply. Maneesh became disturbingly aware that Shah had now obtained control over his life.

As they entered the compound of Shah's apartment house, he muttered in the same stern tone, "Park the car near the right wall. Lock it and hand over the key to me, then move over to your car and wait there. I will send your wife down. You need not come up." Maneesh was terribly worried about his wife but he dared not argue. He meekly followed Shah's directions.

Rashmi opened the door in response to the insistent rings of the bell. It was nearly three in the morning. Both the women had talked and talked till they could not resist the onslaught of slumber and dozed off in the coach where they were lounging. "Got so late! We were worried if there was an accident or something," she remarked inquisitively. Ignoring her probing observation he said brusquely, "Send that woman down. Her husband is waiting near the car." Pushing her aside, he hurried to the bedroom and closed the door behind him. Manju had also woken up to the sound of the bell, and was now sitting in the coach sleepily looking at the couple, not comprehending what was happening. Rashmi, knowing as she did the ways of her husband, calmly explained to her that Maneesh was expecting her downstairs.

Manju saw Maneesh standing near the car, his face ashen with fear. "What's the matter Maneesh? Mr. Shah was also very tense. Why were you so late? Met with an accident, or got into some other trouble?" She fired a volley of questions as she opened the door and climbed into the passenger seat. Maneesh started the car and took off ignoring her questions. "What's the matter? Why don't you answer my questions?" Manju persisted, intrigued.

"Don't ask any questions. Let's get out of this place first," Maneesh said briefly as he pulled the car out of the gate and headed home.

Maneesh drove silently, though somewhat unsteadily. He did not utter a word till they reached home. The sullen look on his face worried Manju. Maneesh was a transmuted man, she could sense that. Usually calm and composed, and sure of himself he was now jittery. In the privacy of her bedroom she, persisted with her questions, albeit gently to get him to speak out on what troubled him so much. Ultimately he spoke. Though he had promised Shah not to divulge what had happened even to his wife he had to unburden himself if only to reduce the tension that had built inside him. Briefly he narrated the grisly tale to her and how Shah had trapped him. Manju was remorseful. She was conscious that Maneesh had got into this predicament entirely because of her indiscretion, though he was too much of a gentle soul to rub it in. She decided to stand by her husband and help him, though she did not have the foggiest idea how she could do it.

Two days later Maneesh nervously read a small item in the newspaper that said that a dead body had been washed ashore in the Ghodbunder creek. It was obviously a case of homicide as, the body bore a bullet wound but police investigation was hampered because it had not been identified. Thane police were investigating the case.

A few days later, when Maneesh's mind had considerably eased and he was able to focus on his work, his telephone rang late in the evening. It was Hasmukhbhai Shah. His voice bore traces of the same viciousness which Maneesh had noticed after the murder. His face fell, much to the chagrin of Manju who was watching him. Shah told him that the body had not been identified till then. "I read it in the newspapers," Maneesh blurted.

"That's an old story. I am telling you the latest," Shah scowled. "And listen. This means that the police would not be able to fix the identity unless you gave them the clue."

"I promised you that I would not do any such thing," Maneesh said docilely.

"I can't be very sure," Shah sneered, and then added, "Listen, tomorrow is Sunday, a holiday for you. We are meeting at eleven o'clock in the morning at the Delight restaurant in Bandra. So be there on time."

"What is it for?" Maneesh asked.

"Don't bother about it right now. You will come to know tomorrow. Don't try to avoid," Shah hung up, giving no opportunity to Maneesh to quiz him further.

The next morning Maneesh dutifully presented himself at the Delight restaurant at the appointed time. Shah was already sitting at a corner table. With him was another person, much younger and better dressed. When Maneesh joined them Shah introduced the other person as his business partner. Maneesh was at a loss as to what it was all going to lead up to, when the other person spoke, "My name is Sadiq Seth. I'll be frank with you. You are a highly educated person, and would understand what we are into. Mr. Shah, as perhaps you know, runs a chemical factory in Saki Naka industrial area. He also manufactures Mandrex tablets as a side product. We are his sole customers. We smuggle them to South Africa, which provides us with a very profitable and lucrative market. I control this part of the operation on behalf of Aneesbhai, who is the chief. The gentleman whose dead body you drove the other day and later dumped into the Ghodbunder creek was our agent in South Africa..." At that juncture Manoj made a bid to interject, wanting to correct the statement but Sadiq stopped him with a firm wave of his hand. "So, what I was saying was that that gentleman tried to be smart, in fact he duped us by spiriting away a consignment saying that it was lost in transit. But we have our ways of finding out the truth. He was called here to explain. My position as guarantor was clear. Either he pays for it or Hamuksbhai does not get any payment from me. In our trade loyalty counts, and the participants have only two choices, either they go along faithfully or get a bullet into their nut. In this case the issue is settled now, so let's not talk any more about it." He concluded his long exposition on seeing the waiter approach them for an order. He also took the initiative, perhaps to impress upon Maneesh that he was the boss, and ordered cutlets and coffee without so much as seeking the preferences of his companions.

Maneesh was perspiring profusely under his shirt and was very close to a nervous breakdown. He was totally flabbergasted and at a loss how to react, because he just couldn't understand how they intended to fit him in their sordid affair. He knew, however, that he could not rebel and ask them to go to hell. He was dealing with a bunch of ruthless racketeers for whom murder was perhaps a matter of routine. The fear of meeting the African's fate made him tongue-tied. He chose to sit meekly, looking down at the tabletop, trying to steel his nerves to face whatever lay ahead.

"You don't have to get so worried Dr. Maneesh Mathur. We are not going to eat you up for no reason. I just gave you our background because we want to be friends, that's all," Sadiq said. His tone was now gentle though the viciousness in his eyes had not diminished.

"No not that," Maneesh said tamely. "I am really not able to understand what you intend doing with me. I only tried to be helpful to Mr. Shah that night, and have promised him again and again that for me it's a closed chapter. I have sealed my lips. What more do you want of me?"

"Ah, don't get so worried my friend. We trust you, both Mr. Shah and me. Isn't that so, Hasmukhbhai?" Sadiq asked turning to Shah. Shah nodded mechanically.

"If that's so why have you called me?" Maneesh asked, emboldened by the assurance.

"Oh, didn't I tell you, I wanted to meet you and become your friend? In fact I wanted to thank you for helping Hasmukhbhai clear that mess," Sadiq said sharply.

The cutlets and coffee arrived. Maneesh gulped the cutlets and drained the coffee down his throat, as if he had not eaten for days though he had no appetite. He hated every moment that he had to spend in their despicable company. Luckily for him the moment he finished Sadiq said to him, "Dr. Mathur you may leave if you have other commitments but remember what I said. For our part we would like to stay on for a while to discuss business matters." Taking the cue, Maneesh rose in his seat and murmuring something inanely by way of excuse and thanking them for the hospitality, made himself scarce.

Two months later, when Maneesh had started feeling certain that the Shah—Sadiq experience was behind him, and that he was perhaps too harsh in his judgement of Sadiq, he received a telephonic call late in the evening. "Hello, Dr. Mathur, how are you?" It was Sadiq.

"I am fine. Thank you," he replied softly. A pall of gloom descended on him.

"It's a long time since we met last. Please come over to New Oberoi Hotel tomorrow at ten-thirty in the morning. I shall be waiting for you in the lobby. For you to readily recognise me I may tell you that I shall be wearing a steel gray safari suit. As for me, I will have no difficulty placing you though we have met only once. I have your photograph taken on the occasion of our last meeting, in fact yours and mine together. I always carry a camera in my handbag on such occasions, you know. Shah took it for me when he briefly went to the toilet," Sadiq said with an audible chuckle, leaving him with no choice to decline.

"Okay," he said feebly, and hung up.

As Maneesh climbed the portal of the New Oberoi Hotel the next day exactly at eleven o'clock, he saw Sadiq sitting at a distance in the lobby. He was obviously eyeing the entrance because he spotted Maneesh the same instant and stood up to beckon Maneesh by a gesture of his hand. Maneesh timorously approached Sadiq and sat down on a chair opposite him. Sadiq was, however, all smiles. He made polite enquiries about the well being of Maneesh and his family, and pointing to a young man in a lounge suit sitting by his side, said in a hearty voice, "Mr., I mean Dr. Maneesh Mathur, meet my good friend Dr. Mirza. He has just landed from Dubai and is very keen to meet you." The suave looking man made a gesture of half-rising in his seat and extended his hand to grasp Maneesh's limp one.

"How do you do, Dr. Mathur? Sadiq was all praise for you, so I said, I must meet you during my current visit to Mumbai," said Mirza, with gusto. As Maneesh was trying to collect his wits while mumbling a reply, Sadiq proposed, "Why don't we move over to the restaurant in front? That's a better place to talk, I suppose." As if to show the way, he got up and started moving towards the restaurant door—the others followed in silence.

When they settled down at a secluded table Sadiq impatiently summoned the waiter and placed order for chicken sandwiches and coffee. He did not believe in the niceties of consulting his companions about their preferences, or perhaps this was his way of showing Maneesh that he always called the shots. Having disposed of the waiter Sadiq opened the conversation again, "Dr. Mirza is a renowned scientist like you, Dr. Mathur, therefore, I thought you would also like to meet him and exchange views. I am no match for people like you when it comes to matters scientific."

"Where do you work, Dr. Mirza?" Maneesh had by now mustered enough courage to formulate a cogent question.

"Oh, I work in Dubai. We have a small lab, small but well equipped I may say, where we conduct research on application of nuclear technology, especially in the field of food preservation. I know you people are quite advanced in that field." Maneesh nodded. The waiter deposited the sandwiches and coffee in front of them and withdrew.

"Are you working in the same field?" Mirza asked Maneesh.

"Not really. I work on the nuclear reactor at the moment, but some time ago I did work there. Yes," Maneesh said, and then repented his indiscretion.

"That's lovely, I can learn a lot from you, I am sure," Mirza said enthusiastically.

"Err, yes. We can exchange views. Mine would be outdated though. Unfortunately they don't allow any outsiders to visit our establishments unless cleared at the highest level," Maneesh said apologetically.

"I understand. I understand Dr. Mathur. That's everywhere. But we can always talk, if you do not mind, that is."

"Of course, one can always talk though I wonder what use it would be to you. You people must be quite advanced in the technique. It is of so much relevance to you in your hot country," Mathur said tentatively.

"Well, its relevance to us is undisputed, but to say that we were advanced would be an exaggeration."

The two talked for a while, dodging and sidestepping pointed questions from either side, while helping themselves to sandwiches and coffee. Maneesh was now less apprehensive and talked with greater ease. Sadiq finished his coffee hurriedly and said, "Well, I must get going now. I have an appointment to keep. As it is, I am of a different grain. Don't much understand what you are talking about. My main job was to introduce you two, and that I have done." He rose in his seat, placed a hand on the shoulder of Maneesh and said almost in a whisper, "I am sure, you two would be good friends, but don't forget the old ones. I shall be in touch." Turning to Dr. Mirza he said, "I am sure, you will take care of the bill. Don't let Dr. Mathur pay. I will be offended."

"Don't you worry on that count. Dr. Mathur is our guest. Goodbye," he shook hands with Sadiq. Maneesh followed him reluctantly and shook Sadiq's hand.

When he had left Mirza took out a small box from the portfolio he was carrying with him, and pushing it towards Maneesh, said, "This is a small gift from a budding friend. I am sure, you would not mind accepting it. There's a Cross pen set for you. What can one offer to a scientist but some writing material?" he said with a chuckle. "There is a pair of ear rings, amethyst set in silver for Madam. We get very good amethyst in Dubai. And of course there are Swiss chocolates for the little prince. I am told you have a sweet five-year old who wants to follow in the footsteps of his illustrious father." Maneesh was amazed to learn how much Mirza already knew about his family.

"No, no Dr. Mirza, I can't accept them. They are too expensive," he protested, embarrassed.

"There you are wrong, Dr. Mathur. You have no idea how cheap things are in Dubai when compared with outside. They say, if you want to purchase Swiss chocolates, purchase them in Dubai. They are a lot cheaper than in Switzerland. And secondly, we have a tradition in Dubai that I must not violate. Whenever we go out, we must carry presents for the people we meet. I have brought several other gifts for my friends and acquaintances here. You are not the only one. Please have it. I shall be extremely pleased."

By now Maneesh's defences were down. He quietly accepted the gift packet wondering how he was going to explain it to his wife.

Dr. Mirza paid the bill and both left the restaurant together. Mirza took leave of Maneesh on the plea that he had to go to the toilet but not before extracting a promise from Maneesh to meet him again when he visited Mumbai next. For good measure he obtained from Maneesh his cell phone number, so that he would not have to bother others for getting in touch with him.

Fifteen days passed without Sadiq or Mirza contacting him. This was long enough for Maneesh to rationalise and salve his conscience, as it were. He was now less afraid of Sadiq though he was well aware how ruthless and deadly he could get, and that he could annoy him only to his peril. It was the entry of Mirza and the presents he brought that seemed to change the complexion of the relationship. Not that Maneesh was hankering for the gifts or that he felt overly happy, receiving them from a stranger, but they helped to highlight the human side of the emerging relationship, or so he reasoned. He was now considerably at ease, in fact implicitly looking forward to his next meeting with Mirza to which he had already consented.

It was Saturday night. Maneesh had had his dinner and was lounging around in his sitting room, talking to his son Ashish whenever the child was sufficiently distracted from the cartoon serial he was intently watching on the television.

All of a sudden, the mobile phone chirped. It was Sadiq at the other end. "How are you Dr. Mathur?" he enquired, to begin the conversation.

"Fine. Thank you," Mathur replied feebly. He was still very apprehensive about Sadiq's designs on him. He also realised that Mirza was hand-in-glove with Sadiq, for he had given his cell phone number only to Mirza.

"You remember that African fellow? Well, his relatives are creating problems. They have petitioned their government saying that he often visited India and therefore, the Indian government may be moved to make serious enquiries about his whereabouts. Being of Gujarati origin, he also has some relatives in Mumbai. They may also get active. But don't get overly worried. So long as you continue to be our friend we will guard your interests."

"Thank you very much indeed," Maneesh heard himself say. This was surrender, he realised but the news had given him a rude shock and rekindled unpleasant memories of that night. He was already sweating profusely and his hand that held the tiny phone was shaking involuntarily.

"I thought, I must let you know. Good night," Sadiq disconnected abruptly.

Maneesh sat down in a sofa, stunned by the message that Sadiq had just conveyed to him. He was again made acutely conscious that his freedom, in fact his life was now at the mercy of these desperadoes. He continued to sit there, lost in his gloomy thoughts unmindful of the occasional questions his son asked. Luckily for him his wife did not make appearance in the room, otherwise his crestfallen countenance would not have escaped her attention.

Fifteen minutes or so had passed when the mobile phone rang again. Maneesh switched it on nervously and said tamely, "Hello, Mathur here."

"Hi, Dr. Mathur. How are you? Glad to hear your voice again. I am Mirza," the other voice said volubly.

"How are you, Dr. Mirza?" Maneesh responded with some enthusiasm.

"I have come down to Mumbai. A business trip, you may call it. Remember your promise? Well, let's meet tomorrow.

It's a Sunday, so I am sure you can spare some time. Will lunch or dinner suit you? I should be only too happy if you could make it."

"You see Dr. Mirza, I too would have been happy to join you for a meal but it so happens that some relatives of my wife's are coming to us for lunch and then in the evening I have promised my son to take him to a puppet show."

"I quite understand. A family man has his engagements especially on holidays. Then let us meet over a cup of tea, at eleven in the morning, same hotel, Old Wing this time. I am sure, you are not going to say no," Mirza insisted.

Sadiq had already made Maneesh malleable. He could not put up more resistance.

"All right," he said lamely.

"That's decided then. Lobby of Old Oberoi. Thank you and good night, Dr. Mathur," Mirza hung up.

Despite his wife's protests Maneesh left for the hotel on time promising her to return well before the guests arrived. Maneesh was hugely relieved to see that Mirza was alone, and Sadiq the very sight of whom he abhorred, was nowhere near. Mirza greeted him ebulliently and led him to one of the hotel's exclusive restaurants. Unlike Sadiq, Dr. Mirza showed the courtesy of asking Maneesh as to what he would like to have, but forced upon him several varieties of pastry, despite his protests. Mirza started the preliminaries with the humid weather that Mumbai was having those days and cleverly manipulated the conversation to Maneesh's job in the BARC. The absence of Sadiq and a scientist like himself for company impelled Maneesh to be more relaxed and open. He, however, wondered why Mirza was so interested in the actual job he was doing, rather than irradiation of food products, which was Mirza's primary concern. He did not have to wait long to unravel the mystery.

When they were halfway through downing the assorted pastries and tea Mirza suddenly asked "How did the little prince like the chocolates?"

"Oh, he devoured them," Maneesh said, brightening up.

"I am sure, he did. They are so tempting even I can't resist them," Mirza certified.

"Must be. He did not give a bite even to his Mummy by way of taste," Maneesh added. "Here are some more for him," said Mirza, pushing a box of chocolates towards him and before Maneesh could say something in protest he asked, "What's his name, by the way?"

"Ashish, Ashish is his name," Maneesh replied.

"Ah, Ashish. What does it mean?"

"Ashish means blessings," Maneesh supplied the meaning. "Wonderful. That's a lovely name. A true blessing of God, a son is. Isn't that so Dr. Mathur?" Mirza asked.

"In a way yes," Maneesh replied tentatively. He wondered if Mirza was going to ask him about the gifts he had brought last time for him and his wife, but he didn't.

After gulping a mouthful of tea Mirza spoke again. He said solemnly, "You see, Dr. Mathur. We have met only twice but I have started liking you immensely, not only as a scientist of high calibre but as a human being too, which I value more. Possibly providence willed that we meet, otherwise in normal circumstances it is unthinkable that we would ever run into each other."

"True, very true," Maneesh interjected, not comprehending what was to follow.

"I will be very frank with you. I believe that it's only on the foundation of honesty and truth that enduring friendships are built. And I mean to build such a friendship with you."

"I am with you."

Mirza looked at him with a hint of a smile, which puzzled Maneesh.

"I will tell you how I came to know about you and why I have come all the way here to meet you. I am indeed a scientist as you would have by now affirmed, but I am not from Dubai though I often go to Dubai, because we have a consultative contract for the irradiation facility they are building. I belong to Pakistan Atomic Energy Commission, now on loan to another department, the ISI, but I continue to be associated with the project because I have been in it since the beginning. Our department people often meet Anees who is the boss of Sadiq whom you have already met. We need not go into the reasons. It is actually Anees who is financing the setting up of the facility I just mentioned to you. Naturally therefore, I also meet him whenever he wants to get a feedback from us. During one such meeting he mentioned to me that an Indian nuclear scientist like me had become a thorn in their side, and they were thinking of eliminating him." On hearing this Maneesh was so shaken that the fork with which he was eating the pastry slipped from his hand.

"Now don't get overly worried. Call me Good Samaritan or whatever you like, but as a scientist I thought that nothing could be more calamitous than bumping off a scientist for reasons that had nothing to do with his vocation. I, therefore, pleaded with Anees to introduce me to the scientist, that is you, and leave it to me to ensure that you bring no harm to his men. His point was that he did not want to spend energies of his men reminding you every now and then to remain quiet, so the easy way out was to bump you off." Mirza stopped his narration perhaps to gauge the effect his disclosure was having on Maneesh. Maneesh was of course perspiring profusely. He had no interest left in eating what was in the plate before him. Mirza liked what he saw. His desire was to make him so pliable that he ate out of his hand.

"But I have promised them time and again that I would never utter a word to anyone and I have so far kept my word. That should convince them of my sincerity and dependability," Maneesh bleated sheepishly.

"I know, you would keep your word, but who can convince these gangsters? Yes, gangsters, for, that is what they are in reality. But don't you worry about it. It is now my word. I am your guarantor. That's the only thing they understand. They want someone else to stand surety so that they can wring his neck. It's now my neck that is at stake."

"Why did you have to do that for a stranger, that too a foreigner—and an Indian to boot?" Maneesh asked innocently.

"My dear Sir. It's not a question of you being a stranger or an Indian. It's a question of a scientist keeping the honour of another scientist."

"Thank you, thank you indeed," Maneesh said, expressing his gratitude.

"But Dr. Mathur, the question that exasperated Anees still remains. How do I remain in touch with you, especially because I cannot frequently come to your country. I have made these two trips at considerable risk to myself. This obviously cannot go on," Mirza said with great vehemence.

"That's true. What do you propose then? We can perhaps correspond and remain in touch so that you feel reassured," Maneesh made a simple suggestion.

"No Dr. Mathur. Let us be practical about it. You are well aware that I cannot come to India under normal circumstances. Human nature, being what it is, one does not know what pressures and considerations would weigh with you in the future. You would perhaps escape though I am not so sure about that, knowing as I do the capabilities of Anees inside India, but I surely will have to pay with my life being your guarantor."

"What are you driving at? I am really not able to follow."

"Simple enough. It is what we may call, transference of the hook, the accountability. Hereafter, Dr. Mathur you shall be accountable to me instead of Sadiq and his band of desperadoes. I am sure, you would like to deal with me rather than those shady characters."

"Without doubt."

"I am glad to hear that. But then I must have my pound of flesh for sticking out my neck and taking so much risk on your account."

"What do you mean?"

"It's a straightforward proposition. Dr. Mathur, you give me access to whatever you are doing at the BARC. In fact my bargain is for whatever is happening in the whole department in which you are working. I quite realise that because of restrictive security you might not be able to obtain anything from other departments in your outfit so, for the present we will forget about those departments," Mirza said with a flourish of generosity.

That was a bolt from the blue. Maneesh had been completely taken in by the smooth talk of Mirza, whom he had started regarding as a high-minded scientist motivated by sheer sympathy for a fellow scientist.

"You mean Dr. Mirza, I make you accessory to all the secrets that I do not even discuss with my colleagues? If I am caught I will lose my neck," Maneesh said agitatedly. He was shocked beyond measure by the nature of the demand.

"No, you don't lose your neck for that Dr. Mathur, but you surely would if left at the mercy of those gangsters," said Mirza coolly. "I will tell you how you will never be caught. Simply disclose your password to me, and leave the rest to me. Later on your endeavour should be to obtain the passwords of your colleagues. You don't copy anything. You don't carry anything outside the security gates. You don't stick your neck out. Therefore, there would be no question of your neck getting stuck anywhere. You follow me?"

Mathur clutched his head in both hands. He was totally confounded. An uneasy silence fell between the two. Mirza was not the one who would hasten matters and spoil the game. He was experienced enough to know that it took time for such propositions to sink in, and therefore, the target must be given time to think and rationalise, to conceptualise his defences and work out his probable gains and risks. He coolly beckoned the waiter and asked him to fetch the bill. When the waiter disappeared, Mirza gently addressed Maneesh who was still sitting silently as if in a trance. "Dr. Mathur, I can well imagine what is passing through your mind. But weigh my harmless suggestion against the risk you are presently facing, and then come to a conclusion. And yes, I forgot to mention a very important point. You are not going to do all this gratis, otherwise that would amount to my blackmailing you. We shall pay you generously. If you let me have your bank account either in this place or your native Allahabad, I shall ensure that money is deposited in your account from time to time depending upon the value of the information I am able to cull out from your network." In reply Maneesh simply gave him a blank look.

"I will give you some time to mull over the proposition and give me your decision. I will not be able to come here again. Sadiq who is getting impatient to know the decision one way or the other, will contact you after seven days. Please simply tell him if you have decided to be friends with me. He will not pester you with more questions. Should you decide to follow my suggestion, I will find a way of working out the modalities of taking the follow-up action. In fact, I should be grateful if you would write down your personal e-mail address for me on this paper," Mirza produced a small piece of paper and a pen from his pocket and placed them before Maneesh.

Maneesh picked up the pen as if in a daze and wrote the address but gave no verbal response. Mirza paid the bill and stood up. "Shall we leave now?" He asked Maneesh.

"Yes," Maneesh mumbled faintly and got up.

Both came out of the restaurant together but without exchanging a word. When they reached the lobby Mirza extended his hand and said, "Shall we say Khuda Hafeez for the present? Insha Allah, we will have a fruitful relationship." Maneesh shook his hand limply and giving him an inane smile rushed towards the parking lot. He wanted to get away from Mirza as fast as he could.

When he reached home around one o'clock the guests were already there. His wife, Manju was anxiously awaiting his arrival. She became worried when she saw the leaden expression on his face and noticed the nervousness in his gait. Forcing a smile at his guests and muttering some unintelligible excuses for being late, he rushed to the bedroom. He very much wanted to lock himself inside and give vent to the tumult and agony that had built within him. The thought of ending life as a sure way of escaping from the unbearable, heartrending distress crossed his mind more than once. Perhaps sensing his mood Manju closely followed him giving him no chance to lock the door from inside. Instead of wanting to know what had delayed him so much, she spoke to him in a gentle voice asking him if he needed anything to freshen up. She waited for him to get ready and brought him out to be with the guests. During the lunch Maneesh tried to act a good host but did not much succeed.

As soon as the guests departed Maneesh went to the bedroom. Manju followed him after dispatching Ashish to the neighbour's house to play with their children. She saw Maneesh sitting on the bed clutching his head with both hands, a sight she was getting used to of late. She asked him what the matter was, and tried to pull his hands away. Instead of telling her anything he started crying like a child. She let him cry for a while and then gently persuaded him to calm himself and face whatever fate had ordained with grit and fortitude. Her words of courage had their effect on him. He composed himself and told her all that had passed between him and the wily Dr. Mirza.

"So, what do you propose to do now?" she asked. "You have a week to decide but I think you must make up your mind right now. Miracles are not likely to happen in seven days that would salvage the situation for us."

"You are right Manju. I have to choose between the devil and the deep sea, and might as well do it right now. There is, however, one more alternative, an escape I might say, that I have been pondering over for some time," he said glumly.

"No Maneesh, never ever think on those lines. Think of what will happen to Ashish. His future is in your hands," said Manju, sensing what he had in mind. "We must face the situation boldly."

"Very well said, but what is the choice before me? Succumb to that rascal Mirza's wicked proposal and betray the trust reposed in me, and be called a traitor by the whole country. No, I can't do that. My parents will be ashamed of me. Even Ashish when he grows up will loathe calling me father. The alternative is to put my neck on that gangster Sadiq's guillotine and let him chop it. Even then people will say all sorts of nasty things about me. In either case, what will happen to you people?"

"Maneesh, I have a feeling that there is a third alternative and that alternative isn't the same you mentioned a little while ago," Manju said gravely. "Why don't we explore it?"

"What's it you are talking about?" Maneesh asked, not comprehending what she was hinting at but with hope and curiosity in his eyes.

"Do you recall, when we joined here you had a long session with the security chief? He had alerted you against the various pitfalls that you were likely to encounter, and advised you to first come to him and make a clean breast of everything the moment you thought you had done something indiscreet, or if someone had approached you with an unholy proposition, rather than put it under wraps and later come to grief when eventually exposed. You came home and told me all that because he had said that even the wives had to be careful, because an approach can be made through them too."

"Yes, yes, I remember," Maneesh said with a distant look in his eyes. He was recalling his first interview with the security chief. "What do you propose we do now?"

"Simple enough, follow his advice. We go to Mr. Ravindran tomorrow and tell him everything. Surely, he will be able to think of something that would protect you from the harm they are threatening to do."

"No, that would be risky. Suppose he does not believe me and instead suspects that I had already compromised the department's secrets. These police chaps are very suspicious by nature. I will be then in deep trouble without having done anything of the sort. Besides, Sadiq's threat would still be looming large over my head. Will he be able to save me from those scoundrels?" Maneesh protested.

"Don't be unreasonable Maneesh. Mr. Ravindran is known to be a very responsible and professional man. He will never do anything so rash. He has close contacts with the police. He may, for all I know, arrange police protection for you. Whatever it is, that misery would be much less than what you are suffering right now. Besides, you won't be alone when facing the gangsters, I am sure of that."

"Are you indeed?"

"Yes, I am."

"Okay then. As you say. I will contact Mr. Ravindran tomorrow," Maneesh acquiesced.

"Why delay matters? Why don't you ring up right now and seek an appointment? You have but seven days at your disposal."

"But it's Sunday to-day. He may not like it," Maneesh protested again, but Manju was determined. She wanted to strike the iron while it was hot. Who knows, Maneeesh might change his mind tomorrow, she thought. She therefore, picked up his cell-phone lying on the side table and checking up Mr. Ravindran's home number, dialed it. Soon Mr. Ravindran came on the line. Manju handed over the phone to Maneesh gesturing him to speak.

"Good afternoon Sir, I am Dr. Maneesh Mathur. I am sorry, I am disturbing you on a holiday, but I am very disturbed concerning some official matter, which would be, I thought, your concern too."

"It's all right with me. Go ahead," Ravindran, the chief of security in the Department of Atomic Energy said amiably. His friendly tone gave courage to Maneesh.

"Can I come and see you first thing in the morning tomorrow Sir?" he asked.

"Yes, come over to my office. I will be relatively free. Be there by ten-thirty," Ravindran said after a pause.

"May I bring along my wife also, Sir? She too is in a way concerned."

"Yes, bring her along if you want to. No problem," Ravindran was for too experienced in the field to discourage any such approach. Maneesh thanked him profusely and hung up. He felt extremely relieved, in fact elated by the positive response he had received from Ravindran.

Seeing him smile after a long while, Manju too was pleased. Her hunch had given them a good start.

"Let's not now worry. I am sure, Mr. Ravindran will find a way out for us," she said, joyfully giving a hug to Maneesh to lift his spirits further.

The next morning Maneesh and Manju were at the DAE office near the Gateway of India at 10:15 sharp. Maneesh took leave for the day to avoid seeking permission to leave office, which would have made many a tongue wag. Ravindran called them in soonafter he arrived. He ordered coffee for all three of them and until such time it was brought in, talked to the couple making polite enquiries about their family and background. Once the coffee was served and the attendant out of the way Ravindran turned to Maneesh and said, "So, let's hear what's eating you, Dr. Maneesh Mathur." Maneesh froze. Gloom enveloped his countenance. The faculty of speech seemed to desert him. He started faltering in search of words. Realising his plight Manju butted in, "May I make a beginning, Sir, since it all started with me? My husband will pick up from where I end."

"Very well. Go ahead," Ravindran consented. Manju then told him how she got acquainted with Rashmi Shah, and carried the story till the end of the party at Rashmi's house, and then looking up at Maneesh said, "Now my husband will tell you what happened thereafter, first hand." By then Maneesh had collected his wits. He then narrated the story further till his previous day's meeting with Dr. Mirza. He felt extremely relieved when he finished and glanced at Manju for approval. "This is the life and death problem I am facing now, Sir," he said looking up at Ravindran.

"Not you alone. Say we are facing. I am with you in it henceforth," Ravindran said supportively. Manju gave a pleased 'I told you so' look to Maneesh, and said, "We are very grateful to you, Sir for empathising with us."

"In fact you deserve to be congratulated on your courageous decision to come to me straight away. Very few in your position would do that. Believe me, no harm will come to you. We will fix those scoundrels squarely and in time. But let me first collect the right kind of players." Ravindran then asked his secretary to connect him to Mr. Mundkur, chief of the counter-intelligence unit of IB. When Mundkur came on line Ravindran said, "Mundkur, here's a very challenging case for you. Can you come over to my office right away?" On receiving an assurance from Mundkur he hung up and said to the Mathur couple, "Will you please wait in the visitor's room till Mr. Mundkur arrives. He is the right person to take charge of the operation, and a very competent person too. So have no apprehensions about him. I will call you in the moment he arrives. In the meantime I will attend to other matters." Maneesh and Manju rose and made for the door.

Mundkur arrived in less than twenty minutes. Khot his assistant, was with him. Ravindran sent for Maneesh and Manju as soon as the two were seated. "Mundkur, meet Dr. Mathur and his wife, Manju. Dr. Mathur is a bright and conscientious scientist of our organisation, but right now he is in a nightmarish situation. Dr. Mathur, this is Mr. Mundkur. He is a specialist in this business. I believe he will take charge of your case. I may assure you, you will be in safe hands if he does." Ravindran said, introducing them to one another. Mundkur and Maneesh shook hands. Manju nodded.

"It's better Dr. Mathur, if you told him your grisly story yourself. Don't omit any details," said Ravindran, to initiate the discussion. Maneesh began. It was much easier for him now to repeat what he had told Ravindran a little while ago. When he had finished, Ravindran asked Mundkur, "What do you think of it? How do you propose to proceed?"

"Several factors are involved in it. There's the ISI espionage attempt, then there is the blackmail attempt by the gangsters who are also in the international drug business, and of course there's the murder of a foreigner that till to-day remains undetected."

"Yes of course. It's a complex case that has to be viewed in the present and the future tenses because Dr. Mathur is under active threat and must decide one way or the other before the week ends," Ravindran observed.

"I suggest, if it's okay with you, that I take Dr. Mathur with me to my office. We will then work out the strategy how to meet the threat. I will have to call the City police also because an unsolved murder case of theirs is involved, and we require their assistance too whenever executive action is called for."

"That's fine with me. I suggest Dr. Mathur you go with them. If you want the desired results you must go the whole hog. As for Mrs. Mathur, I don't suppose they would need her presence. She can be dropped at your place on the way. Isn't that so Mundkur?"

"Yes, we don't need her."

"Okay then, good luck to you. And yes, I will apprise the Chief about the happenings, so Dr. Mathur you don't have to worry on that account." Ravindran shook hands with all of them and escorted them to the door of his office room.

When the group reached Mundkur's office he rang up his friend Inspector Sawant of the City Crime Branch. "Sawant, you have an unsolved murder case of a foreigner on your hands, I understand."

"Yes, there is. Transferred by Thane police. So?" Sawant asked.

"If you come over immediately I will give you the solution. It's now your turn for a change to come to my office. Hurry up if you don't want to miss the bus."

When Inspector Sawant arrived, Mundkur called his assistants and apprised them of the facts. "Two options are available to Dr. Mathur," Mundkur began his analysis. "He either accedes to Mirza's demand and thereby becomes an ISI mole in the BARC, or he says no to him and then prepares himself to receive Sadiq's bullet in the head. If we want to trap Mirza then Dr. Mathur will have to tell Sadiq when he rings him up on the coming Sunday to obtain his reply, that he is agreeable. There is, however, no guarantee that Mirza would immediately appear on the scene though the temptation would be very high. He has already made it clear that he would find it difficult to come. In my opinion he has already stuck his neck out much more than is good for a foreign intelligence officer without diplomatic cover. Obviously the circumstances demanded it. They had to send a scientist to rope in a scientist. The same compulsion no longer operates while working out the mechanics of operation. Mirza has already placed his demand, which forms the basis of Dr. Mathur's involvement. Further modalities can be worked out by e-mail or at a risk, on phone. Mirza has access to both. Will it, therefore, be safe for us to believe that Mirza would fall for the bait?" Mundkur looked around at the assembled officers to seek their reactions.

"Mirza is the real big fish. It would be a grand thing to nab him," Bhadang, Mundkur's other assistant, was the first to give his preference.

"Tempting indeed," Khot said. "But supposing he does not come calling and prefers to negotiate by wire then how do we grapple with the ensuing imbroglio?"

"If you ask me," said Inspector Sawant. "As an executive policeman I would go in for the bird in hand, that is, pin down Sadiq. Further, Hasmukh Shah cannot be left roaming the streets now that we know that he killed that Gujarati from South Africa. As long as Mirza does not turn up we cannot touch Shah, if nabbing Mirza is the objective. God knows what further mischief Shah and Sadiq would be upto in the mean time." There were nods of understanding from others.

After a good deal of deliberation an action plan was worked out. Mundkur then called in Maneesh who was waiting in an adjoining room and gave him an outline of what he had to do. "To-day onwards Dr. Mathur your security as well as the security of your family will be our concern, that is of the City police and the IB. You need have no misgivings about it. But to end this agony for you we must neutralise those scoundrels. In that operation we expect you to play a part and play it well," said Mundkur.

"I already feel reassured. I will do whatever you ask me to. Please have no misgivings about it," Maneesh assured. With so many competent looking men to take care of him he no longer wore a morose look and readily agreed to do the bidding.

Sadiq rang up Maneesh late in the evening on Sunday as anticipated. Maneesh greeted him with affected warmth. "So what's your reply?" Sadiq came straight to the point.

"Why don't we meet in a day or two according to your convenience Sadiqbhai? I wish to get a few points clarified from you before making up my mind," Maneesh suggested in a persuasive tone. This came as a surprise to Sadiq but he did not fall for it straightaway.

"It's very simple. If I were you I would go along with what Mirza proposed. But I leave the final choice to you. You have to simply tell me whether your reply is yes or no, and you could do so on the phone as well." Maneesh, however, persisted pleading that saying no was inviting certain death but knowing the tremendous risk involved in saying yes he wanted to work out certain modalities for which his assistance as an interlocutor was essential. Finally Sadiq agreed to meet him. "Okay, okay. If you are so insistent we will meet tomorrow at six in the evening at the New Oberoi. Does that satisfy you?" he asked. He did not want to spoil Mirza's game otherwise it was against his grain to entertain even entreaties from an intended prey.

When Mundkur learned about the outcome of the meeting he was extremely pleased though they had less than twenty-four hours to prepare. He and Sawant were certain that Sadiq would cover himself adequately as a measure of precaution though he might not anticipate a trap.

"Bhadang, please place your watchers all around the hotel in such a way that they are able to cover every entry and exit and spot any suspicious looking persons that may be hanging around. They could be Sadiq's men ready to rush in for support. And Khot place your men inside likewise to cover similar persons. We should be in a position to neutralise them in time," Mundkur instructed Bhadang and Khot, in anticipation of Sadiq's every possible stratagem. Murthy, his technical assistant, asked Maneesh to dress himself in a loose fitting full-sleeved dark sports shirt and slacks and attached a slim tape recorder to his belly and taped a thin microphone below his collarbone connecting it to the tape recorder. He taped yet another microphone to his left wrist in such a manner that it would never show. Maneesh was advised to keep that hand ahead while Sadiq was speaking so that his words would be clearly recorded. Mundkur then gave him a final briefing. "In your conversation please cover the whole episode including the murder," he advised. "The main poser that you should put to Sadiq for him to convey to Mirza would be what protection would you be given if you came under suspicion in your espionage activities? The second would be, will Sadiq guarantee your safety against Hasmukh Shah getting panicky or impatient and bumping you off? All said and done he was no longer in the picture. The idea Dr. Mathur, is to make Sadiq talk on the murder as well as the espionage proposal, do you follow?"

"Yes, yes. I follow," Maneesh assured him.

To every one's relief Maneesh played his role with confidence, wearing all the time, the look of a person in torment. Sadiq came on time. He made one of his assistants who had accompanied him to sit in the lobby while he went inside the restaurant with Maneesh. When Sadiq and Maneesh emerged from the restaurant, Mundkur's men accompanied by Sawant's Crime Branch Commandoes were all over them. For good measure and to beguile Sadiq, they rounded up Maneesh as well only to release him later.

Enchantress

Ursula Gomes, 28, crestfallen and disconsolate, had come seeking shelter with her father, chef in a Goanese restaurant in the Karachi harbour. Her husband, Ronny Gomes, was himself a cook on a Panama registered merchant ship. They had been married four years ago but had hardly spent much time together. He was frequently at sea cooking for the ship's crew, and philandering when the ship berthed at a port. When the stories of his libertine behaviour inescapably reached Ursula's ears, she sulked and quarrelled with him whenever he returned to Karachi. The proverbial last straw came in the shape of a letter she received a week ago from Ronny in which he had told her in unmistakable terms to forget him altogether. He had taken a Venezuelan woman as wife and had no intentions of returning to Karachi anytime in the future. Deprived thus of the financial support she got by way of the occasional money he sent her she had but one alternative available to her and that was to return to her father.

Her father was not happy at the prospect of supporting a daughter all her life, or try and get her married again which was a very difficult proposition, given the fact that it was a tiny Goanese community that Karachi harboured. He, therefore, looked the other way when Lieutenant Karim Khan of the Pakistan Navy befriended her and eventually took her as his mistress. It was not that Ursula was sitting idle at home. She had completed her high school education in a convent school and was quite bold. Therefore, she soon took up job as a waitress in the restaurant in which her father served. That's how she came in contact with Lt. Karim Khan. When Karim Khan was transferred to Islamabad he took his legitimately married wife with him but not Ursula. He had hired a small dwelling for her when he found it difficult to carry on his liaison with her under her father's roof. He now promised to send her a monthly dole and to visit her as often as official duty could bring him to Karachi. Lt. Karim Khan kept his promise, and Ursula found the new arrangement financially viable but not much to her taste. She was a woman of active habits, a bit adventurous one might say. She had dreamt of visiting distant lands when she married Ronny but that was not to be. Now as mistress of the naval officer she was denied even the opportunity that would satisfy her social instincts.

Her forced idleness and near confinement to the house added to the restlessness that she experienced, after the departure of her lover. Once when Karim Khan was on a visit to Karachi and spending the night with her she complained to him about her inert life and lonely existence. "I am sick of sitting idle in the house doing practically nothing. The only thing that sustains me is the thought of your returning to Karachi but that is also getting scarcer," she said plaintively.

"Look, Ursula. I understand your suffering, but I have my limits. I am a government servant and must obey government orders. I try to make your life as comfortable as I can. I also seek every opportunity to visit Karachi so that I can be with you. As things stand, I have no hopes of getting a transfer back to Karachi in the near future," Karim Khan tried to explain his predicament.

"Does that mean that life for me will continue to be the same dreary loneliness?" She asked angrily.

"Well, yes and no. I already explained to you my compulsions. But I have not been insensitive to your suffering. I really love and care for you, believe me."

"What is the use, if things can't change for me?" she asked in a dismal voice.

"No, things can change. That's why I said yes and no. If you go along with what I propose, life will be full of adventure and thrill for you, and it will also incidentally bring me credit," he made a beginning.

"What's your suggestion?" She asked eagerly.

"Look, my bosses have been for the past several months suggesting to me to find out some suitable competent person who loves adventure. Their idea is to send that person to India to settle down in Mumbai, where all the important Indian naval establishments are located, and supply us information. I thought you would fit the bill wonderfully well. You have the Goanese background, which will make it easy for you to merge with the local population. You know, there are thousands of Goanese in Mumbai. And then you already have some experience of working in a restaurant."

"My God, you are a clever devil. What a cunning way of getting rid of me!" She interjected.

"Oh, no darling. Believe me. That's not the idea at all. You spend only a few years in Mumbai. When you return triumphantly about which I have no doubt, I will be here. We shall again be together. My people will put a good chunk of money in your account in advance and thereafter from time, to time, so that when you return you will have a comfortable bank balance. So much money in fact that I might be tempted to borrow from you!" he elaborated, painting a rosy picture.

Ursula did not reply. He was keenly observing the changing expressions on her face. When he realised that the proposal he had just made was taking root, he thought of leaving her alone to let her mull over it. Before leaving he again assured her, "Ursula, I tell you in all honesty, I thought of this idea in your, in fact in our, best interest. Give a thought to it. There's no hurry. Only don't talk about it to any one, not even your father. This would be a highly secret mission. Any premature leakage would mean the end of it, and harm to both of us. I will come back again tomorrow. Give me your reply then."

The next day when Karim Khan visited Ursula in the evening he found her in a sombre, contemplative mood. This did not augur well for his mission. Instead of asking her directly if she had made a decision, he went all over the whole scheme again assuring her all the while that nothing but good would accrue to her at the minimum risk. Karim Khan soon realised that his fears were misplaced. Ursula had more or less made up her mind to give his scheme a try. All day she had ruminated over her present life and the prospects that awaited her in the foreseeable future. 'What was she at the moment?' she asked herself and answered, 'Mistress and captive of a naval officer who could abandon her any day.' Her father was getting old and not keen on taking on her responsibility, otherwise he would not connive at her liaison with Karim Khan. Besides, she belonged to a hopelessly small minority without any godfather. The alternative was to go back to the restaurant clearing tables and serving dishes besides meeting lewd and amorous advances from the sailors and naval men who patronised the restaurant. Karim Khan would certainly abandon her should she refuse the offer, she was sure of that. In comparison the opportunity to live a life of freedom and adventure in the land of her forefathers about which she always had enormous curiosity, stood out as an immensely attractive proposition. What made her heart sink, however, was the unfamiliar nature of work that involved considerable risk to her personally. Self-doubt and fear of failure raised their heads every time she felt elated at the thought of the nice time she would have. But when Karim Khan extolled the virtues of the job for the second time she decided to take a plunge.

"For your sake and your sake alone, I am inclined to venture into this frightful business," she eventually told Karim Khan. "But two things cause me great anxiety."

"What are those?" Karim Khan asked eagerly. He was happy that she had walked into the trap. He had two objectives of his own in persuading her to undertake this out-of-the-way risky job. He was getting tired of her, besides she was a drain on his resources. Sending her out on a job like that would almost mean getting rid of her for good. He also saw in it brighter career prospects for him in the new vocation he was assigned to. Karim Khan had joined the celebrated but much feared ISI. He knew that he would surely ingratiate himself with his bosses if he could, within months of joining the organisation raise a female agent—a pioneering feat—and induct her into India which was their prime target. He was, therefore, prepared to give her a long rope, and meet all her reasonable conditions.

"If I get caught what happens to me? Who will save me?" She asked.

"And the second?" Karim Khan asked without answering the first query.

"What happens to me when I come back?" Ursula put her second question.

Karim Khan was greatly relieved on hearing the two questions that made her dither. What he had to do was to convincingly bluff to her on both counts, which he did with great elan.

"My dearest Ursula, how can I ever think of abandoning you to the wolves? First, I shall ensure that you never get caught. I will train you so well that not even the devil can unravel your secret. These Indians are a lousy lot. You can fool them in no time. As to your second question, I must confess, I feel terribly hurt. With me around, that question should not arise at all. You will return to my arms. We shall live together happily ever after. But this is not all. You are going on an important government mission and the government will look after you well monetarily. I guarantee you that. Does that satisfy you, darling?" He asked, to be sure.

Though Ursula took his promises with a pinch of salt, especially of waiting for her, she felt comforted that she would have some money of her own in the end. When she expressed her agreement, Karim Khan was overjoyed. He literally lifted her off her feet and waltzed on the small sitting room floor. In the end he told her that he would carry the good news to his bosses and, all going well, return after a week when their training would begin in right earnest.

Exactly seven days later Lt. Karim Khan knocked on the door of Ursula Gomes late in the evening. He had a brief case in one hand and a rucksack in the other. Ursula found him beaming with excitement when she opened the door. He carefully closed the door behind him and embracing her with the fervour of a long lost lover said, "How are you Madame Ruby Coello? Congratulations on your new appointment."

"Ruby Coello? What are you talking? Have you taken one too many already?" Ursula asked, bewildered.

"Yes, that's the name you shall take when you go to India. It's better you get used to that name here itself. I shall call you Ruby Coello hereafter so that it does not sound strange to you," Karim Khan said quite seriously. "I am here at your service from tonight for seven days. We start our first lesson by going over your new life story."

"First tell me what did your bosses say?" Ursula asked inquisitively, ignoring his proposal.

"Oh, they were mighty pleased. In fact one of them said that he would like to interview you. I said nothing doing. I was afraid that after seeing your lovely face he might give a go by to our scheme and snatch you away from me. I insisted that they remain satisfied with seeing your photograph only, and I had my way," he said with mischief in his eyes.

"You may be pleased to know that while you are undergoing training preparing yourself for the role you would be playing in India, you would be paid ten thousand rupees a month. Your salary will be doubled when you are actually launched. Ten thousand will be deposited in your bank account and the other ten thousand you shall be paid in cash in Indian rupees. In addition your house rent, taxi and entertainment expenses will be taken care of separately. You need have no worry on that count. Are you happy now, darling?" He asked.

"Yes," she said equably.

"If your training starts today, your salary also starts today. Let's therefore, get cracking right now," he said impatiently. She had no choice but to accede.

They elaborately went over the story that he had written down on a sheet of paper. She was to be Ruby Coello, originally from Mapusa in Goa. Her grandfather was in the service of a Sardar from Gwalior and therefore, the family settled down there. She had her education in a local school. She later served as a waitress in a restaurant and had now come to Mumbai in search of better prospects.

"This will explain your Goan origins as well as your lack of familiarity with it," he clarified. "You will be sent to India on an Arab Dhow. You will be escorted by Hafees, a trustworthy old hand at this business, so you don't have to worry about your safety. He will transfer you near the Indian shore to a fishing trawler that will land you on the seacoast near a place called Murud. Hafees will then put you on the train that will take you straight to Goa. Once on the train you are on your own. When you reach Panaji that is the capital of Goa, you will have to find accommodation for yourself in a middling hotel. I have in my bag all the literature about Goa, your ancestral land. Study it carefully. You will then feel confident."

"Don't you think that's dangerous?" She asked almost in panic.

"No not at all. I will guarantee your safety on the sea. This is a naval operation. Anyone playing foul will be reduced to shreds, and they know it full well. So, have no worry on that count. As to your safety on ground, much depends on how you prepare yourself. Unlike here, Indian society is pretty free and heterogeneous. With money in purse—and I assure you, you will have plenty of it—you can freely move about without difficulty."

"What do I do in Goa?" She asked, reassured by his words.

"Goa is the land of your forefathers. It's a small but lovely country. I wish I could come along with you. Roam about and see the whole of Goa. Visit Mapusa that is the place your family is supposed to come from. Be friendly with people to get to know their culture, their peculiarities and sensibilities. But mind you, don't get too friendly with any one. Otherwise as the Indian habit goes, they would embarrass you by asking too many personal questions. That may even expose you."

"In short I become a real Goan," she interjected.

"Yes but not quite. Remember that your family is supposed to have migrated to Gwalior two generations ago. This is necessary because there are too many Goans in Mumbai, and everyone has relatives back home in Goa. Since your family migrated long ago you have no connection left with Goa, not that you know of at any rate."

"I get it."

"Good. After spending two weeks in Goa you travel to Gwalior via Mumbai. Stay at Mumbai en route for two days just to get acquainted with south Mumbai which will be your field of activity and where you would eventually settle down."

"My trip to Gwalior is to get to know the city, I suppose?" She anticipated.

"Not merely that. Of course you should get to know the city well. You are supposed to have spent the whole of your childhood there. You must visit the school you were educated in, the locality in which you lived and all the historical places and landmarks. We have chosen this place for you because not many people from Gwalior would be found in south Mumbai."

"I see your point," she nodded.

"You are going to stay for two months in Gwalior."

"Two month? Why that long?" She asked, not comprehending the purpose.

"After acquainting yourself with the city, as I mentioned earlier, you will search for and get a job in a restaurant that takes waitresses. Don't haggle over the salary they offer you. Your idea is to generate credentials that would help you get a suitable job in Mumbai, your final destination," he clarified.

"From Gwalior naturally you move over to Mumbai. You will stay in a hotel to begin with and search for a one-room accommodation in south Mumbai, particularly Colaba area. If you engage an estate agent he should be able to get you a suitable place, of course at a price but that shouldn't worry you. We shall provide for all that."

"Will I get accommodation that easy?" She expressed her doubt.

"You will have to. You must. Simultaneously you will search for a job of a waitress in a restaurant that is frequented by sailors and naval personnel. We will give three months for that. You must choose your place carefully. The success of your mission depends on that. If you can't get into such a place in one go it does not matter. Take a job in a less suitable place but move over at the first opportunity," he made the purpose clear to her.

"Hmm," she grunted.

"I think darling, this is enough for to-day. We will resume tomorrow. Until then you study your life history," he concluded the session.

The next seven days saw him train her in all aspects of the tradecraft, a term used in the business of dirty tricks to indicate the cunning ploys that a spy and his master use to ferret and communicate secret information. Simultaneously he took care to chirp encouraging words into her ears and paint a sunny picture of her adventurous life in India, to keep her resolve firm. One day he brought a laptop computer and a cell phone and spent the whole day in teaching her how to use them. "Look dear, secure communication holds the key to your safety and the success of your mission, so you must practice diligently," he impressed upon her time and again. He taught her how to make use of them to send e-mail which would be her main mode of communication saying that later she would be trained to use a mobile internet terminal that combines those two gadgets plus provides other facilities. When she had mastered the procedure of sending e-mail he gave her an e-mail address and said, "You are going to send all your communication from India to this address. To make sure that you don't make any mistakes you must send messages to this address right now and every day so that I can correct you if there is any error in your handling. This will also enable you to remember it accurately," he told her while insisting that she send several messages in his presence.

When Karim Khan was satisfied that Ursula was reasonably confident of conducting herself in the new role, he gave her lessons on the organisation of a navy and the kinds of warships and weapons it generally uses. Later he took her on a round of the naval base to let her see things for herself. The last lesson of hers was to learn by heart what she was to find out about the Indian navy. Happy that she had fared well he took her out for a grand dinner at an expensive restaurant on the last day, and asking her to continue practising relentlessly in his absence, took her leave. He was to return one month later when she would be dispatched on her mission.

When he showed up again as promised he insisted on going through all the lessons all over again, in her interest as he repeatedly told her. He took her out to make purchases for her journey. Ursula was excited. She wanted to make lots of purchases but he forbade her. "You will carry only two dresses, my darling," he told her with a tone of finality. "And those dresses shall not have Pakistani labels. In fact you will carry nothing with you with Pakistani markings."

"How do I manage in just two dresses?" she asked incredulously, deeply disappointed that he had put a wet blanket on her shopping plans.

"Oh, I never said that. You fill your wardrobe to your heart's content when you settle down in India. Any Pakistani clothes in your baggage would be a giveaway, please bear that in mind," said Karim Khan, firmly.

On the last day he brought a small India-made suitcase in which she was to carry her meagre belongings. Its bottom was covered with an old issue of an Indian newspaper. Below it was kept Indian currency sufficient to see her through till she finally returned to Mumbai to find a dwelling. "Now remember well, darling. Do not even by mistake throw away the newspaper. It contains the name of the havala dealer in Mumbai and the code word that would enable you to collect money from him after you reach Mumbai. You discard it, you go without money," he warned her. In response to her bewildered look he said, "Simply hold the top right corner of page number two close to a burning electric lamp for a few minutes and the details would slowly emerge in print as if from nowhere. Those are written in secret ink." To prove the veracity of what he had just said he produced another newspaper piece and gave her a demonstration.

The suitcase pocket had an Indian passport bearing her name. He showed her the passport and said, "This is your passport, my dear. It would establish your identity as an Indian whenever required."

"I am happy I have some solid document to establish my identity," Ursula said, taking the passport in her hand and browsing through it.

"The passport could prove to be your life saver. Please listen carefully. If you come under suspicion anytime, fly immediately to Kathmandu. Your Indian passport would dispense with the requirement of a visa. You could thus leave instantaneously. From Mumbai you should fly to Delhi, Patna or Kolkata and from there catch a flight for Kathmandu. Once in Kathmandu you should contact Taj Travels. You would then be in safe hands. They are our people. They would make arrangement for your onward journey to Karachi. Is that clear, darling?" Karim Khan asked.

"Yes, very much so," replied Ursula, without enthusiasm. The thought was dampening.

As a special concession he also gave her telephone numbers of a hotel in Panaji. She could be reasonably sure of getting accommodation in that hotel, and need not feel lost on reaching Goa. When she asked him if she was not to carry any of the gadgets she was taught to use, Karim Khan said with deep concern in his voice, "Oh, no. I don't want to send my beloved to the wolves straight away. Should a mishap occur those gadgets would expose you."

"Then why was I taught their use?" Ursula was intrigued.

"Be patient my dear, be patient. I will unravel the whole mystery to you in a moment," he said. "I have given you the London e-mail address. From every place you reach in your sojourn you will send a brief e-mail conveying your welfare in the code language I have taught you. Remember that that's the only manner in which you can communicate with us. You can use any cyber café to send the e-mail. As soon as possible open a Yahoo and a Hotmail e-mail account and inform us about the particulars. Let each account be in a different name. This will enable us to guide you from time to time. Check your e-mail at least once in a week. Follow these instructions carefully."

"If that's the arrangement those gadgets don't come into the picture at all," she asked impatiently.

"Wait, wait. I am coming to that. When you settle down properly in Mumbai, that is, get a room on rent for yourself, you will naturally tell us about it. Exactly one month thereafter you will get a postal cover that will contain nothing but a cloak room receipt of Kalyan railway station. Kalyan as you would soon discover on reaching Mumbai, is a railway junction about an hour's journey from Mumbai. Against the receipt you will collect a small suitcase from the railway station. Take care to collect it immediately. I suggest, you visit Kalyan railway station in advance to find out where the cloak room is located so that you do not flounder on the day you go to actually retrieve the suitcase. The suitcase would contain all the gadgetry that you have been using here during your training. Is that clear now? Are you happy?" He asked in the end.

"Yes. That's a good idea."

Karim Khan was greatly relieved when Ursula alias Ruby went through all the paces confidently and without a mishap. She got employment after a brief struggle in a restaurant in Colaba that was the favourite of naval ratings and petty officers alike. Her charm and ready amiability earned her many friends. She, however took care never to take any one to her room. Those were her inviolable instructions. As her friend circle increased she realised that her job as a waitress put severe restrictions on her time and freedom. Her masters back home were very pleased with the information that she sent frequently, therefore, they readily agreed when she proposed that she be allowed to purchase a tea stall not far from the place where she was working. With money readily coming through the havala channel and the façade of bank loan, she could easily outbid others who had an eye on it. She renovated and upgraded it and gave it a new name, Crab and Cola, proclaiming that crabmeat dishes was its specialty.

Her old friends and admirers as well as several others flocked to her neat little joint, so much so that as the reputation of her preparations spread, even young naval officers started making forays, much to her advantage and the delight of her masters.

The Chief of Military Police was an angry man. He banged the table with his fist, giving vent to his impotent fury and bellowed, "Damn it, can't we do anything against that Goanese tease? Bah! The way our chaps swarm round her. It infuriates me."

"I am afraid Sir, we can do precious little in this matter beyond what we have already done so far," his deputy counselled sedately. "She has done nothing that can be regarded as illegal, even objectionable. As for the naval chaps they also have not violated any regulations. It is true that they flock to her restaurant but they go their only when off-duty. Some of them take their wives too with them. Once or twice our people noticed her going to a picture with a naval fellow but even that cannot be officially objected to. We did advise the naval commanders to dissuade their men from patronising her restaurant but they expressed their difficulty, which is genuine."

"Tell me, why do these fools go to her wagging their tails. Is she that amorous?" The chief asked.

"I must admit that she can easily lay claims to good looks and a good figure, but she is not a flirt though she does seem to take it sportingly when some one takes a bit of liberty. The food she serves is said to be really delicious. She has a very fine Goanese cook, and she herself supervises cooking," the deputy enlightened the boss.

"Pretty tough situation. I am not inclined to look the other way because I strongly feel that there is more to it than meets the eye. Can our chaps not find out more about her and her activities?" He asked the deputy.

"I am afraid, we have gone as far as we safely can. Our men are not trained to make such sensitive enquiries."

"Do you mean to say, we just keep quiet?" asked the chief indignantly.

"No Sir, I don't mean that. We can ask the Intelligence Bureau to look into this case. They are the right people to handle such intricate matters," the deputy suggested.

"Hmm. I think you are right. We will ask them to pick up the threads."

"Yes Sir. We would then know for sure whether she is a vivacious but innocent restaurateur or a cunning temptress playing a deep game."

"That's right. I know Mundkur, the chief of the counter-intelligence unit, nice chap. I think, I will go and see him tomorrow and request him to nose about and let us know what he makes of it," the chief nodded his concurrence and then after a pause spoke to his personal assistant on the intercom, "Raman, please make an appointment for me to see Mr. Mundkur of IB tomorrow, preferably in the afternoon. I am sure, you have his number."

"Yes, Sir."

When the chief of Military Police finished unburdening himself, Mundkur assured him that he would do all that was within his competence to unravel the secret of the vamp that had caused him so much mental agony. Mundkur collected all the particulars that the chief had about the woman and her establishment and promised to get in touch with him when he had something interesting to report.

As soon as he was alone Mundkur sent for Khot, his trusted lieutenant. Since he was from Sawantwadi that was close to Goa he thought that Khot would be the right person to get close to her and also detect discrepancies in her behaviour. When Khot arrived, Mundkur asked him to take a chair and said, "Khot there's an interesting case for you. A femme fatale from Colaba causeway is playing havoc with the naval chaps, it seems. Everyone is bending over backwards to earn her favours. I want you to see what sort of a woman this one is and what she is up to. The chief of Military Police was here a moment ago. He smells a rat but is not able to establish anything. That's why he came here to seek our help," Mundkur briefed his assistant, and added with a twinkle in his eyes, "But please take care that you do not yourself succumb to her charms."

"You know me well Sir," Khot replied with a smile. "What would you like me to do?"

"First, detail two men to keep a discreet watch on her eating place, and two men to keep a watch on her flat from the time she returns home till she leaves for work the next morning." A plan of action had already taken shape in Mundkur's mind. "The men at the restaurant should carefully note who are her regular customers, how she behaves with them and whether any special relationship can be discerned. This watch should be mounted for a week. That should give us enough data to draw some conclusions."

"Sir," Khot nodded.

"Thereafter you introduce yourself into the scenario."

"Sir?"

"Yes, you visit her restaurant posing as a naval officer. That's the only way one can get a closer look at her and what's really going on. I will ask the Military Police chief to lend you a set of uniform of a Petty Officer. He will also provide you a companion for your first visit. I am sure, he would have some one who has recently joined his outfit and is not yet widely recognised by others," Mundkur elaborated.

"Why in uniform Sir?"

"That will help her spot you as a newcomer and as a naval officer at that. She will take initiative to talk to you to know more about you. Call yourself Suneil Kamath and tell her that you have recently arrived on posting from Kochi—you have already visited the place once or twice, so you know something about it—and that you were posted in the signal section. My hunch is that she will get interested in you. Thereafter you can go in civvies, only take care to occasionally don your uniform. Get as friendly as you can without getting emotionally involved—and I am making a serious suggestion. When you are dealing with a young woman who is not averse to using her physical charms, a man on the job has to be very vigilant."

"I understand, Sir," Khot said.

"When you have made a fair assessment of her we shall decide upon our next move. This should keep you busy for a month and more. In the meantime I shall get her telephone placed under surveillance. She has one at her restaurant. One doesn't know if she has another at home. Both will have to be observed. And yes, I am arranging for your attachment to the signal section of the navy for a couple of days. You must familiarise yourself with its working otherwise you may make an ass of yourself talking to her."

"That would indeed be fine, Sir," Khot said brightening up for, he was a bit worried on that count.

Khot's watchers reported that she never left the restaurant while it was open. She was indeed very friendly with her naval customers and seemed to know every one by name. If a new customer arrived she made it a point to get introduced to him. They had by now identified her regulars whom she allowed to spend more time than the eats they ordered warranted. Invariably she hung around with one of the last customers and even ate with him. It was quite likely that she did not charge him. In contrast she spent a very lonely life at home. No one visited her nor did she go out anywhere on her own. If she went out with anyone in the evening, which was not frequent, she always met him at a neutral place outside her lane and returned alone at night.

It was now time for Khot to make entry. He did the job remarkably well. She did spot him as a newcomer, and made polite enquiries about him and his companion and saw to it that they were served promptly. When Khot asked for the bill she came over to him and said, "With the compliments of the management. Thanks for visiting."

"Oh, no. You will ruin yourself if you feed people for free," Khot protested.

"Don't you worry. I am sure you I would have many more occasions to entertain you. I will charge you then." She said nonchalantly. But when Khot insisted on making payment she did not protest too much and accepted the money. Thereafter Khot stopped by alone several times taking care to keep a decent gap between any two calls. He could clearly see a determined effort on her part to be friends, and also encouraged her. Slowly, almost imperceptibly she started casually asking him questions about his job. Khot played his part well. After apparent initial hesitation he started answering her questions. It was obvious that her knowledge and interest in naval matters were much more than an average person would have.

When Khot apprised Mundkur of the progress he had made till then, Mundkur said, "The time to take the third step has arrived. It's going to be a very sensitive step and so we must plan it with great care. I have a report from the police. The result of telephone interception is very disappointing. She has no telephone registered in her name or at her home address. They had to therefore, remain content with whatever the restaurant telephone yielded, and it yielded precious little."

"That means we do not bank on this avenue. What do we do next, Sir?"

"I am afraid Khot, you have to now take a step forward in your, shall I say amorous, relationship with your new girlfriend," Mundkur said in all seriousness.

"What do you now propose I should do?" Khot asked apprehensively.

"I said one more step forward. You must persuade her to go to see a picture with you. She is known to have gone for late night shows with other guys, so not a very difficult proposition I suppose. We could take a chance when she went out with someone else but then we won't have much notice, besides we won't know how long she would stay away from the flat."

"What's the purpose?" Khot asked.

"I thought, you would have guessed already. We want to search her flat stealthily in her absence. If she is collecting information about naval matters she must transmit it to someone else. Therefore, a communication system must exist and that can exist only in her flat. That's why she keeps all her friends away from it. Unless we search her apartment we won't know for sure that she is a spy, to tell you frankly," Mundkur explained.

"I get your point Sir. I will try, and I have a feeling I will succeed," Khot said.

"You only feel that way. I am confident of it. She surely would fall for your persuasions. She would perhaps see in it an opportunity to get something really meaty from you in return for the warmth of her company," Mundkur said in a lighter vein.

Two uneventful weeks passed. Mundkur waited patiently for Khot to come to him. He did not want to hurry him. He was aware that such delicate matters had a dynamics of their own, a period of incubation, as it were, therefore, endurance was called for. Though Khot was not used to this kind of love game Mundkur had confidence in his basic competence. Eventually the day dawned when Khot gleefully broke the news to Mundkur no sooner the latter reached the office. "Sir, you would be glad to know that I and my newfound girlfriend Ruby, are going the day after to see a late night show at the Excelsior, that's in the Fort area," Khot said, blushing despite himself.

"Congratulations! Congratulations, young man," Mundkur said exuberantly, shaking Khot's hand vigorously. "At long last you have succeeded. It is for us now to play our part while you keep your ladylove busy at the theatre. Let me see; your location at the Excelsior would give us a warning time of just ten minutes. I would have preferred a farther cinema theatre but one can't tailor-make these things."

"I had very little choice Sir, because Ruby was keen on seeing the picture that was running in that theatre," Khot clarified.

"I appreciate that Khot, you have done a good job."

Mundkur decided that when Khot picked up his friend from the main road where she was to meet him, Shivkumar Jain, an officer from Khot's group would follow the couple in a taxi. He was to inform Mundkur the moment the couple went inside the theatre and then mount watch outside. His most important job was to contact Mundkur and warn him, no sooner Khot and his lady companion came out of the theatre to go home.

The moment Jain informed Mundkur that Khot and his friend had entered the cinema theatre, Mundkur and a technician from his office who was good at picking locks and identifying electronic gadgets reached the vicinity of the building in which Ruby lived. They waited for Ruby's neighbours to retire for the night and quietly approached her flat, keeping a man outside to warn them in case something unusual happened. The technician did not take much time to unlock the door. Both entered the flat, taking care to close the door behind them and immediately started systematically searching the small sitting-cum-bedroom in the dim light of the torches both carried.

The room was sparsely furnished, therefore it did not take them long to rummage through all the things that were there. The bed did not conceal any secrets. The wardrobe was full of clothes and little else. In the bottom shelf Mundkur found an old vanity bag tossed in a corner. When he inspected its contents he found a passport in it that was little used. It was an Indian passport bearing Ruby Coello's name. Mundkur quickly took down its number and date and place of issue before replacing it in the bag, which he carefully deposited wherefrom he had picked it up. The room did not yield anything else that could interest them. Mundkur was perplexed. "If the woman is in the murky business she must have a means of secret communication. What could that be? We haven't come across anything so far," he remarked to his companion.

Now only the kitchen and bathroom were left. They entered the kitchen that was in reality a small strip of room. Mundkur went through the kitchen cabinets fitted to the wall but without luck. The technician simultaneously worked on the cabinets that were below the kitchen platform. When the cabinets containing utensils and other kitchen accessories did not yield anything he turned almost in desperation to the corner chest that housed the gas cylinder. To his amazement he noticed a small dark packet-like thing taped to the inside of the black cudappah stone top. Anyone opening the shutters of the chest in the normal course by bending a little would miss it entirely. Only when one went down on one's haunches could it be seen. He whispered to Mundkur about his find. Mundkur asked him to first carefully observe its position and the manner in which it was strapped before dislodging it. The technician took out the packet, which was in fact a flat box, with great care and opened it with Mundkur peering from above. It contained a gadget that the technician, after turning it over on his palm, identified as a Mobile Internet Terminal. He explained that it contained a mobile phone, e-mail and messaging on the move and several other features. Mundkur was happy. "That's it. The smoking gun evidence. This establishes the real nature of her work." He took down the mobile number and other particulars before asking the technician to re-fix the packet in the same manner as it was before. Later they searched the bathroom but it was as innocent as the sitting room.

When they came out locking the flat behind them it was nearly midnight. Before they could hit the main thoroughfare, Mundkur's mobile phone chirped. It was Jain informing him that Khot and Ruby had come out of the cinema hall and were looking for a taxi.

"Ah," Mundkur remarked with satisfaction. "A good job done and well in time. Now Madam Ruby Coello can come home and have a good sleep, happily dreaming about the nice time she had with dear Suneil Kamath. We are off to our homes too."

The next day Khot entered Mundkur's cabin wearing a worried look.

"Why what happened? Did you have a quarrel with her or what? Why do you look so haggard?" Mundkur asked on noticing the expression on Khot's face.

"No Sir, nothing of that sort happened. But I ask you earnestly, when is my role-playing going to end? I am in deep trouble," Khot gasped.

"What's the matter?"

"First she tried to get fresh with me. Normally it should be the other way round but I was keeping myself in check. I was till the end not sure if she had lost control over herself or she was only acting, because in between she used to ask pointed questions. I detested both. One was extremely trying for my self-control and the other for my skimpy knowledge of the signal section. If that's not enough, she extracted from me a promise to take her to the musical extravaganza that's going to be staged at the Andheri sports complex next week. That has caused me real worry," Khot lamented.

"You don't have to worry about it, Khot. Ring her up tomorrow and tell her in a worried tone that your father is seriously ill and therefore, you are leaving for your hometown immediately. You don't know when you would be able to return but would get in touch with her the moment you came back. Also appropriately apologize for not being able to take her to that musical programme. After that just forget about her."

"Why Sir?" Khot asked, brightening up.

"That's because we were successful in our mission. I must thank you for facilitating this delicate operation. If you had not suffered her for three hours we would not have been able to rifle through her apartment. We got some very significant stuff," Mundkur confided.

"Is that so, Sir? That's really great," Khot exclaimed.

"To take you into confidence, we got her passport and what's more, a very valuable piece of evidence—her communication system—which would support our contention that she was spying for some country."

"I am really happy."

"Khot, it's your unusual efforts that have finally paid off. She is such a clever woman that I was wondering how we were going to nab her. She does not go out to meet anyone; she does not collect any documents; she does not make any payments, and yet she is a prolific purveyor of vital intelligence about practically everything under the Navy's roof in Mumbai. But our stratagem paid off, and you played a very delicate role in it," said Mundkur, complimenting Khot.

"Thank you, Sir," Khot acknowledged.

It took Mundkur just two days to find out from his IB colleagues in Bhopal that the Bhopal passport office had not issued any passport in that series and that no passport had been issued in the past five years to anyone by the name of Ruby Coello. The woman obviously carried a forged passport, which raised in Mundkur's mind a legitimate question, 'Was she Indian at all?' He also found out that Ruby's cell phone connection was from AT&T, which she operated on the strength of pre-paid card that cuts out so many formalities. The cell phone was not in her name. This was damaging evidence but not clinching enough to establish that she was spying.

Happy that he was able to get enough evidence that pointed to her being a spy, Mundkur was now busy collecting evidence that would establish it as fact. She did not use the cell phone to contact anyone, therefore, getting any evidence of incriminating conversation was out of the question. The Internet communication that she may be having—and she must have it otherwise what use is all that equipment? he argued to himself—offered the only hope. It was a highly technical matter and he was sure that the IB technicians who were working on it would succeed in hacking into her communication channel before long, and they did indeed succeed. The text of the messages disclosed that she was spying for Pakistan's ISI. He now wanted some more time to collect enough intercepts that would give him definite clues about her accomplices and collaborators in the Indian navy but that was not to be.

While Mundkur and his men were busy, disaster descended upon them like a ton of bricks. After waiting patiently for Kamath alias Khot to return from his hometown Ruby started making enquiries with other naval officers who patronised her restaurant. She was either really smitten by the love bug for, all said and done Khot was a good looking handsome young man, or she was worried that Khot had taken offence at her behaviour that day when they went together for the cinema show—one could not be sure. To her surprise and frustration, none seemed to know signalman Kamath personally, to be able to give her information about his whereabouts.

Then it so happened that a new naval officer made his appearance at her restaurant. As was her wont she made polite enquiries about him and what he preferred to eat out of the fare she had to offer. She was overjoyed when he told her that he was from the signal section. It was a godsend opportunity she thought, and made solicitous enquiries about Kamath. "You know Mr. Kamath. Such a nice person, My favourite customer," she said to him endearingly.

"Mr. Kamath? Which Kamath are you talking of? There's no Kamath in my section. I know all of them by name," he replied in astonishment.

"He might have been recently transferred then," Ruby said, more to console herself than to convince him.

"Can't be. I would know. I have been working in that Section for the past one year and more," he was vehement. A chill went down her spine. Was it a trap in which she had foolishly got herself ensnared? She kept her cool and went back to her counter. There she went over all her past encounters with Kamath, dispassionately dissecting his behaviour, his responses to her questions and suggestions, and above all his last conduct. The retrospection convinced her that Kamath was an imposter who had befriended her with a purpose and that purpose could only be to expose her. She was now genuinely frightened. Alone in an alien country and a grave crime on her head she could think of no other way but to flee. Though lunchtime was approaching she told the head server, "I am not feeling well, John. I am going home. Must rest for a while. Please look after the customers while I am away. I shall be back in an hour." The next moment she was out in the street making for her apartment.

An hour later the leader of the watcher team that was keeping an eye on her rang up Mundkur. "Sir, she left the restaurant around twelve-thirty, which was very unusual, and taking a taxi went straight to Crawford market. We followed her but she moved about fast on foot going from one shop to another making purchases. She seemed to be in an awful hurry. What she actually purchased we could not see. Lastly, she visited a travel agency on the Mohammedali road, and then went straight home."

"Where's she?" Mundkur asked briefly.

"At the moment, in her apartment," the watcher replied.

"Keep a sharp eye on her. Don't let her hoodwink you, and remain in touch. I would like you to keep me posted of all her movements promptly," Mundkur directed.

"Sir."

Mundkur sat bolt upright in his chair on hearing about her having visited a travel agency. 'What was she up to? Has she suspected a trap? If that's true then she must be preparing to flee and flee fast. That's why she left the restaurant at that

busy hour and went shopping. There was no time to lose.'
Mundkur pondered. His mind worked fast.

"Listen carefully," Mundkur told the watcher. "I expect
her to leave her apartment in a short while. Follow her closely
when she does. Please remember, time's precious and we must
not lose her."

"We are on absolute alert, Sir."

"Keep me informed of every move of hers. I want a minute-
to-minute report," Mundkur emphasised and hung up. While
he was working out in his mind the next move the watcher
rang up again. "She is leaving her apartment just now. She
is wearing a purple salwar-kameej and carrying a largish
handbag," he said.

Mundkur sent for Khot and told him, "Khot, I have a
feeling, your ladylove is about to bolt. We should not allow
her to escape from our clutches. She has done enough damage
to deserve severe punishment."

"What makes you think she is running away Sir?" Khot
asked.

Mundkur briefly narrated to him what the watcher had told
him and added, "In all probability she will catch an afternoon
or evening flight. We must nab her before she does that."

"What are my instructions, Sir?" Khot asked
apprehensively. He fervently hoped that his boss wouldn't ask
him to test his charms again on that wily woman.

"I know what your fears are, No, I am not about to ask
you to do any such thing. You are the one who has seen her
closely. Therefore, you can spot her quickly. I want you to
proceed to the airport immediately. I also suggest that you
take Gayatri and Sweta with you. They will be able to pull

her out even if she is in the midst of a flock of females. In the meantime I will ask Bhadang to find out which flights are leaving Mumbai this moment onwards to-day, and who are the unaccompanied women passengers on them. So, get those two girls and proceed to the airport. Before you reach there, I should be able to furnish you with information about the women passengers. Once I tie up the loose ends I shall also join you."

As Khot rose in his seat to take leave, Mundkur's phone rang. It was the watcher again. He was frantic. "Sir she left the taxi at the Churchgate railway station and went inside. We followed her at a distance. Instead of going to the ticket counter or platform she went to the ladies toilet. We had no choice but to wait outside. We waited for full fifteen minutes but she did not emerge. Having no clue as to what she would be doing inside all that time I asked a sweepress to check inside but she found no woman of that description. We are extremely sorry, Sir, but what do we do now?" He asked nervously. Mundkur became grave. Missing her at that juncture was the last thing he wanted to hear but he was not the one to get upset or flabbergasted in a moment of crisis. His mind was now working fast. He asked the watcher, "Did you see any burqa-clad woman leaving the toilet?"

"Come to think of it, Sir, I have a feeling that a woman in black burqa did come out of the toilet about five minutes after Ruby entered but I won't be absolutely sure. Besides I don't suppose she was carrying any bag with her."

That was good enough for Mundkur to conclude that Ruby had played a clever trick on them. Once inside the burqa no one would recognise her nor would any one be brash enough to ask her to remove it. She had obviously purchased the burqa when she went to the Crawford market.

"In a way that makes our quest simpler," he remarked after apprising Khot of what the watcher had told him. "Now in the passenger list Bhadang would have to hunt for only Muslim women passengers that are travelling alone, and for you Khot only those women passengers who are wearing a burqa. Doesn't it make our task easier?"

"That's true Sir. But spotting her under the burqa is going to be a well nigh impossible task," said Khot.

"I don't suppose so. When you go to the airport you would realize yourself. For all I know there might be only one woman wearing a burqa. In a worse case scenario there might be more. In that case use your ingenuity. You have plenty of it. Now you must get going. Hurry up." Mundkur dismissed Khot and sent for Bhadang.

When Bhadang arrived he said to him, "Bhadang. I want some quick enquiry made. Time is of essence. I want you to find out in the next fifteen minutes what are the flights that are leaving Mumbai within the next four hours and the unaccompanied Muslim women passengers on them. Cover all airlines and all destinations. I am now leaving for the airport. I would expect a call from you en route."

"Yes Sir. I shall get this information for you as fast as possible and inform you on the mobile," Bhadang promised Mundkur and withdrew. Mundkur also left for the airport after alerting the airport police chief.

"While Mundkur's car was racing along the western express highway Bhadang contacted him. "Sir, here's the information you wanted urgently. Two single female Muslim passengers are travelling by Jet Airways to Kolkata. They were separately booked. Their names are Farida AfzalBeg and Shirien Kanchwalla. The flight will be leaving in an hour's time. Further, only one similar passenger is booked on the IAC flight to Delhi that leaves at six-fifteen in the evening. That's all Sir,"

"Thank you Bhadang. That's really a quick job. Now I must disconnect," Mundkur cut off the connection, got in touch with Khot and passed the information on to him. "Khot," he added, "Attend to the Kolkata flight passengers immediately. They might be passing through the security check. I am not yet clear why she should want to go to Kolkata but we will ponder over that later. If both women are burqa-clad use some ruse that would enable you to see their faces from a distance. If only one is wearing it then that's our quarry. Detain her with the help of the airport police, if need be. I shall be there in fifteen minutes."

Khot and his two female associates rushed to the security check enclosure. As predicted by Mundkur, passengers booked for Kolkata on Jet Airways were passing through the door frame metal detector and then frisked by policemen. To their consternation they found two burqa-clad women in the queue. Both were cleared by the security and hung on for a while in the throng of the passengers. Khot had to do some quick thinking. He consulted his companions to find out if they had any ideas. They could not suggest anything that would solve their riddle without running the risk of inviting the ire of the passenger if she were not the right one.

While they were thus huddled together not sure how to proceed, announcement was made on the public address system asking the Kolkata-bound passengers to proceed to the aircraft. There was no time to waste. All three rushed forward still not sure what to do. The passengers had lined up in a queue again at the exit gate. Khot who was watching both the ladies from a distance suddenly exclaimed aloud, "The shoes, the shoes. Get that woman who is ahead in black burqa." His companions gave him a perplexed look, not comprehending what he was saying. Realising their bewilderment Khot, who had by now collected his wits, explained, "Do you see the shoes that the first burqa-clad woman is wearing—those beige ones with two black stripes across? Those are the shoes Ruby wore frequently. They are perhaps her favourite. She is Ruby I am sure. You both flank her on either side and ask her to step aside telling her that you are from the security and have some clarification to seek. Then bring her here to me."

Gayatri and Sweta did as directed by Khot. The woman in burqa protested but had no choice. As she turned back and moved a little distance accompanied by the two women, she saw Khot standing in front of her, smiling. Her worst fears had come true. "You scoundrel!" she screamed and collapsed in the arms of her escorts in a swoon. Accompanied by Inspector Kulkarni of airport security, Mundkur arrived in the nick of time to hear Ruby's outburst. He quietly patted Khot on the back, and beckoned the two ladies to move Ruby who was now showing signs of regaining consciousness, to a nearby police post.

Audacious Venture

It was a well-attended party that Vice-Admiral Punecha, the Chairman of the Mazgaon Docks, threw in honour of the visiting Defence Minister. The Minister had especially flown down to Mumbai with a host of Defence Ministry officials for the launching of a new frigate that the Dock had successfully built. Vice-Admiral Punecha had proudly mentioned during the launching ceremony that it was the most modern warship in its class in the world, a boast that was well justified in the opinion of knowledgeable people.

Punecha had taken care to see that all officers who had contributed to the success of the project were invited to the party. It is thus that Bhaskar Bhargava, the head of the Design Division and his assistant Rajesh Mathur, along with their spouses found themselves mixing with top civil and military officers on the spacious lawns of the Vice-Admiral's official residence. As often happens in these parties, the menfolk drifted together, regrouping themselves into small bunches according to their official status. The women for their part did likewise, flocking according to the ranking of their husbands.

There was, however, a small, rather motley group of the wives of all the officers who worked in the Docks in which eventually all such ladies would seek refuge, once they finished the officially expected rounds of other groups. It is to this group that Rama Bhargava and Meena Mathur meandered, though separately.

Usha Bhatnagar was already there. She was Meena's close friend. Naturally, Meena approached her on joining the group, and lightly patted her on the shoulder to attract her attention.

"Hello, Meena, we have been waiting for you, but you were busy with big bosses. And why not? I would do the same if I were wearing a gorgeous sari like yours," Usha, garrulous as usual, said mischievously.

"Don't bother about the sari. It's not a new one. Tell me instead how I look," Meena tried to divert her attention from the sari.

"Oh, haven't any of those V.I.P.s you were talking to told you already? My dear Meena, you look smashing as always, but that sari adds to your charm. Where did you get it? It's an excellent French Chiffon, that much I know."

Rama Bhargava who was standing nearby listening to the tete-a- tete of the two younger ladies stepped in. "Yes Meena, where did you get it, it's exquisite. I also immensely like French Chiffon," she remarked. This made it impossible for Meena to dodge the issue. After all, Ms. Rama Bhargava was the wife of her husband's immediate boss.

"Oh, I didn't purchase it. It was a Diwali present from Altafbhai, a good family friend," Meena replied sheepishly.

"Must be a big businessman, to give a sari like that," Rama remarked sharply.

"Yes, he is in the export business, a big executive in a foreign export company," Meena added needlessly but perhaps to explain the foreign origin of the expensive sari.

"How did you come to know him. In our kind of job we don't come in contact with such business people," Rama continued her cross-examination.

"Oh, we came to know him through my father-in-law. He later invited us to dinner at his place," Meena added innocently.

"Oh, I see," Rama remarked icily. Usha was sorry for her friend and felt a little guilty at having first broached the subject. Taking advantage of a lady joining the group, she pulled Meena away from her boss' wife. When out of earshot she said, "I am extremely sorry Meena. I started it all. I never realised that she was listening. Anyway, you should not have mentioned that Altafbhai or whatever was his name. I only hope she does not go broadcasting it everywhere." Soon dinner was announced and the two friends made a beeline for the tables where food was laid.

Rama Bhargava did not spread the juicy bit she had extracted from Meena Mathur among other wives, as feared by Usha Bhatnagar. Instead she used it to work up a huge grievance against her husband. It had become a common practice in the Bhargava household, that whenever the couple returned from an evening party or dinner, Ms. Bhargava would unleash a commentary on the evening's events, critically appraising the hosts and every couple that had attended the gathering, and in the process run her husband down sometimes criticising his mannerism, sometimes his excessive attention to other women, or whatever caught her fancy. Mr. Bhargava knowing his wife's propensity had built a fairly impregnable rampart of silence against her verbal onslaught. He did the same that night. Picking up a nondescript magazine he buried himself in it. However, he pricked up his ears when he heard the tale about some Altafbhai giving an expensive sari to his assistant's wife as a Diwali present. He set the magazine aside and asked, "Which Altafbhai? What did she say he does?" His wife misunderstood the import of his query.

"Not an ordinary shopkeeper or trader like your grocer who sends half a kilo of commonplace sweets to you as Diwali gift. He is a badasaab in a foreign trading company that is engaged in exports," she said tauntingly. Not her derisive gibe, but what she said made him anxious.

"What else did Meena tell you about this man Altaf?" he asked inquisitively.

"Why, you want to go and ingratiate yourself with him? If you are so keen you should have asked her yourself. Did you not notice her sari? What were you doing all the while?" Rama Bhargava was again on the offensive.

"Look, you have been repeatedly telling me you want a transfer from this place. I was therefore, all the time hanging around the Joint Secretary who has come along with the Minister. He is the one who can do it if he means to."

"What did he say?" she asked, cooling down.

"Well, he gave a promise of sorts. I will remind him again tomorrow. They are all coming to our establishment in the morning," Bhargava, re-assured by the gentleness in her tone, gave her some additional information.

By this time Ms. Bhargava had changed into nightclothes. Sobered by the thought that her husband, about whose extracurricular capabilities she had grave doubts, had at long last done something for getting a transfer, she soon fell asleep. But Mr. Bhargava could not. What his wife had told him about his assistant's cordial relationship with a businessman of a foreign company caused him great anxiety. He had served for more than two decades in defence-related organisations and had thus became sensitive to security needs. His concern was further exacerbated when he recalled that Rajesh Mathur was visibly unhappy ever since he had been superseded. He personally liked the young man but could not do much to help him because somehow the Vice-Admiral had developed reservations about his capabilities. Therefore, when Rajesh offered to help him with his chores he let him handle several files that should not have normally gone to him, taking it as his effort to ingratiate himself with the superiors. He now wondered if it was not a huge blunder on his part. This thought made him more restless. He was in a quandary what to do. His conscience did not permit him to sleep over the matter ignoring what had come to his notice. He could not report the matter straightaway to the Vice-Admiral whose immediate reaction would be to haul him over the coals for being careless about his subordinates. Maybe the Vice-Admiral would take some drastic action against Rajesh in anger, while it is possible that the whole thing was a product of his imagination and Rajesh was perfectly innocent.

He pondered over the dilemma for a long time, when suddenly a possible solution occurred to him that made him smile. He knew Mundkur, the chief of the counter-intelligence unit in the Mumbai office of the Intelligence Bureau. He had come in contact with Mundkur a year ago in connection with a case and was well impressed by his professionalism and discreet handling of sensitive matters. He thought, Mundkur would find out the truth tactfully if he could be persuaded to take interest in the case. He decided to contact Mundkur in the morning before going to the office and apprise him of his apprehensions. This put his mind at rest and he dozed off to sleep in the wee hours of the morning.

"Good morning, Mr. Mundkur. This is Bhaskar Bhargava from Mazgaon Docks. Sorry for ringing you up so early in the morning but there's something very urgent I want to talk to you about," Bhargava rang up Mundkur after making sure that his wife was out of the way.

"That's okay with me. When do we meet?" Mundkur asked in a businesslike manner, sensing that Bhargava was indeed very anxious.

"Really speaking, at the earliest but there's a problem. I cannot tear myself away from the office. A host of Defence Ministry officials are visiting us this morning, and I cannot afford to wait till they leave," Bhargava presented his difficulty.

"Where do you live, Mr. Bhargava?"

"Napean sea road."

"Then do one thing, instead of taking the usual Walkeshwar road which I presume you would be taking every day, go by Kemp's Corner."

"Okay, no problem. But how does it solve my problem?" Bhargava asked.

"When do you usually leave for the office?" Mundkur asked, ignoring Bhargava's query.

"At eight-forty five because I must reach my office by nine-thirty."

"Okay, today leave at eight-forty and be at Kemp's Corner by eight-fifty. You will be then on time for your office. I will be standing at Kemp's Corner on the footpath in front of the Chinese restaurant that you face as you take right turn at the corner to go south. For quick recognition I shall be in a blue safari suit. Pick me up and then tell me your story. Drop me at a convenient place en route when we finish talking. Is it clear to you?" Mundkur asked in the end.

"Yes, clear. A marvellous idea I must say, Mr. Mundkur," said Bhargava, in admiration.

"Then see you at eight-thirty at Kemp's Corner," Mundkur repeated the vital details for Bhargava's benefit and hung up.

There was no difficulty spotting Mundkur. Bhargava briefly stopped the car at the curb and opened the door. Mundkur hopped in closing the door after him. As soon as they hit the main road Mundkur said, "Now tell me what is bothering you so much Mr. Bhargava."

Bhargava gave an account of all that had happened the previous night and also frankly expressed his misgivings.

"Your suspicion, Mr. Bhargava is not at all misplaced, going by the circumstances you just now described," Mundkur said in an encouraging tone. "I must compliment you on your sense of duty. For my part I may assure you that I would do my best to get at the truth, and quickly. Give me a tinkle at seven-thirty in the evening. By that time our men would have collected enough dope on this mysterious Altafbhai and his outfit."

"That would be wonderful."

"We will then be in a position to decide if further probe was necessary or it could be ignored as an innocent indiscretion on the part of your assistant."

Bhargava nodded in affirmation.

"Please drop me near the Churchgate railway station and then proceed. My car would be waiting somewhere nearby," Mundkur instructed.

Mundkur got out of the car as smoothly as he had got into it and disappeared in the crowd of office goers.

Bhaskar Bhargava impatiently waited for the evening to come. The moment it was seven-thirty by his watch he rang up Mundkur. "Mr. Bhargava, I think we are going to have a job on our hands—you and me. Let's meet tomorrow. It's a holiday for you. Why don't we meet at the Nish restaurant on the August Kranti Marg at eleven-thirty. It's not very far from the place where you live and is not much crowded either at that hour. We can therefore, talk at leisure and in comparative privacy," Mundkur suggested. Bhargava was left with no choice but to agree. Not that he did not want to meet Mundkur. In fact he was dying to hear what Mundkur had found out. His problem was that he had promised to chauffeur his wife to the market. He did not want to plead with Mundkur so he decided to face his wife, come what may.

"It would suit me fine, Mr. Mundkur," he told Mundkur, limply.

"Excellent. See you then tomorrow at Nish at eleven-thirty. I will be waiting for you at a table for two at the far end of the hall. Good night." Mundkur articulated briefly and disconnected. He was not used to talking more than required.

When Bhaskar Bhargava entered Nish restaurant, Mundkur was already sitting there. He beckoned Bhargava to join him and immediately ordered some eats and tea after ascertaining the latter's preference. Once the waiter was out of the way, Mundkur straight away broached the subject.

"As I mentioned to you on the phone we have a very testing time ahead. At least that is my gut feeling."

"What precisely do you mean?" Bhargava asked, not comprehending the real import of Mundkur's remark.

"You see we were quite lucky in being able to locate your worthy assistant's generous friend. Altaf Hussain is otherwise a common name but luckily for us there is only one Altaf in the foreign trading community in Mumbai. Mr. Altaf Hussain is a dashing guy, and the mainstay of the West Asia Trading Corporation. This is said to be a Kuwaiti company that is chiefly engaged in exporting rice and other cereals as well as fruit and vegetables to the Middle-East and importing carpets, dates and the like into India from there. Altaf Hussain carries the designation Trade Promotion Officer that obviously allows him freedom and opportunity to move around and meet people. While the company's office is located in the Fort area, our quarry lives with his family in one of the Jolly Maker buildings in Cuffe Parade. He is a Kuwaiti passport holder but we are not sure if he is really a Kuwaiti by birth for, he does not have the looks of an Arab. He is also very fond of giving parties and attending parties. That's how he met your assistant." Mundkur paused to observe Bhargava's reaction.

"Strange, very strange. Rajesh is otherwise not a party going man. He is supposed to have been introduced to Altaf by his father who is a lawyer, practises here in Mumbai though the family actually hails from Uttar Pradesh."

"Oh, that fits one more piece in our jigsaw puzzle. I suspect that this Altaf Hussain is either from U.P. or his family hails from U.P. For all I know he might even be a Muhajir. These people usually seek out people from U.P. and befriend them."

"Quite possible. Lucky that he did not hunt me out. You know I am also from U.P." Bhargava said sheepishly.

"That's probably because unlike your assistant, you do not have a freewheeling relative here. Anyway, let's give some thought to how we should proceed from here. We will now be keeping both under observation and at the same time find out more about this company's activities as well as Altaf Hussain's background, though my feeling is that he is anything but a simple business executive. As for you, I suggest, Mr. Bhargava, that you keep a wary eye on your assistant's activities in the office and keep him away from sensitive matters, especially if they are not his direct concern. Please also find out if he has of late befriended some one else from a different section or division. He would do that to cull information that is not readily available to him in his section. And please do not take any one into confidence, not even your Chairman at least for the present." Mundkur completed his briefing.

"It's good that you mentioned our Chairman. I was wondering whether I should not tell him."

"No. Right now you don't have to tell him anything. If our hunch comes true we will find the right moment to tell him what is going on in his outfit. We will cover you properly, have no worry on that count," Mundkur assured Bhargava. After a brief pause he added, "Incidentally Mr. Bhargava, can we have a good photograph of your assistant Rajesh Mathur, maybe from his dossier or identity card records? That would help our officers identify him quickly."

"I can do one better The launching ceremony of the frigate has been completely video taped. There's a focus for full one minute on him in it when he was introduced to the Defence Minister. It will give your men his total profile. I can easily procure a copy for you." Bhargava smiled in self-appreciation.

"That would be excellent. Please give me a ring as soon as you get it. I will have it collected from you."

It was time for them to depart. Mundkur briefly repeated the instructions to Bhargava and asked him to be in touch with him. He then beckoned the waiter to bring the bill.

The next day in office Mundkur allocated tasks to his officers. Khot and his group were to trail Altaf Hussain and also make enquiries about the expanse and types of his activities. Bhadang and his team were to keep watch on Rajesh Mathur's movements. Each group was to report to him the developments, first thing in the morning when Mundkur came to office.

Seven days passed without any group reporting any exciting development that could connect the two targets. Khot of course had found out that Altaf Hussain threw dinner parties at his residence at least once in a month to which he invited Indians from diverse fields and vocations, and that he had an expensive way of living. In contrast his trading company did not appear to be transacting much business.

On the eighth day when the full team assembled in Mundkur's cabin Bhadang opened his account somewhat hesitatingly. "Sir," he commenced, "My men noticed a rather bizarre thing about Rajesh Mathur yesterday. He left his office around five-thirty in the evening in his car, which is his usual practice. Our men followed him. Instead of going home he went towards the President Hotel at Cuffe Parade. There's a public park there close by. It's called Colaba Woods. He parked his car at a distance and entered the park. After strolling for a while in a listless manner he settled down on a bench. He then got up and went to the lawn that is on the southern side of the park. He walked on the lawn for a few minutes and sat down near a palm tree. It was not clear if he was waiting for some one or had come only for fresh air. He changed his sitting position once or twice. Must have spent about ten minutes there. He then got up and went straight to his car and drove straight back home. There weren't many people on the lawn at that time, so our men couldn't go close enough to see what he was actually doing there."

"Ah, there seems to be much more to it then meets the eye," Mundkur remarked, and asked Khot if he had anything to report.

"Sir, in the light of what Bhadang has reported just now what I have to tell you assumes considerable significance." Khot began.

"Is that so? What have you got in your bag?" Mundkur asked.

"Sir, my men shadowed Altaf when he left the company office at about four-thirty. First he went to Strand bookshop and browsed through some books. Did not purchase any. From there he went home. It was five-thirty when he reached Jolly Maker building. Around six-thirty he was seen leaving the building in his car. He had his two children with him. He went to Colaba causeway where he purchased an assortment of chocolates from a confectionery shop. He then drove to the World Trade Centre, and parking his car near the Casablanca building took the children to the Colaba Woods. First they went to the children's section and later roamed around a bit. They finally settled down on the lawn that is on the southern side of the park. Instead of occupying a central patch they sat at the edge where there is a row of palm trees girdling the lawn. Altaf took out chocolates from his pocket and gave them to his children. He also helped himself to some. For a casual observer it was a perfect scene of a father enjoying the evening in the company of his children. After a while he gathered his children and returned home."

"We are very close to putting two and two together," Mundkur interjected, "What we have to ascertain is whether Rajesh and Altaf took their positions under or near the same palm tree. For that purpose I suggest that you both, Khot and Bhadang, send a man each from your watcher teams and let them pin point the spot. They may also examine it closely to find out if any tell-tale marks exist that would suggest the use of the spot as a Dead Letter Box to pass material."

"Yes Sir, that would be a clear indication of their clandestine relationship," Khot remarked.

"And with very sinister implications for the Mazgaon Docks and of course the country," Mundkur completed the observation and added, "Now get cracking. We are on the threshold of a big breakthrough. Can't afford to lose time."

After about three hours the two watchers who visited the park together confirmed that both the quarries had sat under precisely the same palm tree. Unfortunately they noticed nothing of significance on the ground because the gardeners had watered the whole area in the morning. Mundkur immediately requested the Commissioner of Police to place

AUDACIOUS VENTURE   **153**

the telephones of Altaf and Rajesh Mathur under observation, and also asked his men to be extra vigilant now that the hunt for the big game was on.

"Nothing of significance was noticed in the tapes of their telephonic conversations. I got the latest report a little while ago. The Cyber Crime Cell of the Crime Branch has likewise reported that though both have Internet connection they don't seem to be using it for contacting each other unless they have worked out some devious way. It will take a lot of time and effort to discover it, if there exists any. For the present there is no alternative to intensifying our vigil. I am sure as hell that they must communicate periodically now that the business is thriving, and that secrets passed from the Docks would be mostly in the form of documents, their photo-films and so on, and occasionally, written reports. We have discovered one way of indirect communication. They would use it again perhaps at some other place in a different manner. And take it from me, one of these days they must physically meet sub rosa. We should be waiting for that opportunity so that we can catch them together." Mundkur was briefing his officers after they drew a blank for the tenth consecutive day.

"Our sights are set, Sir. We know whom we have to catch and in which situation. Every endeavour of ours would be directed towards that end." Khot paraphrased Mundkur. Bhadang nodded his concurrence.

It was the Wednesday of the week that followed Mundkur's exhortations to his officers to be on the look out for the right opportunity to nab the twosome. For the two watcher teams the whole day passed like any other, nothing different from the routine. Both Altaf and Rajesh attended their respective offices and left for home in the evening. Khot's team that was trailing Altaf saw him enter Jolly Maker building where he lived, and parked itself at a strategic place some distance away. The only thought uppermost on the minds of the watchers was the approach of nine o'clock, when the night shift watchers would relieve them. All of a sudden they saw Altaf's car coming out of the building gate. It was seven-fifty. Altaf was alone in the car. They followed him at a safe distance.

Altaf cruised leisurely by the Madam Cama road and took a left turn where the road meets Marine Drive. While the watchers' car was negotiating the turn he turned left again taking the road that passes in front of the new wing of Hotel Oberoi. When the watchers' car reached that road Altaf's car was nowhere to be seen. They therefore, lingered for a brief while at the crossroads wondering whether he had gone straight ahead or turned left again to skirt the Oberoi hotel. All of a sudden one of the watchers noticed Altaf emerging from the basement-parking place of the hotel. They could not immediately move lest he noticed them and therefore, watched him from their car as he entered the hotel lobby. Two watchers went inside the hotel in search of Altaf. They carefully scanned the lobby and the restaurants but could not find him. They went to the basement car park as well. His car was very much there.

The team leader who had stayed back in the car hurried to inform Khot and Mundkur on the mobile phone that they had lost track of Altaf. "He is obviously on a sly errand," Mundkur observed. "Please continue the search for him but don't leave the hotel. He was bound to return to retrieve the car."

While the search for Altaf was going on at the Oberoi, the leader of Bhadang's watcher team that was maintaining a vigil at Rajesh Mathur's building rang up Mundkur. "He left his house at eight and after parking his car by the roadside on Marine Drive, entered Hotel Oberoi. Two watchers have also followed him inside the hotel to keep a track of him," he reported. It was clear to Mundkur that the time for action had arrived, though rather suddenly. He told both the teams to keep on their respective trails, and that he was himself reaching the hotel within minutes.

Mundkur asked Khot and Bhadang to join him immediately and bring Gayatri Monappa and Sweta Pande along. The women may have a role to play should action become necessary, he told them. Mundkur also rang up Inspector Sawant of City Crime Branch, his old friend and a trustworthy police officer. "Sawant, want some real action? Here's an opportunity. Please reach Mantralaya with two sections of your men and at least two fast cars. I will explain to you the action plan when we meet," he said, in a business-like manner.

While Mundkur was about to reach the Oberoi he got a message from the team trailing Rajesh that he came out from the hotel after sitting for a while in the lobby and was now moving in his car towards Churchgate. For a moment Mundkur thought that a golden opportunity had slipped from his hands but he was not one to give up so easily. There had to be a meeting between the two, he reasoned with himself. It is not unlikely that there was some mix up. But then going by the rules of the spy game, they would converge again at the alternative meeting place which could be found out only by closely shadowing Rajesh. He, therefore, warned the watcher team not to lose his trail under any circumstances and decided to remain himself with the Altaf's watcher team till some definite indications were available about their next place of meeting.

After about ten minutes, Mundkur got the message that Rajesh had gone straight to the Gateway of India and was now strolling towards the Radio Club that was at the farther end of the boulevard. Mundkur was sure that Rajesh was whiling away the time before the moment for the next meeting arrived. The question before him was, what would be the place? He was reasonably sure they would now have dinner together. That would give Mundkur and his team sufficient time to carry out the blitzkrieg, but first he must plan for such an exigency.

Around nine o'clock Mundkur got a tinkle from the team that was following Rajesh that at ten minutes to nine he had got into his car and was going back towards Churchgate. Mundkur asked his officers to get into the cars and wait for further instructions. A few minutes later his cell phone buzzed again. It was the watcher team leader reporting again that Rajesh had parked his car near the Braborne stadium and then gone inside the Gaylord restaurant. 'So, that's the place where he would now be meeting Altaf.' Mundkur muttered to himself.

Mundkur asked Inspector Sawant on the phone to proceed at once to Eros cinema theatre and meet him in front of the building. He asked Altaf's watcher team to stay put, where they were in case the latter returned to pick up his car. "Come on. Let's go quickly to Eros cinema." Mundkur told his driver. Inspector Sawant was already waiting for him when Mundkur arrived. After briefly telling Inspector Sawant his further plan of action Mundkur asked him to stay put till he received a call, and started for Gaylords restaurant on foot. He beckoned Khot and Bhadang to accompany him. When they were nearing the restaurant one of the watchers met him near the stadium. He pointed out a red Maruti car, saying that it belonged to Rajesh. Near the entrance of the restaurant they met the other two watchers. They confirmed that Rajesh was inside sitting at a table with Altaf. Keeping the others, behind Mundkur entered the restaurant premises to discreetly survey the setting. A couple of minutes later he emerged from the restaurant, beaming. "The right moment to act," he whispered to Khot and Bhadang. "You two stay here, keeping a vigil on both of them. Don't hesitate to act at once should the need arise though I don't suppose they would part company that early. Under no circumstances should they be allowed to leave the restaurant. I will return in a few minutes. Till then hold the fort." Mundkur went back to where Inspector Sawant and others were waiting for him.

"Sawant," said Mundkur on reaching the place near Eros cinema where Inspector Sawant was waiting for him. "The right opportunity to nab them has arrived. They are together in the restaurant eating. But let's first place your men at strategic places so that those two blokes can't escape even if they try to."

"Oh yes. I have already done some thinking on it while you were away," responded Inspector Sawant and quickly explained to Mundkur where he would be placing the men."

"That's excellent. Let's order them to take positions. There's no time to spare," said Mundkur approvingly. Soon every possible point of escape was effectively blocked.

For their part Mundkur, Inspector Sawant and the two ladies, namely Gayatri and Sweta who had been asked to stay behind, moved on to the restaurant. "No change in situation Sir." Khot said in a low voice.

"Suits us fine, now you two, Khot and Bhadang remain where you are but please be on the alert. Please rush in the moment you hear a commotion inside the restaurant. We would need your assistance." Mundkur gave parting instructions.

The foursome then entered the restaurant posing as two friendly couples. Mundkur and Sawant went to the manager's cabin and taking him into confidence, arranged that the table next to the one at which Altaf and Rajesh were sitting, would be allotted to them the moment it was cleared. The manager agreed and instructed the steward accordingly, introducing the two to him as his personal friends. Within a few minutes the steward ushered them in saying that the table had been tidied. They went inside chatting, as if the two normal couples out for a dinner together.

When the steward brought the menu cards Mundkur fumbled as if for his glasses inside a small handbag he was carrying with him. What he in fact did was to position the bag in one corner of the table in such a manner that a small hole on its side, that coincided with the lens of a highly sensitive video camera that was inside the bag, faced the two targets who were sitting next to them. In the meantime Sawant declared that he would settle for orange juice. The two ladies cooed their agreement. "Okay, in that case I too shall have orange juice," said Mundkur, giving up the search for spectacles. Sawant placed on order on behalf of them all. As soon as the steward left with the order they started studying the menu cards again, discussing various dishes among themselves.

Rajesh threw a few furtive glances at the two young ladies at the next table and then ceased to evince interest. Something far more serious was weighing on his mind. Altaf watched them warily for a while, sizing up the two fit looking men but his suspicion was allayed by the fact that there were two ladies in the group. He eyed them too, but his attention was soon claimed by the steward who came to take order for dessert. "What would you like to have for dessert?" Altaf asked Rajesh. "Vanilla ice cream with strawberry" Rajesh indicated his preference. "Okay, I shall have the same." muttered Altaf. "Two vanilla ice creams with strawberry," he told the steward in a louder tone who promptly scribbled the order on his notepad and disappeared.

Taking advantage of the lull Rajesh took out a small cigarette case from his breast pocket and quietly pushed it towards Altaf. "Altafbhai, this is a small contribution for the occasion. Hope you like it," he said in a low, hoarse voice. At that moment Mundkur who was watching them from the corner of an eye drained the remaining juice from the glass and brought it down with a thud. That was a signal for others to act. Inspector Sawant and Gayatri immediately rushed to either side of Altaf while Mundkur and Sweta flanked Rajesh.

Altaf and Rajesh were both stunned. It was Altaf who gathered his wits first and asked in an irritated tone, "Who are you? What do you want?"

"We are police and you are under arrest," Inspector Sawant replied sternly, placing his hand on Altaf's shoulder.

"So what? You can't behave so atrociously. We are two friends dining here. What's wrong in that?" Altaf simultaneously tried to rise in his seat asking Rajesh to do likewise, but Inspector Sawant who was strongly built, and Gayatri, who was a karate black belt holder, together pushed him down. Rajesh was so flabbergasted that he did not make any move. Hearing the commotion, Khot and Bhadang also rushed in, after asking the watchers to call the two cars that were stationed at a distance. They helped in dragging Altaf and Rajesh to the entrance of the restaurant. Altaf was vehemently protesting but the hold on him was so firm that he could not do much. The captives were thrust separately into the two waiting cars where burly armed policemen flanked them. Mundkur asked the drivers to proceed straight to Crime Branch office and himself followed them in another car.

By the time their vehicles reached the Crime Branch office, Mundkur had worked out in his mind the line of action he would now adopt. Therefore, as soon as everyone alighted he asked Khot and Bhadang to take the two prisoners to two different rooms and thoroughly search their persons. He decided to tackle them separately from the very beginning so that they did not draw sustenance from each other. He requested Inspector Sawant to depute some police officers to assist Khot and Bhadang, for the legal aspect of the case would have to be handled by the police.

"I suggest Sawant, you tackle this fellow Altaf at the moment. He may need some rough handling, just to soften him a bit," Mundkur suggested.

"As you like. I am game. The chap is also making a nuisance of himself, talking about his legal rights as a foreign national."

"That's the real reason why I want you to deal with him, so that you can take care of those legal hassles as well with the assistance of your legal advisor."

"Okay, okay. I will straighten him out. No problem," Sawant agreed.

"As for interrogation I suggest we concentrate on Rajesh first. He is likely to break down much easily and thus provide possible evidence to corner Altaf." Mundkur defined his strategy.

Within minutes Khot reported that he had recovered a Goldflake cigarette packet from Altaf's breast pocket. It did not contain any cigarettes but a mini cassette that is normally used in a dictaphone. Mundkur knew that Rajesh had passed on the packet to Altaf. As a matter of fact he had given the signal for action as soon as he noticed the transaction. "Let's see if the cassette contains anything incriminating that would help us charge both of them with a serious crime. Right now we have precious little." Mundkur said. He called for a mini tape recorder and played the tape, while the other officers listened. They were greatly elated to hear the contents, which were office memos, notes and even letters read out by Rajesh.

"Obviously, this is how instead of filming documents, they were passed by Rajesh to Altaf. A clever way, I must say. We are very lucky indeed to lay hands on the tape. This is actually smoking gun evidence that clearly establishes that Altaf was working as a spy master for a foreign country—I am not very sure that it is Kuwait—and Rajesh is the mole he has created in the Mazgaon Docks to ferret out their secrets." Mundkur interpreted the existence of the tape for the benefit of his colleagues.

"Now, Khot and Bhadang, you must hurry to the houses of these two blokes. They must be thoroughly searched. And of course you will have to search their office cabins also. All these tasks must be completed before daybreak. That will give us enough time to prepare documents to seek police custody remand for them. We will face stiff opposition from their lawyers. Rajesh's father himself is a lawyer, and I won't be surprised if some prominent city lawyer holds a standing brief for Altaf or his company. To gain access to Rajesh's cabin, I will have to seek the Admiral's permission. I will take care of that while you are searching their houses. Now, get busy, fast. Take adequate number of Crime Branch officers with you. Altaf's house in particular will have to be rummaged thoroughly. Get in touch with me the moment you find anything interesting," he said. Inspector Sawant also completed the arrest formalities shortly thereafter and dispatched the two guests to two different rooms on the third floor of the Crime Branch Lock-up.

By four-thirty in the morning both the search parties were back in the Crime Branch office. Their booty comprised: a small transistor radio recovered from the side table that was next to Rajesh's bed. A dictaphone, a small camera with folding tripod from the locked drawer of his desk in the office. A compact transmitter from the study of Altaf, and 19 Kgs of black plastic stuff packed in packages of one kilogram each from the loft over the bathroom of the servant's quarter attached to his apartment. A quick check up with the Forensic Science Laboratory led to the stunning discovery that the black plastic stuff was indeed the deadly RDX.

"It's not very clear at the moment, to what precise purpose all these things were being put by these chaps. Their interrogation alone would reveal us the truth. Together, however, they provide damning evidence against Altaf and his accomplice," Mundkur observed after examining the finds.

"Let's get ready for the interrogation then, but, ah, we must first obtain their police custody remand." Inspector Sawant responded. He did not have much difficulty in obtaining police custody remand for both of them for five days. This, they thought, would give them enough time to unearth all the ramifications of the case.

That night when Rajesh Mathur was brought into the interrogation room, Mundkur, Inspector Sawant, Khot, Bhadang and a couple of expert interrogators from the Crime Branch were already seated around a table. Mundkur asked Rajesh to sit down. The latter meekly occupied the chair that was meant for him, keeping his gaze riveted to the floor.

"Yes Mr. Rajesh Mathur, how do you find your new quarters? You are going to be our guest for five long days, so make yourself comfortable. That's the best we can provide. You are perhaps used to a lavish style of living, and why not? With free flow of money coming from our dear Altafbhai in exchange for selling the country's secrets, for betraying the motherland." Mundkur opened the interrogation. Rajesh did not respond.

"The country entrusted you with its defence secrets because you hold a responsible position of trust. The Defence Minsiter honoured you only the other day little realising that you were double-crossing, selling national secrets for money. And what about your family? Your old father, he has such a fine reputation as a lawyer. He will have to hang his head in shame. Your wife and your children, people will jeer at them in the streets. Did you ever think of that? "

"No Sir, I am terribly ashamed of myself now. I almost unknowingly walked into it," Rajesh softly mumbled. He was deeply hurt at being called a traitor.

"You were present in the court, Mr. Rajesh, when we presented the evidence we have against you both. You are an educated man, and a lawyer's son to boot. You would have by now realised that we have some very damaging evidence against you, and whether you co-operate or not we are determined to get more. But let me tell you, our main target is this enigmatic Altaf. We will crack him too. We have broken greater crooks. So, if you really feel remorseful about betraying the country and want to make amends, you can co-operate with us in fixing this scoundrel who lured you into this murky business."

"What do you want me to do?" Rajesh asked.

"Very simple. Tell us the whole story. It will save us a lot of bother. In any case we are going to get it out of you, but if you tell us on your own without suppressing vital facts or trying to dupe us it will go a long way in our taking a softer stance towards you." Mundkur made the proposition.

"I will Sir, but one request. Keep my family out of it. The sin is mine and mine alone."

"That's a promise." Mundkur.

Rajesh asked for a glass of water and drained it down. Then sinking back into the chair he began, "It all started very innocently some eight or nine months ago. My father met Altaf Hussain at a dinner at a common friend's house. We hail from UP. He claimed that his family was originally from UP. Therefore he showed warmth and affinity. Later he invited my father as well as my wife and me to his house for a dinner. They appeared to be a friendly sort to us. A month or so later, he invited us again at his place along with our children for the birthday bash he had organised for his son. One thing led to another, and I found myself invited by Altaf for lunches at periodic intervals. I took it only as a friendly gesture. One day he asked me for our departmental telephone directory pleading some excuse. I was a bit reluctant because our directory is marked confidential, but he convinced me that no great harm would be come to me, and I agreed. Later whenever we met he would ask me a few questions about the goings on in Mazgaon Docks, and I would reply taking them to be casual questions.

"Here I may tell you that just about the time I met Altaf I was overlooked for promotion in my set-up and was very upset about it. When I confided to Altaf he sympathised with me. Thereafter he would passingly broach that subject whenever we met and curse my seniors for being so unjust. One day he invited me for lunch at an expensive restaurant and made a proposition. He said that denial of promotion means denial of higher status and denial of extra remuneration. While nothing could be done about the abnegation of higher status, he could compensate for the other if I helped him. His idea was that I should give him information about the happenings in the docks in the form of periodic reports and in turn he would make me generous payments which I could use to make my family happy. I was taken aback but he argued that I would not be required to do anything out of the way to oblige him. He asked me to take my own time and decide.

"I mulled over the proposal for some weeks and finally decided to do his bidding. Then a regular relationship developed. He told me that it was not proper for us to meet frequently and taught me how to pass my reports indirectly. A few days later he invited me to a hotel where a stranger who was perhaps his colleague taught me how to use a camera to photograph documents and a mini tape recorder in which I could read documents, noting etc. and which I could carry, upholstered, secretly under the arm when I went for a discussion or meeting. Later in a separate meeting, Altaf gave me a few pieces of a peculiar contraption that looked like a metallic syringe. I was to conceal a film roll or cassette into it and bury it at a predetermined spot either in the Kamala Nehru park or the Colaba Woods park. If it was a document we were to exchange similar looking bags in a shop. Altaf also gave me his personal telephone number and a code. I was supposed to ring up that number and ask if it was a particular number that was only slightly different but that difference would indicate what kind of material I wished to pass to him. Altaf would say, 'wrong number' and hang up. He gave me a tiny radio and said that the following day I would hear on the radio, which had a fixed frequency, *raag malkauns* for just one minute at six-forty five in the morning. The instrument on which it would be played would determine the place where I had to deposit the material or meet. The whole thing was worked out in detail. Therefore, it worked perfectly well.

"About a fortnight ago I developed an impression that my boss Bhargava was no longer comfortable with me. Earlier he trusted me with every thing, which facilitated my collecting information for Altaf but now he would not pass files to me. I, therefore, got a bit apprehensive and wanted to seek Altaf's counsel. When I passed a film roll to him through the Colaba Woods transfer point I also included a brief note in it asking for a personal meeting. The following day I heard the *malkauns* tune on Sitar, which meant that we would meet in the lobby of Hotel Oberoi at 8 p.m. I went there on time but did not find him. I went to Gateway of India to kill time and then proceeded to Gaylords restaurant which was our alternative place of meeting at 9 p.m. You caught us there. The vital mistake I committed was, disregarding his instruction never to pass any material during a personal meeting. I was afraid and wanted to suggest to Altaf that he permit me to keep quiet for some time. I had already some material with me recorded on the tape and thought of passing it onto him since there would be no communication between us thereafter. You have got that tape now which has sealed our fate." Rajesh ended his narration and concealed his face between his two palms.

"How much did he pay for this work?" Mundkur asked. Rajesh had so far made no mention of the payments he received.

"Ten thousand a month."

"Plus expensive presents from time to time." Mundkur supplemented.

"That's true, but that was not very frequent after he started paying me regularly."

"That will do for the moment, Rajesh." Mundkur signalled the end of the session.

The following night it was Altaf's turn to face the interrogation team. No one in the team expected it to be a cakewalk, but they had not anticipated Altaf to be such a tough nut either, especially because there was so much damning evidence against him. For every incriminating evidence or circumstance he had a ready answer, so much so that even placing the RDX packets seized from his flat before him did not unnerve him. Starting with disputing that it was indeed RDX he went on to claim that the place where it was found was not under the control of his family since it was a servant's quarter. He even suggested that the police might have planted it there to involve him. But he was dealing with people who were seasoned in the game and had enough material up their sleeve that would implicate him.

The interrogation team had to work for three nights and almost three days before it could piece together the whole story, with reasonable certainty that it was the truth. Put succinctly it ran as follows:

Altaf Hussain's real name was Mohammed Saifuddin Qadri. He belonged to a Muhajir family that had settled down at Multan. After completing his high school education he joined the Army where within a short time he rose to become a Major. While he was doing a stint in the Directorate of Military Intelligence his services were requisitioned by the Inter-Services Intelligence. That was some four years ago.

One day the Chief of ISI called a meeting of a handful of young officers that included Major Qadri. He told them that he was in search of bold officers with initiative who could fend for themselves in the most trying situations. Elaborating, the Chief said that ISI officers were posted abroad under diplomatic cover as members of the embassy staff, so that if they were caught running spy operations by the host country they could claim diplomatic immunity. This was valued very much by ISI officers who were posted to hostile countries. But it had the disadvantage also. They were quickly identified by the counter-intelligence agencies and neutralised, thus considerably reducing their utility. The Chief wanted to try a new experiment. He wanted to send officers in the guise of a businessman or executive to these hostile countries. They would have no diplomatic cover but would enjoy more freedom to operate. Since this involved considerable risk as, if caught they would have to face the consequences according to the law of the land, the Chief wanted people to volunteer. They were supposed to offer their candidature in a private communication to the Chief. Finally two officers were selected, Qadri was one of them.

A few months later he was asked to proceed to Kuwait and join a trading firm named West Asia Trading Corporation. It was a company floated by some Kuwaiti nationals in collaboration with Pakistani traders, but with secret ISI funding. Qadri was asked to familiarise himself with the working of the Company and also to acquire the mannerisms of a business executive. The company was trading mostly with countries in the sub-continent. Qadri spent over a year in Kuwait doing the Company's work and became in every manner a business executive.

About eight months ago he was told that he had been transferred to the Mumbai office of the Company. While he was getting ready to move to Mumbai he was asked to meet a gentleman in Karachi. When he reached the given address he was greeted by an ISI officer who told him that his main brief in Mumbai would be to collect intelligence about naval establishments, that's why his office as well as residence would be located in south Mumbai close to those establishments. He was then sent for a month-long attachment to the Pakistani naval headquarters at Karachi where he was trained in naval matters and instructed about what information he should collect about the Indian navy. He then went back to Kuwait and travelled to Mumbai on a Kuwaiti passport that was furnished to him by the ISI.

He got an early break in Mumbai. While he was wondering how to make a beginning, Advocate Mohammed Yunus whom the Company had given a standing brief, threw a party. Qadri was of course invited, so were several prominent people of Mumbai. At the party he met a lawyer, Mathur by name whose family hailed from UP. During casual conversation Qadri learnt that Mathur was a widower and that his son who lived with him was working as Deputy Manager in the Mazgaon Docks. A golden opportunity had come his way so early, and he decided to exploit it to the full. Within a fortnight he threw a party himself, despite his wife's protests and invited Advocate Mathur along with his son and daughter-in-law. This is how he came to know Rajesh Mathur.

Thereafter he focussed his attention on Rajesh Mathur. Before long he realised that Rajesh was fond of good food and could not resist the temptation of eating at an expensive restaurant if he got a chance, and that he was frustrated with his job because he had been overlooked for promotion. Both these circumstances suited Qadri fine and he exploited them to the hilt. Eventually Rajesh agreed to supply him vital information about what was happening in the Docks. The ISI headquarters were extremely pleased with the quick progress he had made and sent a technician to Mumbai, who trained Rajesh in the use of various gadgets that would facilitate collection and transfer of information.

Things had quickly settled down to the routine, with none visualising any mishap when about a fortnight ago there was a frantic message from Rajesh who wanted to meet Qadri. It seemed that his boss had suddenly started ignoring him. Earlier at Qadri's instance Rajesh had ingratiated himself with his boss by offering to lend a helping hand even in matters that did not concern him directly. That gave him access to a wider area. The change in his boss' demeanour worried Rajesh. He wanted to seek his advice and suggest that they stop work for a while. That's when they were caught together.

As for the RDX, the designs were very sinister. When the ISI headquarters realised that Rajesh was completely under the thumb of Qadri, they conceived an ambitious plan. They wanted to totally cripple the Mazgaon Docks that built modern warships, at an opportune moment in the future. Qadri was instructed to build a network of accomplices at the workman level inside the Docks with the help of Rajesh. He would either win them over himself or introduce them to Qadri who would then try his usual tricks to make them amenable. Their job would be simply to implant RDX primed devices at prescribed vital locations. They were to be detonated simultaneously with remote control that Qadri would handle from outside. A timeframe of one year was given to Qadri for this operation. RDX was being supplied to him in small one kilogram packets concealed in the shipments of black dates that his company imported from Kuwait for supplying to local wholesale traders. Qadri discreetly removed them before the consignments were distributed, and stored them on the loft in his own apartment wherefrom they were recovered.

It was in wee hours of the morning of the fifth day when the interrogation team completed constructing Altaf's statement. Yet some minor missing links and contradictions remained. That was the last day of police remand. Both accused had to be produced in the court at 10 o'clock. Mundkur therefore, gestured to Bhadang to bring in Rajesh. His idea was to confront them both, as the last measure to smoothen out their respective statements and fill the small gaps that still existed.

A few minutes later Bhadang came running back. Checking himself outside the door he motioned Mundkur to come out. When Mundkur joined him he took him aside and in a worried, hushed tone requested him, "Could you please come to Rajesh's cell?" Apprehending that something was amiss, Mundkur followed him without asking any questions. The two policemen who had accompanied Bhadang to escort Rajesh to the interrogation room were standing in front of his cell glum faced and silent. Bhadang stopped when he reached them and gestured Mundkur, who was close behind, to look inside the cell. When Mundkur turned his gaze inside the cell a grisly sight met his eyes.

There at one end of the room below the only window the cell had hung Rajesh Mathur's inert body. His trousers were missing from his groins. Instead, one sleeve of the trousers was wound round his neck and the other was tied to a steel bar of the window grille. He had apparently committed suicide during the night. Mundkur dispatched one of the policemen to fetch Inspector Sawant and then turning to Bhadang, asked in even tone, "Why should this happen? You were talking to him everyday, while we were busy with the other fellow."

"Sir, when I met him last, that is, yesterday afternoon, he was in a depressed mood. His father had come to see him a little earlier. When I routinely asked him if he was all right he started crying uncontrollably. After a while when he cooled down he said that what you had told him during the questioning had come true. His father was now a broken man. He told him that he had stopped going to the court because he could not face the taunting questions of his colleagues. Rajesh's sons also had to be withdrawn from the school, and his wife had locked herself up in the bedroom. She refused to meet even her parents. Every one in the family is in terrible agony and for all this misery and humiliation, Rajesh said, he alone was responsible. I tried to comfort him but he was inconsolable."

"He must have then brooded over it alone in the stillness of the night and decided to end his life." Mundkur concluded. By that time Inspector Sawant had arrived. Turning to him Mundkur said, "One more problem for us, more particularly you. A death in police custody. He punished himself preemptively." He then briefly told Sawant what had happened and added, "We have to get busy with the formalities of the court. I suggest Sawant, you put an officer in charge of the dead body and carry out legal procedures. The custodial death aspect can be faced later. Right now we continue on the old track. In fact, I was expecting to get the confession of this chap recorded before a magistrate, if all went well. That would have been another strong piece of evidence against the main culprit."

"You are right. I will ask Inspector Ghaisas to attend to this new case while we start drafting the remand application and preparing papers for the court," Sawant echoed his agreement.

When Mundkur, Inspector Sawant and the Legal Advisor where huddled together in Sawant's room, Inspector Mohite of the criminal intelligence cell that specialised in collecting intelligence on organised gangs, darted in, "Sorry, gentlemen, for butting in like this but I have a very important information to share that cannot wait."

"No, no, it's fine. What's it that you want to tell us so urgently? We have to take the accused to the court at ten, therefore we are in a hurry," Inspector Sawant responded.

"I know that but what I am about to tell you has a direct bearing on the case that's why I barged in." Mohite emphasised the urgency of his mission.

"Please do take a seat and tell us all about it," Mundkur said pushing a chair towards him.

"Thank you," Mohite said briefly while sitting on the chair and commenced, "Now listen carefully, I have a very reliable information that Shakeel's men are going to intercept your convoy while you are taking the prisoner to the Arthur road prison from the court, after the hearing is over. By activating the right contacts they have ensured that you would not get further custody remand, and now I understand that you were also not seeking extension of police custody. That settles the issue. The attack will be between the court and the prison."

"What's the purpose?" Inspector Sawant asked impatiently.

"Shakeel has contacted his trusted men in Mumbai several times since yesterday. He has instructed them to rescue this Altaf Hussain at any cost. They have been asked not to worry about the cost in terms of men lost. Shoot the policemen also if necessary," Mohite disclosed, and then asked out of curiosity, "Who is this famous Altaf Hussain in reality? Must be an important person otherwise such a risky operation won't be launched."

"Oh, he is an ISI officer, but don't tell the press as yet. Is there anything more you have up your sleeve?" Mundkur asked, now a worried man.

"Oh, I see. That explains it. One more thing. The instructions to these people are, to take him safely out of the city. Later on, he would be taken care of by some other people. We have not been able to get any dope on the actual plan that has been hatched, perhaps because it's not yet disclosed to others. But I suppose this is good enough for you to plan your counter-strategy."

"Oh, yes. This is more than enough to work out our strategy. Thank you, thank you, indeed. That was a wonderful piece of intelligence you gave. Please do not hesitate to rush in again if you have anything to add," Mundkur thanked him from the bottom of his heart. One of the accused had been taken away by death, he did not want the other to be taken away by Shakeel. That would be too disgraceful. This was one more emergency in hand that could not be passed to any one else. He requested the Legal Advisor to complete the remand papers and left the room with Inspector Sawant to plan the counter-operation.

"You see, there are four different ways of reaching Arthur road prison from the court premises, and we can take anyone of them to take the prisoner to the prison." Mundkur started his briefing as soon as Inspector Sawant collected the chiefs of the Special Operations Squad and the Commando Unit. "So, if I were planning the rescue operation I would find out the segments that are common to all the four. In other words, the roads that cannot be avoided whatever route the convoy takes. If I lay the ambush on one of these segments I would be sure of coming across the convoy. Therefore, while planning a counter offensive we must be ready to face the ambush at one of these places. Luckily for us in this case, such segments are only two, one that emanates from the court and the other that goes to the prison. Is that clear? Do you agree with me?"

"Yes, yes, that's a very sound argument," One of the listeners said.

"Now, we can neutralise the court-end segment which is short, by heavy deployment of armed police, but we can't do the same for the other segment. That is too long, and crowded, we won't be sure even if we saturate the whole of it with policemen."

"That's true," Inspector Sawant interjected.

"We therefore, prepare ourselves for an encounter in this segment. Will it be all right if we keep armed men in a jeep as vanguard, followed by the vehicle in which the prisoner will be travelling, of course accompanied by armed guard followed by two jeeps, one carrying the commandos and the other a small contingent of SOS sharp shooters? Or you want more men?" Mundkur looked around for comments.

"No, a larger group would create confusion." The Commando chief opined.

"In my reckoning," Mundkur continued. "They will allow the front vehicle to pass and then intercept the main vehicle. They will not shoot indiscriminately at this vehicle, for fear of killing the man they want to rescue. The attack would be on the front and rear vehicles to hold them at bay while some of them go close to the main vehicle and pull out the prisoner. I have a feeling, he would be holding himself in readiness for, he would have been tipped off by his lawyer under instructions from the higher-ups. We cannot prevent that, therefore, we take that eventuality into account while planning. The SOS shooters are here to ensure that the prisoner does not fall in their hands alive. He has been found in possession of RDX and that is enough for you to shoot him down if he tries to escape. I need not elaborate more. I hope I am clear on that point?"

"Yes, yes." They echoed in unison.

"Inspector Sawant and I shall be following the convoy in a car at a distance, and shall rush in too," Mundkur concluded.

As the prison came in sight, a pick-up van that was coming from the opposite direction suddenly swirled and dashed against the vehicle in which Altaf was travelling. The next moment four persons sitting in the van vaulted out and rushed towards the stranded vehicle. Simultaneously there was firing on the other vehicles in the convoy from armed men who emerged from a car that was following the pick-up van. But the occupants of these vehicles had already jumped out and taken positions. They returned fire. The driver of Altaf's vehicle was badly injured because of the impact and therefore, could not manoeuvre the vehicle. The four men opened the doors of the vehicle from both sides to pull Altaf out. One of them shot the guard who was sitting next to Altaf. A split second later Altaf emerged from the vehicle, supported by a rescuer. Instantly there was a volley of fire at them and both collapsed in a pool of blood. The SOS sharpshooters had done their job. The commandos also managed to shoot down the remainder. The whole blitz lasted hardly a minute, at the end of which five persons lay dead on the road. Altaf was one of them.

"What an end to a sordid adventure!" Mundkur muttered, bending down over Altaf's body to have a closer look.

Unsuspecting Couriers

"HELLO, GOING TO INDIA AGAIN. NEED ANY ASSISTANCE?" Bashir Khan heard a voice behind him. He turned round to see where the question came from. A paunchy man in his mid-fifties was standing before him, amiably grinning. He was holding an artificial leather portfolio under his arm. Before Bashir Khan could reply the man said again, "Don't you remember, I helped you with the formalities last time you were here for a visa?" Bashir Khan did recall that he had sought the assistance of a visa agent, but he did not remember if he was the same person. He mumbled something, not denying the claim but not accepting it either. Gul Mohammed, the visa agent, was a dynamic, aggressive man. He put his arm round Bashir's shoulders and led him away from the crowd of visa seekers. Bashir did not resist. Having arrived at Islamabad from Karachi the previous evening, he had come early in the morning to the visa section of the Indian High Commission only to find that the queue of visa seekers like him had already assumed a serpentine shape. The CID policemen were first checking every person before allowing him to approach the visa section. Many were pulled out by them for further questioning. Bashir was not sure when his turn would come, therefore, when Gul Mohammed assured him that he would save him of that trouble he readily agreed to follow his advice.

True to his word Gul Mohammed not only got him exempted from the CID check but also managed to get the visa application deposited before the end of the specified period. Bashir was indeed grateful. "I am indeed grateful to you, Sir," said Bashir when his application reached the Indian visa officials. "How much should I pay you? I mean what are your normal charges?"

"Oh, no charges. I was only trying to be helpful to you because I liked you," Gul Mohammed said, brushing aside the suggestion. "Now that you are free why don't you join me for a cup of tea? There's a restaurant over there. Let's sit and chat a bit." Bashir did not refuse, though he did not understand why Gul Mohammed was taking such an interest in him. While they were having tea, a sophisticated-looking young man joined them. Gul Mohammed introduced him as Major Naqwi. Thereafter Major Naqwi took the reins of conversation in his hands and questioned Bashir at length about his family background, what he was doing for his livelihood and why he wanted to visit India. Unaware that he was now face to face with an ISI officer for whom Gul Mohammed worked as a 'Talent Spotter', Bashir answered all questions unreservedly, if only to be on the right side of the man in authority which he thought Major Naqwi was.

Bashir told him that he had cleared the tenth standard, but later abandoning his studies, he had joined his elder brother in running a canteen on contract at a vocational training institute at Karachi. It was not a very paying proposition as they were not making much profit. His father was a retired railway employee who had settled down in a suburb of Karachi. His family hailed from a village near Jalgaon in Maharashtra State of India. His father joined the GIP Railway during the British period and served at Bhusawal for a number of years till 1947, when he opted to migrate to Pakistan. He later joined the Pakistan railways at Karachi and eventually purchased a small house in the suburbs. All the brothers and unmarried sisters—seven in all—were living with the father.

"What's your purpose of visiting India unless it is to dig up your father's old relatives?" Major Naqwi asked him the moment Bashir paused. "No, Sir, that's not the reason. I got married a year and a half ago to a girl from Bhusawal. She is in fact distantly related to me. I am now proposing to visit my in-laws with my wife and newborn son."

"I see, that's interesting, your acquiring an Indian bride." What do you propose to do after returning from India, continue to work with your brother in a non-paying business?"

"I have no definite plans, Sir. Jobs are not easy to come by, but if I get a good job I would only be too willing to go in for it rather than slog in the canteen under my brother." Bashir replied, wishing ardently that Major Naqwi takes pity on him and makes an offer.

As if reading his thoughts Major Naqwi said, "I can be of help in getting a job for you. It would be exciting as well as paying. Besides, you and your wife would be able to visit your relatives in India any number of times."

"Really Sir? What's the job like?" Bashir asked excitedly. He thought his wife would be extremely pleased.

"It's simple enough. When you now go to Bhusawal you find a house on rent in the town, pay a deposit as well as rent in advance, which I am told is the practice, and take possession. On expiry of the visa period, you go to the office of the Superintendent of Police, Jalgaon and obtain a departure note from them, but instead of going to Attari outpost to catch a train for Lahore you roam about for a few days and return to Bhusawal to the house you have already rented and settle down there. To the inquisitive relatives you give out that you wanted to start a garment export business and were trying to obtain a resident visa. Is it okay with you?" asked Major Naqwi gazing pointedly at him. Bashir was in deep thought weighing the pros and cons of the bizarre proposal. He did not reply.

"Now listen, what you will get by way of remuneration," Major Naqwi continued. "You will be paid eight thousand rupees while in India. In addition, rupees five thousand would be deposited in your bank account in Pakistan every month. Don't you think it's a good salary?"

"It is Sir," Bashir conceded. "I would be only too happy to do any job if I am paid that much money." He had now made up his mind. He was sure that his wife would be delighted with the prospect of living once again at a place where she had grown up, and that too independent of the in-laws.

"What would I be expected to actually do, Sir? You really want me to start a garment export business? I know nothing about it," he asked diffidently, as a late thought.

"Well, that would be your front. What you would be actually required to do can't be explained in a meeting like this. You come tomorrow to this address—" Major Naqwi gave him a slip of paper that contained the address—"and we will brief and train you for the job."

Bashir nodded his acceptance while pocketing the piece of paper.

"Well then, see you tomorrow. I must leave now. I have some other engagement," said Major Naqwi, getting up. After he left, Gul Mohammed congratulated Bashir on netting an excellent job and further drove into his ears the benefits of adhering to the right decision he had made. He wanted to make sure that Bashir did not change his mind.

Bashir was quite happy with the proposal, though he was foggy about what his job really was going to be. The next day he reported at a house on the outskirts of Islamabad as directed. Major Naqwi was already there to receive him. There were a couple of more men who were introduced to him as his instructors. The instructors gave him lessons in security and then about identifying military personnel, military formations and the various kinds of weapons and other hardware they often use. Once he reached a satisfactory level of learning, he was tested and certified by the instructors as ready for the job. Major Naqwi then interviewed him to satisfy himself and briefed him about the job to be done in India.

"The defence production factory at Varangaon, which is not far from Bhusawal, is going to be your main target." Major Naqwi told him. Bashir had already heard about the Varangaon factory during his previous visit to his father-in-law's place. "Your main job would be to create sources in the factory and obtain from them documents that would show the specifications, numbers manufactured and places of dispatch, in fact any document that would throw light on the working of the factory, please etch it in your mind," Major Naqwi emphasised. He gave Bashir a telephone number on which he could contact him by ringing up from a reliable STD/ISD booth. He also gave him rupees five thousand to meet his initial expenses. "Your visa is ready. Gul Mohammed has already obtained it for you. Therefore, now that your training and briefing are over you had better return to Karachi and collect your wife and child and proceed to India. Our men will help you organise your travel." Major Naqwi told him before wishing him good luck and taking leave.

Bashir had no difficulty locating a modest three-room block with the help of his relatives for which he would be required to pay rupees two thousand rent per month in advance and a deposit equivalent to three months' rent. When Bashir informed Major Naqwi about it the latter congratulated him and asked him to expect a money order for rupees ten thousand. The promised money order arrived within a week. It was sent by someone from Mumbai.

To Bashir's utter delight he discovered that a second cousin of his wife's—Sajjad Khan by name—actually worked in the Varangaon factory. Taking advantage of the circumstance he made a social call on him along with his wife, and painted a rosy picture of what he was doing in Pakistan. "I am in garment business," he told Sajjad Khan. "My main clientele is in the Middle East but I am not content with it. I see that India provides a vast market. I am seriously thinking of opening an office here too." He laid the groundwork for his future stratagem. Sajjad Khan was impressed.

"Really? You mean to say you will be exporting garments from Pakistan to India?" he asked innocently.

"Yes, why not? We have some novel designs and excellent craftsmanship. I am also thinking of exporting Indian garments from here to the Middle East and even to the far-east." Bashir laid it thick. By the time Bashir and his wife left Sajjad Khan was fawning over them, in the hope of getting some opening for himself.

As the visa period of forty-five days came to an end, Bashir followed the instructions given by Major Naqwi when he was sent on the assignment. He left Bhusawal with his wife and child in time after obtaining a departure note from the district police office at Jalgaon. They went to Delhi and Ajmer Sharief and returned after a fortnight to begin the second chapter of his assignment. On his way back from Delhi he brought some readymade clothes. Some he sold to people in the neighbourhood to establish that he was indeed in the garments business, and some he presented to relatives making it a point to go to Varangaon for the purpose. Sajjad Khan and his family members were extremely pleased when they discovered that Bashir's second visit to their house brought some nice clothes for them. They were people of very modest means, for, Sajjad Khan worked at a low level as a helper. Bashir spun a lot of yarn as to the several business contacts he had in Dubai and how he was going to utilise them for promoting his garment export business.

Sajjad Khan was greatly impressed by the picture that Bashir had painted about his Dubai connections. The following Sunday he visited him at his house in Bhusawal and after the preliminaries, broached the topic for which he had come. "I am very keen Bashirbhai, to visit Dubai to try my luck. Could you help, since you have so many contacts there?" he asked submissively.

"No problem. Tell me whenever you are in a position to take off." Bashir assured him airily.

"What do I need to do by way of preparation?" Sajjad asked. He had not given a thought to this prerequisite.

"The first requirement is a passport and the second is of course money. Do you have them in your pocket?" he asked. Sajjad Khan did not have either.

"Don't worry. I will try and help you out," Bashir assured him. It was now Bashir's turn to pay a visit to Sajjad Khan. He got an application form for passport that he had obtained from an agent in Bhusawal, filled by Sajjad Khan, asking him to leave the rest to him to get him a passport.

For solving the second requirement, namely of money, Bashir put up a suggestion to Sajjad Khan for his consideration. "I could arrange handsome payments for you from a good friend of mine if you could secure some documents from the ammunition factory you are working in," he suggested, keenly watching Sajjad Khan's reaction to the proposition. To his pleasant surprise Sajjad agreed without demur.

"If that fetches me money I will do it," Sajjad said slowly but deliberately. "I am prepared to do anything that would take me closer to realising my dream of going to Dubai."

A fortnight later Sajjad Khan paid a nocturnal visit to Bashir and gave him two transfer memos that he had pilfered from his office. Bashir could not make out much as to their importance but nevertheless congratulated him on his endeavour. For good measure he paid him one thousand rupees from his pocket and asked him to be at it, and bring more documents.

After Sajjad Khan left, Bashir went to a Public Call Office and contacted Major Naqwi on the phone number he had with him. He was worried that the Major might get annoyed with him for disturbing him late at night but, to his great relief the latter seemed happy at the progress he had made in such a short time. "Ring me up again tomorrow night around the same time," he asked Bashir. "I will then give you further instructions." When Basher dutifully contacted him again Major Naqwi told him, "Pack the memos given to you by Sajjad Khan in a sturdy green cover, the type used for sending heavy material by post, and write on top in red ink, 'For Ibrahim Seth', and proceed to Mumbai immediately. In Mumbai, check in at Hotel Rahat in Dongri. Give your name as Rafiq Patel—remember well Rafiq Patel. Then contact me from a PCO at night."

"If I don't get accommodation in that hotel where do I go?"

"Don't worry on that count. I will take care of that. A room would be made available to you if you give the correct name." Major Naqwi assured him, and hung up.

Bashir caught the first available train that was going to Mumbai. He had no difficulty securing a room in Hotel Rahat. The receptionist nodded knowingly and handed him a room key the moment he gave his name as Rafiq Patel. He freshened up and went out in search of a PCO. When he rang up Major Naqwi, he himself answered as if he was anxiously waiting for his call. Major Naqwi obtained from Bashir the number of his hotel room and asked him to wait in the room itself. "What do I do with the packet I have brought with me?" Bashir asked impatiently.

"Have patience. Let me complete," Major Naqwi said sternly. "Within the next couple of hours a young man, Shafi by name, will approach you in your room. He will be wearing black trousers and gray shirt and carrying a brown grip. He will introduce himself as, Shafi, an assistant of Latifbhai. You should ask him if Latifbhai had returned from Mecca to which he would reply, 'yes, a fortnight ago'. Shafi will ask you if you had brought a parcel for Ibrahim Seth. That's the time when you should hand over the green packet to him. Is it clear to you, my friend?"

"Yes, it's quite clear," Bashir replied briefly.

"Shafi would in turn give you a white envelope containing rupees five thousand. You should give four thousand to Sajjad Khan and keep the remainder one thousand for yourself as defrayal of the expenses you would have incurred. Contact me from Bhusawal after two days. Good luck," said Major Naqwi, and disconnected.

Exactly two hours later there was a knock on his door. Bashir eagerly opened it. The hotel boy was standing in front of the door with a young man by his side who gave him a smile when their eyes met. He dismissed the hotel boy and invited the man in. The drill as indicated by Major Naqwi followed. Within minutes the young man, who had introduced himself as Shafi, left after collecting the packet, which he carefully placed in the zippered handbag he was carrying. Bashir opened the white envelope that Shafi had given him and counted the money. He had already given one thousand rupees to Sajjad Khan from his own pocket. He decided to pass on another one thousand to him as an incentive and keep the rest for himself. Before leaving Mumbai, Bashir went to the Regional Passport Office and submitted his application for an Indian passport giving his name as Sajjad Khan but affixing his own photograph. He threw away the application form that Sajjad had given him.

Two days later when Bashir contacted Major Naqwi he expressed his disappointment at the material he had sent. "There was nothing very valuable in it," he told Bashir. "Please impress upon Sajjad Khan to get really good stuff. In the meantime please try for someone who had better access." Bashir visited Varangaon that evening and told Sajjad Khan that if he wanted money he must not pass on rubbish to him. "My friend is upset that he paid you so much money. In future, he has asked me not to pay you anything unless he has first examined the papers," he told Sajjad Khan, and made that an excuse to pocket the additional one thousand rupees that he had thought of paying him.

"I am a small minion, you must realize that, Bashirbhai. I have no reach to better quality stuff. It's invariably classified and therefore, exclusively handled by senior officials," Sajjad Khan pleaded submissively. A good source of money was about to dry out for him, and he was greatly frustrated.

"Can you not find someone who could give you those papers? I mean don't you have anyone among the supervisors who could be persuaded to pass on classified papers against payment? The money would be substantial, as you very well know," Bashir persevered. Sajjad Khan pondered for a while and said, "Come to think of it, my immediate superior, Joseph Mathew would perhaps take the bait. I could introduce him to you," he offered.

"What makes you think that this Joseph Mathew of yours would be amenable?" Bashir asked probingly.

"Well, he is extremely fond of the booze and therefore, always short of money, so much so that he often touches small fries like me for petty loans. He is indebted to all his subordinates including me. That will explain to you his precarious financial position," Sajjad elaborated.

Bashir thought that Mathew was a good prospect and readily agreed to meet him. Sajjad Khan, however, had a condition. Bashir should give him a ten-per cent cut of whatever payment he would be making to Mathew in the future, a condition that Bashir had no hesitation in accepting.

Bashir did not have to wait long. The following Sunday, Sajjad Khan came to Bashir's house. "Please come with me right away," he pleaded. "If you want to strike a bargain, now is the time. As you suggested I spoke to Mathew. You would be pleased to know that he not only agreed to meet you but has actually come down to Bhusawal."

"Is it? Where is he?" asked Bashir. He was all excitement at the sudden turn of events in his favour.

"For a change he is accompanying his wife to the church in Bhusawal which she attends every Sunday. He has agreed to meet you after the service when his wife would be talking to other churchgoers."

"Damn good work Sajjadbhai. Let's go."

Both hurried to the church. When the service was over Sajjad Khan went upto the exit door and beckoned Mathew who gave some excuse to his wife and followed Sajjad Khan. The roadside meeting was brief but very productive for Bashir. Mathew agreed to pass on to him through Sajjad Khan whatever classified documents he could keep with himself for a while. Bashir promised to immediately photocopy and return them. Mathew of course wanted the payment to be good. "I assure you, Mr. Mathew, that the payment would be substantial. But I am sure, you would appreciate that the actual amount would depend upon the quality of the material you would supply. My friends are liberal about payment but they don't want to be taken for a ride. They would first examine the stuff and if they find it useful they would promptly send the money that would be appropriate consideration. You will soon realize that they are fair as well as good paymasters," Bashir sermonised.

True to his word, or because he was in dire need of money the following week Mathew handed over a bunch of documents to Sajjad Khan, who came running to Bashir with them. They got photocopies made from a shop whose owner the latter had befriended by then, and returned the documents to Mathew. Bashir contacted Major Naqwi and apprised him of the good tidings. Major Naqwi asked him to follow the previous drill but to stay in Hotel Good Luck in Byculla this time. Shafi would collect the packet and hand over a white envelope that would contain rupees ten thousand.

The whole exercise passed off without a hitch. Soon it became a regular practice as, Mathew getting greedier by the day and with Sajjad as well as Bashir coaxing him, not a single week passed without Bashir making a trip to Mumbai. In the process every one got good money. Bashir kept his promise of giving a ten-per cent cut to Sajjad Khan, but kept for himself forty per cent of the money that was meant for Mathew. Before long Bashir established a network of a photocopier who opened his shop even at odd hours, and a PCO owner who conveyed messages to Bashir from Major Naqwi whenever the latter wanted him to contact him urgently. Bashir had taken care to tell the PCO owner that the caller was his elder brother Sulaiman. Mathew was so prolific and frequent that it became impossible for Bashir to rush to Mumbai every time Mathew loaned documents. Consequently he started combining two or more lots before making a journey to Mumbai. Till then they remained in his house. It was a security risk but unavoidable, Bashir reasoned.

An officer of the Special Branch of Mumbai Police who had once worked with Mundkur when the latter was serving in Mumbai Police, incidentally mentioned to him one day, that during his routine round of hotels and guest houses in Mumbai to check the foreigners' register, he had discovered that Hotel Gulistan in central Mumbai had of late become a favourite of Pakistani nationals. Mundkur who never ignored a tip-off however trivial, immediately asked Khot to develop a contact in the hotel to keep a tab on the goings on there. An opportunity came Khot's way when Kamlakar Kadam, an acquaintance of his, succeeded in getting temporary assignment for three months in the hotel as a receptionist. Khot took out Kadam for dinner and briefed him on what he should look for in the hotel and how he should report his observations to Khot.

One evening, when Kadam was on duty he noticed a young man, portfolio in hand standing in front of the lift, obviously with the intention to go up to some room. A new comer generally approached the receptionist to seek information but this man did not which Kadam thought odd and therefore, asked him as to where he was going. The man brusquely replied, "Room Number 211," and dismissed Kadam's query. But Kadam was persistent. He asked him again, "Whom do you want to see please?" "Rafiq Patel." was the bad-tempered reply he received. Kadam knew that the man who had checked in in Room Number 211 had registered himself as Bashir Khan, but he did not contradict the visitor and simply asked the bellboy to accompany him. Now what had happened was that though Major Naqwi had instructed Bashir to register himself as Rafiq Patel whenever he stayed in a Mumbai hotel, and Bashir did follow his instructions initially, of late he had switched over to his real name as, he found it bothersome to masquerade under a false name for a brief period. The complacency perhaps arose out of a false sense of security that long practice without mishap gives. The young visitor who was actually Shafi knew him only as Rafiq Patel and gave out that name when Kadam asked.

As soon as Shafi and the bellboy disappeared into the lift Kadam picked up his cell phone and narrated the incident to Khot. Smelling a rat Khot promised to send his men. Much before Khot's men could arrive, Shafi had left. When one of Khot's men who had reached the hotel contacted Kadam, the latter told him guardedly, "The visitor has already left. He was in the room only for a few minutes. But the hotel guest—Bashir Khan is his name—is still in his room. He has booked the room only for a day, therefore he may leave soon."

"Will you please point him out to us when he comes out?" requested the watcher team leader.

"Oh, sure. If one of you sit in the lobby it would be easy for me to give you the signal," Kadam suggested. In consultation with Mundkur, Khot asked the team of watchers to remain at the hotel and pick up Bashir when he checked out.

Bashir left by the morning train followed by Bhadang and a team of watchers. It was obvious to Mundkur that Bashir Khan was from outside Mumbai, otherwise he would not have stayed on in the hotel after the rendezvous. He therefore, asked

Bhadang to take charge and follow Bashir to his destination, along with a team of watchers. Their instructions from Mundkur were to stay put at the place and return to Mumbai only when Bashir made another trip, and in the meantime to discover everything about him and his associates and their activities. Bhadang succeeded in establishing the nexus among Bashir, Sajjad Khan and Joseph Mathew. He also found out Bashir's favourite photocopying machine operator and the PCO. He promptly reported his findings to Mundkur, along with the current rumour that Bashir was a Pakistani national. Bhadang and his men were about to round up their enquiries when they realised that Bashir was again on his way to Mumbai. Bhadang informed Mundkur about his trip and their following him. Mundkur organised another team of watchers at the CST railway station to trail Bashir, which it did.

On this occasion Bashir stayed at Hotel Akbar Palace. Within half an hour of checking in he came out of the hotel and made a call from a nearby PCO. It was a brief call. He then returned to the hotel and remained locked inside his room. In the meantime Mundkur's men found out from the VSNL that the call was to a telephone number in Pakistan. They decide to pursue the matter later. For the present it was clear that he was on a secret business and some dramatic developments were about to take place. Mundkur got in touch with Inspector Sawant of Mumbai Police Crime Branch and asked him to join for the final blitz.

They all assembled at a safe distance from the hotel within half an hour. One of Inspector Sawant's officers went inside the hotel, posing as a Special Branch Officer and checked the hotel register. He discovered that Bashir was occupying room number 113 on the first floor. He also found out by casually talking to the Receptionist, that some rooms were vacant on the same floor. Fifteen minutes later Khot and one of Inspector Sawant's officers landed at the hotel in a taxi. Both had overnight bags in their hands. They checked in in room number 116, which was available. They were soon followed by Mundkur and Inspector Sawant who announced to the receptionist that they were business associates of the new arrivals in room number 116, and had come to meet them. Khot ordered tea and eats for them to create an impression that they were engaged in business negotiations. They kept the door of the room slightly ajar, which enabled them to keep a watch on Bashir's room.

When the foursome was about to finish the tea, Khot, who was frequently glancing through the opening in the door alerted the others as, he noticed a young man approaching Bashir's room. From the description earlier furnished by Kadam, they were reasonably certain that the man was Shafi. The time to act had arrived. Khot alerted their men waiting outside the hotel on the cell phone. Shafi knocked on the door instead of pressing the doorbell. After a pause the door opened and Bashir peeped out. On seeing Shafi standing outside, he gave him a smile and beckoned him inside.

The moment Bashir closed the door of his room Mundkur and his companions emerged from their room. Forming a semi-circle in front of Bashir's room, Khot pressed the doorbell. There was no immediate response. He therefore, pressed the bell again. This time Bashir opened the door slightly and asked, "Whom do you want?" None of the team cared to answer. They simply barged in. Taking advantage of the melee

Shafi tried to escape but Inspector Sawant's man was swift enough to nab him by the neck and divest him of his handbag. Inspector Sawant told Bashir in a stern voice, "We are police. Don't make a move. You are under arrest." Bashir was in fact completely flabbergasted by the sudden onslaught and offered no resistance. They next searched his room. A fat white envelope was found tucked under the pillow. His travelling bag did not contain anything of interest. When Shafi's handbag was opened, it revealed a large size green envelope. The green envelope contained a bundle of papers that were photocopies of classified documents that belonged to the Varangaon ordnance factory. The white envelope contained ten thousand rupees in notes of one hundred-rupee denomination.

Bashir and Shafi were taken separately in two cars to the Crime Branch office for interrogation. Shafi was the first to break. "I am a mere courier. I had come to collect the packet at the behest of my master, Latif Seth. Latif Seth is waiting for me in his shop in Kapad Market, Mahim." Mundkur bundled Shafi into the car again and took him to his master's shop followed by a posse of plainclothes men. Mundkur and his team found Latif Seth in the rear room of the shop packing readymade garments in travelling bags, several of which were lying on the floor. Latif Seth was also brought to the Crime Branch for interrogation.

"What's your business, Latifbhai?" Mundkur asked, as soon as the interrogation team surrounded Latifbhai. He was made to sit across the table facing Mundkur and Inspector Sawant.

"I am in readymade garments business," Latifbhai replied.

"What were you doing in the anteroom with so many travel bags around you?"

"Actually my main earnings come from 'Sawari business'. The bags you saw pertained to that activity." Latifbhai elaborated.

"What's this Sawari business you are speaking of?" Sawant interposed.

"I send readymade garments, panmasala in fact all things that are in great demand in Pakistan, with passengers travelling to Karachi. They take them as accompanied baggage in return for a small monetary consideration."

"You must be having someone at the other end to pick them up?" Mundkur asked.

"Yes, the consignment is collected at the Karachi airport by my business partner, Ibrahim Seth."

"Does he send back any articles in return?"

"He sends dry fruit, leather goods, *salwar-kameez* suits etc. There's a good market in Mumbai for them. Ibrahim Seth is on friendly terms with customs as well as immigration people at the Karachi airport, as I am with their counterparts at the Sahar airport. That ensures that the two-way trips run smoothly without a problem."

"Now Latifbhai, come to the point. I want truthful answers from you. Don't forget that Shafi has told us everything about his role in this murky business," said Mundkur, sternly.

"You mean this Rafiq Patel episode? Ibrahim Seth is friendly with a Major Naqwi of ISI, who often helps him get the visa of his friends from India extended. I was also introduced to Major Naqwi by Ibrahim Seth, during one of my business trips to Karachi. At Major Naqwi's behest I would send my shop assistant Shafi to a specified hotel to meet a Rafiq Patel and collect a packet marked to be delivered to Ibrahim Seth. It was in fact meant for Major Naqwi who got it collected from Ibrahim Seth. I have actually never met this Rafiq Patel."

"Shafi also delivered a packet to Rafiq Patel every time he met him, and as we found out now, it contained wads of Indian currency. Did you give that money?" Mundkur asked. "Yes indeed. I did it on Major Naqwi's instructions. He would indicate the amount every time he asked me to send Shafi to meet Rafiq Patel. Major Naqwi promptly compensated the amount through Rehamatulla. He is a *Hawala* dealer." Latifbhai clarified.

"So you used those unsuspecting but money-minded travellers to pass national secrets to the ISI official, along with the merchandise that you smuggled to your business partner." Mundkur said tauntingly.

Latifbhai did not reply.

Mission Bear Hug

IT WAS NINE-THIRTY BY MUNDKUR'S WATCH WHEN HE entered the office that morning. His intention in showing up early in the office was to dispose of files that were awaiting his attention. The usual hustle and bustle of the office was absent for the working officially started only at ten. Mundkur was therefore, surprised to see Sudheer Bhadang in his seat while passing by his room. He was poring over some documents spread across his desk. Mundkur could not resist the temptation of peeping into the room and asking, "Good morning Bhadang. What brought you to the office so early? Something very exciting in those documents you are studying?"

"Something interesting Sir, that may turn out to be exciting," Bhandang replied guardedly.

"Is that so? Can I have an idea?"

"Sure Sir. In fact I was going to report to you what I suspect as soon as I finished examining these documents. That's why I came early to the office. I know that you are frightfully busy these days. So I wanted to meet you before you left the office again for some work."

"That's fine. Come to my room as soon as you have done with those papers. I came early to dispose of some files but files can always wait. Operational needs come first." Mundkur gave him a green signal and left Bhadang's room.

Before Mundkur could dispose of half the pending files Bhadang entered his cabin and started without any preliminaries, "Sir. Two days ago I visited the immigration police office at Sahar airport. It was a routine visit. You may recall Sir, you had given me standing instructions to visit that office every week and scrutinise their embarkation, disembarkation cards."

"Yes, I remember. That's important. It may hold many a clue," Mundkur interjected.

"Sir. While I was studying the embarkation cards I noticed a peculiar thing. As many as seven persons had left for Dubai two days previously by the Gulf Air flight on tourist visa. They were all in the age group of 20 to 30 years. What's more, all the passports were issued by the Mumbai passport office within a space of just two days. My enquiries at the airlines office showed that all the passages were booked by BCG Tours & Travels whose main office is at Lower Parel. The return passage is open, so one is not sure when they would return."

"So, what's the catch in it?" Mundkur asked probingly.

"Seven young males going in one lot only to Dubai, on passports issued almost together appeared fishy to me. They must be part of a racket, I thought and probed further. To my surprise I found that all the seven passports were obtained for them by Lucky Travels within fifteen days. That's indeed remarkable efficiency! Lucky Travels don't enjoy a good reputation. They are hand in glove with some passport officials and manage to get passports issued quickly to people who would otherwise require months. In this lot, some are born in UP and some in Konkan. Police verification itself would take months."

"You are right. What next?" Mundkur asked.

"Now, that's where I come in here to you for guidance, Sir," Bhadang confessed.

"BCG Tours & Travels would surely not give them tickets gratis. Someone must have paid for them. We must find that out. BCG Tours & Travels are not going to tell you the truth if you approach them straight, if there's something fishy about it. You must use your usual methods to find out their bank transactions in the past month and more. Also please ask the immigration police to peruse their records for the past couple of months to ascertain if any other group had left for Dubai in a similar manner. It is quite likely that this was not the first group. When you finish these two enquiries see me again," Mundkur gave his instructions, and indicated to Bhadang that he could go.

Two days later Bhadang entered Mundkur's cabin. He had obtained answers to both the queries. "Sir, no group of this nature had left in the past two months," he informed Mundkur.

"That's a relief in a way. We have perhaps started nosing into this affair right at the beginning. Now what about the financier?" Mundkur asked.

"That's interesting. About fifteen days back BCG Tours & Travels received US$ 4,500 from Dubai by electronic transfer. Obviously that was an advance payment for the tickets for this group."

"Quite likely. But you don't require so much money for two-way air passage to Dubai for seven people. Going by the current fare for group travel I should think that fifteen to seventeen persons should be able to travel in that money to Dubai and back," Mundkur did some quick mental calculations.

"You are right, Sir," Bhadang conceded.

"Bhadang, don't you think, this means that one or two more groups can be expected to travel to Dubai in the coming few days?" Mundkur said with excitement in his voice.

"That is possible Sir," said Bhadang.

"You say possible, I am certain about it. We must alert the immigration police and ask them to be on the lookout. They must also look for this group to return. They may return together or in ones and twos, one can't be too sure."

"I will get in touch with them immediately, Sir," Bhadang nodded.

"Now the next step. While waiting for their return please check up if the particulars about place of residence in Mumbai, occupation etc. given in their passports are correct. Secondly, if BCG Tours & Travels have obtained more tickets for group travel to Dubai in the past few days. That would give some idea about the next group," Mundkur gave further instructions.

"I'll do that, Sir," Bhadang replied, and left Mundkur's cabin.

A week later Bhadang was back in Mundkur's cabin.

"Sir, BCG Tours & Travels have purchased group travel tickets for eight from Gulf Air for Dubai," he told Mundkur. "We may expect another batch of eight to leave shortly. They are open tickets at the moment."

"Perhaps they are waiting for the green signal which they may receive after the first batch returns," Mundkur reasoned.

"One more thing Sir," said Bhadang. "You had asked me to check up if the passport particulars of the seven chaps who have already left, were correct. Their present addresses are correct."

"That's a good thing. You can keep them under observation when they arrive. In fact, I would suggest that you start working right now and create contacts in the neighbourhood who would report on their activities in addition to your watchers reporting the happenings they visually observe. One more thing, Bhadang. When these fellows return ask the immigration police to elicit whatever information they can without giving cause for suspicion, about their activities at Dubai," Mundkur suggested.

Not even a week had passed when Bhadang approached Mundkur again.

"Sir," he reported, "All seven returned last night. They were tactfully questioned but nothing of interest transpired. All of them had the same story to tell. They searched for jobs but did not succeed. They did not bring any valuable articles with them either."

"They were obviously briefed in advance by their mentors," Mundkur opined, "We must now observe their activities very carefully. Secondly, we may now expect the second batch to leave. Put together it is a pretty large group. Some thing big is afoot. Our goal would be to anticipate and be one step ahead. We will meet tomorrow in the morning. Get Khot also for the meeting, and give a thought to the problem in the meantime. I would also mull over it."

"I agree Sir. Some one is behind it and planning a big operation. These people were called perhaps for instructions," Bhadang said.

"You are absolutely right, but the instructions would be very elaborate, otherwise they would not go to the extent of calling them in batches outside India. It's an expensive proposition. I suspect that they are being imparted some sort of training, which is not possible in India. That makes it very sinister. We will have to work fast. So, come prepared with your suggestions tomorrow," said Mundkur. Bhadang left with the promise to come back the following day.

The next day when they met they discussed in detail the various possibilities that existed. At the end of the confabulations Mundkur told Bhadang, "Keep all the seven persons who had returned from the Dubai trip under surveillance. That could give us a clue to their local controller or guide, and also the nature of their activities hereafter." After a pause he added, "Please also establish static observation posts close to their residences to be manned by your trained watchers who would follow their quarries whenever they went out. Secondly, please keep a lookout for the next batch to leave for Dubai."

It did not escape Bhadang's hawk-like acute attention when a few days later another group of eight young men left for Dubai in similar circumstances. He asked the immigration police to watch out for their return, which could be a week or ten days later, and himself got engaged in his group trailing the seven who had already returned.

The watcher team that was keeping an eye on Mohammed Yunus, one of the group of seven, soon made an interesting discovery. Yunus who lived with his family in a one-room tenement in the poorer quarters of Mahim and hawked sundry household articles of daily use in streets across Mohammed Ali road in Central Mumbai, had a mistress living in Dharavi slums. Her name was Gunwanti. Like Yunus she also hailed from Uttar Pradesh. Perhaps they belonged to the same village or at least the district. Gunwanti was a widow who supported her three children by domestic chores in the Wadala residential locality. It was not clear if Yunus lent any financial assistance to her but the watchers had found him visiting her hut almost every alternate day.

When Bhadang apprised Mundkur of this find the latter saw in it a great opportunity to create a useful source. Mundkur sent for Sweta Pande and Gayatri Monappa. He was aware that Sweta's hometown was in Uttar Pradesh. He said to her, "Sweta, here's an opportunity for you to try your professional skills". He then briefly told her what he had heard from Bhadang and said, "Gunwanti is your target. I want you to catch her when she is at home, posing as a social worker. Gayatri will act as your associate. You tell Gunwanti that you belong to a voluntary organisation that helps single women, especially widows with children, sort out their problems. It should be easy for you I suppose, to establish rapport with her because she comes from your state."

"Yes Sir, I am sure, Gayatri and I would be able to convince her of our bone fides," Sweta said, effervescently. She was excited at the prospect of handling a delicate case independently.

"Good, I like that," Mundkur said, approvingly. "First meet Khot. He has information about several women's organisations. He once faced a similar situation. If need be, you and Gayatri visit one of the suitable organisations to get a firsthand impression of their activities."

"Surely Sir. We will then feel more confident to confront the local people." Sweta said.

"That's right. There would be others in the locality asking you questions," said Mundkur. "In the first meeting with Gunwanti ask her only about her problems, and yes, do not forget to ask her if there were other women in the neighbourhood who were similarly placed. If there are any visit them too, at least one or two just to lend credibility to your endeavour."

"Yes Sir," said Sweta in compliance.

"Now Bhadang," Mundkur said turning to Bhadang who was sitting nearby, "You take both Sweta and Gayatri to your room and give them a detailed idea about Gunwanti's location and whatever your men have found out about her background. You should all meet me again after these girls had their first meeting with Gunwanti. We shall then plan our next move."

"Sir," said Bhadang, nodding in compliance.

"OK then, get going," Mundkur said, while dismissing them.

"That's splendid," Mundkur remarked when he learned from Sweta that Gunwanti in fact had several problems, mostly financial and she should only be too happy to receive some pecuniary assistance. She also had a problem managing her children who were manifesting signs of becoming wayward. "It may sound unkind, my expressing pleasure on learning of Gunwanti's tale of woe. I actually feel sorry for her though that's usually the lot of women in that stratum of the society, but in our kind of business we can't afford to be emotional. We have to view the situation exploitatively. We have a potentially important operation on our hands. Her problems are our opportunity though she might also become an incidental beneficiary."

Seeing confusion writ large on Sweta's face Mundkur remarked, "Don't you remember your first lesson in agent raising? You have to ask yourself, what is it that he or she desires most but cannot get? Here Gunwanti's first and foremost requirement is very straightforward and hence easy to meet. She wants money, and we shall give it to her if only to earn her gratitude and put her under our obligation. The problem of her unruly children we shall put for the present on the back burner, that is to say, we shall keep it at the talking-sympathising- exploring stage. This is because nothing tangible can be achieved immediately. Further, for people who are not sure of getting two square meals a day money assumes the greatest importance. So, it's money that would be our channel for winning her over, I mean making her agreeable to do our bidding."

"I get it, Sir," Sweta said. Gayatri also nodded her agreement.

"Now about your next meeting with Gunwanti. Remember that time is of essence for us. I expect things to move fast when the next group returns from Dubai and that would not be long going by the fact that the first lot stayed out only for eleven days. By the time they return we must have already developed our listening capabilities so that we get an idea of what is cooking."

"Sir?" that was Sweta.

"You didn't follow? I shall explain. By the end of the next week you must progress so much in this mission that Gunwanti not only confesses to you about her illicit liaison with Yunus but also agrees to betray him by asking him questions as tutored by you, and suo motu reporting on his movements. We will then be able to get a fair idea of what Yunus and his cohorts are planning to do. Of course we must bear in mind that she would never be able to get for us the whole picture for, Yunus himself may not know it. Much depends on the position he holds in the secret grouping."

"I now follow Sir," Sweta said meekly.

"Sweta, I suggest, in your next meeting that would be this afternoon, you quietly slip some money—say, five hundred rupees—into her palm saying that it was from you personally. Add that you were greatly distressed by her plight and were giving the money to tide over her immediate difficulties such as clearing the past bills of the grocer who was threatening to stop supplies."

"I should think Sir, she would accept the money without much hesitation," Sweta expressed her opinion.

"Bhadang, please advance her the money," Munkur directed.

"No problem Sir. I will give it to her as soon as we go back to my room," said Bhadang.

"Now Sweta, and you also listen carefully Gayatri, because though Sweta is playing the lead role in this act you will have to chip in every now and then in support. You are her associate and companion."

"I am listening Sir," Gayatri spoke for the first time.

"Very tactfully ask her," Mundkur resumed giving his instructions. "If she had a friend or well-wisher and whether he was of any help. If she admits in the first go so much the better, otherwise without giving her offence tell her that you had heard that a *Gaonwalla* of hers, Yunus by name, was playing the Good Samaritan for her, that's why you asked, and so on."

"I follow, Sir," said Sweta.

"Your objective should be to find out how much attached she was to him, whether she would betray him for money—and what is more—fast enough. Please remember that time is not on our side. Do you follow, both of you?" Mundkur asked.

"Yes, Sir," Sweta and Gayatri nodded in unison.

"Secondly, and this is important," Mundkur continued. "Also find out a suitable central spot in her hut where a small transmitter could be concealed without fear of being detected, and more so, how could it be secured there clandestinely. Of course if it were possible to send out Gunwanti for a few minutes when her children are absent the task would be achievable. So create the opportunity. If we are able to fix a transmitter at a strategic place in her hut we won't have to depend on Gunwanti's goodwill and memory to learn what all Yunus tells her in response to her questions."

"I will be looking out for that possibility, Sir, while Sweta is busy talking to Gunwanti," Gayatri volunteered.

"Yes, you better take on that responsibility because eventually you will have to fix the transmitter. You have the requisite technical knowledge. I don't want to push in a technician just for this purpose. That would be a tricky proposition, which may blow our operation," Mundkur clarified the position, and then turning to Bhadang said,

"Bhadang, lend them all the support they need, and bring them back to me as soon as they come from the errand."

Sweta and Gayatri appeared very pleased with themselves when they met Mundkur the following day. Gunwanti had accepted the money without demur, they reported to Mundkur. In fact she felt hugely relieved when the offer was made, and said that God had actually answered her prayers in their form. She was desperate for money but did not know wherefrom it would come. Her youngest child was down with fever for a few days last month, which cost her a neat sum by way of the doctor's fees. The ladies for whom she worked refused to advance her money, complaining that it was her frequent request. At that juncture Sweta broached the subject of her 'Gaonwalla' sympathiser and asked, "Doesn't he lend a helping hand in your moments of distress?"

Gunwanti was taken aback. For good few seconds she stared at them both by turns with a blank expression in her eyes that had an occasional flash of suspicion. It was difficult to read the thoughts that were crowding her not so obtuse mind. Obviously there was nothing pleasant about them. Perhaps she was reviewing her relationship with Yunus, how it all began and what it meant to her today. Maybe she was also trying to fathom the intentions of these two strangers in alluding to her liaison with him. This was the subject none could raise before her without receiving the choicest abuses, so none dared.

Eventually when she made up her mind to speak the vacant expression in her eyes gave place to anger. The next moment she burst out, "That rascal? He is interested in my body rather than in me or my children for that matter. When my husband died I was penniless. The sharks around here got after me but I could sense their intentions and kept them at bay. At that juncture Yunus offered a helping hand. He empathised with my plight and also gave me some money to meet my immediate needs. I accepted the favour from him as he comes from a village that is close to my own in Uttar Pradesh. I did not suspect his evil intentions in the beginning. I desperately needed support and, therefore, leaned on him only to realise soon that he was no different from others. But it was too late. I was much too obliged to him to reject his advances outright. I also needed the prop of a man to feel secure. Since then it has been like that, he has been taking more advantage of me than I getting any substantive assistance from him. My problems are not his concern at all. That's how he behaves." "Why don't you get rid of him?" Sweta asked.

"I would very much like to but I can't. I am afraid that he might physically harm my children or me if I try to jettison him. He is a desperate character."

Finding the ground fertile Sweta hazarded her next step, quite sure that it would meet with her chief, Mundkur's approval. She asked Gunwanti, "Do you know where Yunus had been lately?" Gunvanti did not hesitate to answer now that the barrier had been blown.

"He was absent for more than a week. He told me that he had been to a far off place on an important errand. Beyond that he did not disclose anything," she replied.

"I am keen to know what that job was that had sent him to a distant place. If you can find out this for me you will get a good reward," Sweta suggested cautiously.

Much to Sweta's relief Gunwanti showed no annoyance. She asked without emotion, "What actually do you want me to find out from Yunus?"

"If you are ready to play the game I would coach you about the questions you should ask Yunus when he came to you next. But you will have to be very tactful in asking questions otherwise he would get suspicious. Also you will have to keep your mouth shut, not talk to anyone else." Sweta elaborated. Gunwanti showed willingness to go along. To Sweta and Gayatri she appeared to be intelligent enough not to goof up her assignment.

"Well done. I am so happy you took the initiative. Your judgement that the iron was hot and therefore, it was the opportune time to strike, was sound," said Mundkur appreciatively.

"One more propitious thing happened, Sir," it was now Gayatri's turn to brief Mundkur about her contribution. "Gunwanti offered us a cup of tea, perhaps to express her gratitude for the unexpected dole she received from us. Unmindful of the unhygienic condition of her hut we accepted the offer. Peculiarly, and to our great surprise Gunwanti picked up a small aluminum mug and hurried out muttering that she would fetch some milk from a neighbouring teashop. The children were away perhaps playing in the lane. On our previous visit also they were away. Taking advantage of the situation I inspected the hut carefully. The roof is low and supported by a variety of rafters. The tiny room is informally divided into two areas of use. The left side serves as kitchen and the right side is the sleeping quarters. There are a couple of good spots in the right side of the roof where a transmitter can be easily concealed without fear of detection. If the woman offers tea again next time or we prompt her on some pretext to go out for a few minutes we should be able to do the job."

"That's excellent. I am proud of you two girls," Mundkur exclaimed, pleased with their performance.

Spurred by the praise they received from the chief whom they greatly admired, Sweta and Gayatri carried out with considerable dexterity the delicate task of briefing Gunwanti about the information to be collected from Yunus through tactful questions. They also succeeded in planting a tiny transmitter in the roof of her hut. Bhadang in the meantime arranged with a reliable contact, whose apartment was situated within a hundred meters of Gunwanti's hut, to allow his men the use of a room to mount a listening watch. In one corner of the room they installed an autorecorder that would automatically record the transmissions received from the hut. The leader of the watcher team that trailed Yunus was instructed to switch on the recorder by remote control the moment Yunus entered Gunwanti's hut, and to switch it off as soon as he left it. The results of the first encounter were indeed flattering.

Mundkur was extremely pleased with the success of the scheme, and instructed the two girls to keep in touch with Gunwanti. "Please brief her from time to time—and yes—you must pay her promptly every time she gives you some information. That would bolster her enthusiasm," he told them. "Please also work out a mechanism that would enable you two to meet her outside the locality because your frequent visits would inevitably attract attention which we don't want at this juncture."

Though his design had so far worked well Mundkur was conscious of its limitations. He could not hope to get all the information he would need to successfully forestall the game plan to which those fifteen persons were privy. They were, to be sure, small cogs. The prime movers as well as the main players were yet to be discovered. And that had to be done fast enough, before disaster fell for, he was sure something sinister, something awesome, was being hatched. No one would fork out the kind of money that was being spent on those fifteen lowly people unless high stakes were involved, he argued. Their going to Dubai suggested that the epicentre was outside the country and the main schemers did not want to risk coming into the country. What was within his powers was to foil the plan and nab the players, and that is what he intended to do with all his ingenuity and guile before the time ran out. He sent for Khot and Bhadang.

"You see, we have to act fast in this case, I mean this case of the fifteen blokes which is on our hands," said Mundkur as soon as Khot and Bhadang stepped into his cabin. "It's causing me great anxiety. We must unravel the conspiracy before they act. Something frightful is brewing, I am sure of that. The Gunwanti connection is good so far as it goes but by its very nature it is not likely to yield something very meaty, something that would give us a total picture. We must explore more avenues. Do you have any suggestions?"

"Sir, we have already put under surveillance all the seven persons who returned that day from Dubai. One of them has provided an opening though I concede that it is not enough. What I want to say is that, we shall continue this endeavour and sooner or later we shall get more openings or at least we would come to know about their activities."

"That's fine Bhadang, I don't deny that it has yielded some results but as you have yourself said, this is not enough. Secondly and most importantly, we may run out of time. We do not know enough, and that is precisely my worry. We must penetrate this ring. But perhaps a way may be discovered by constantly watching the movements and visible activities of all those we know are in it, I mean the seven who have arrived and the eight who would be shortly arriving. By the way, I suggest that Khot, you take charge of the second group when it arrives. Bhadang's hands are already full with those seven persons. He won't have more men to spare from his group," Mundkur directed.

"Yes Sir, I will take on that responsibility," Khot said.

"It would really be good. We will then be able to give the case the comprehensive attention that it deserves," Bhadang echoed his concurrence.

"I am happy Bhadang that you appreciate the need to distribute the work in view of the time constraint. Khot, you now get in touch with the immigration police at the airport and see that they maintain a sharp lookout for the second group, which should be returning any day. I would appreciate if they could photocopy a few passports under some pretext. That would give us an idea about how did they spend their time, that is, if they stayed put at Dubai or went elsewhere outside the Emirates," Mundkur advised Khot, and terminated the meeting.

The four Abduls—Abdul Karim, Abdul Sayeed, Abdul Hamid and Abdul Rashid—had made their way into India by vastly different routes but converged at a mosque near Mastan Talao in central Mumbai. This was some eight months prior to Yunus and his group making a trip to Dubai. A year earlier they were strangers but now thick as thieves. In the ISI parlance they were of late often referred to as the gang of four Abduls. All the four belonged to Karachi and its suburbs but had different cultural upbringings. While Karim was a Punjabi, Sayeed and Hamid were Muhajirs but they also had their small distinctness. Sayeed's family came from Uttar Pradesh and Hamid was a Bihari. As for Rashid, he was a Kutty. His family had migrated from Kerala. There was a well-thought out design behind creating this motley ensemble. With their different ethnic backgrounds it was possible for them to hunt freely, given the composite nature of Mumbai's population. They were espied by the talent spotters and selected for their daring and fundamentalist beliefs by Colonel Rafiq Siddiqui of the Inter-Services Intelligence who was about to launch a major offensive in India, Mumbai to be precise, to administer a crippling blow to India's main financial institutions and establishments.

After their formal induction they were taken to Islamabad and quartered in a 'safe house'. For the first two months they were given lessons in theology by a mullah who generated in them enough hatred for other faiths and an ardent desire to sacrifice themselves for the glory of their own faith. They were then taken over by the ISI regulars and taught the fine art of tradecraft. In about six months they were ready for induction into the world of espionage. They were offered handsome salary and promised that, should by mischance they get caught in the foreign country their families would get good compensation and of course, if they laid down their lives that would be in the cause of the faith and they would find a berth reserved for them in the Paradise. The immediate task given to the foursome was to reach Mumbai and settle down there. Later they were to enlist at least a couple of dozen persons instigating them in the name of the brotherhood of the faithful and making offers of handsome monetary rewards.

Karim was appointed their leader perhaps because of his Punjabi descent. Col. Siddiqui was also a Punjabi and showed distinct preference for him. Sayeed and Hamid were flown to Kathmandu on Pakistani passports from where they travelled down as Indians. Karim was smuggled across the Jammu border and Rashid sailed to the western coast in the company of smugglers. They rendezvoused at the central Mumbai mosque where they found the pesh-imam hospitable and helpful. He never asked them many questions and sagaciously gave them a chance to address the Friday *khutba* gathering. This was a welcome opportunity, for the mosque gatherings were going to be their main hunting ground. Money being no problem, they soon managed to get with the assistance of an estate agent, a small flat on rent at a stone's throw distance from Bandra railway station. This became their operational headquarters.

Col. Siddiqui was well aware of Daud Ibrahim's operational prowess in Mumbai, and though he was not averse to making use of it for running his operations he did not want to depend totally on the gangland Don. It was also professionally unsound to expose the whole operation to an outside outfit just to facilitate certain activities. He, therefore, decided to make use of Daud's network only for two purposes. One was to arrange payment from time to time to the gang of four Abduls through

Daud's unofficial banking channel, which was akin to *Havala* operations that the ISI normally used. They were given a secret account number that enabled them to collect money sent to them by Col. Siddiqui. The second occasion to use Daud's facilities would come later.

Abdul Karim in whose name the flat was hired also obtained a telephone connection but always used Public Call Offices for communication with his ISI bosses.

The foursome became regular visitors to the mosque that had given them board and lodging facilities on arrival but did not confine themselves to it alone. Quite often they attended prayers in mosques in Dongri, Pydhonie and even Bandra. Their emphasis, as dinned into their ears by Col.Soddiqui, was to be on exacerbating faith consciousness and to build it into a huge grievance against the majority community that controlled the sinews of power, by highlighting the various ills that beset the financially weak and educationally backward community to which they belonged. The solution lay not in grieving privately but asserting themselves publicly, and the most effective way of doing so was through planned violence that would bring the government to its knees. They were permitted to offer to people who agreed to join the mission a handsome reward of rupees two lakh when the task allotted to them was successfully executed. They were however to be extremely circumspect in selecting candidates lest someone betrayed them.

Their efforts were amply rewarded. An opportunity to do something spectacular for the community and the lure of money attracted many to them. Col. Siddiqui's strategy of looking for suitable young men in the regular mosque goers paid off well. It was easy to take them up the garden path by portraying a rosy picture of what good things would accrue to them if they devoted themselves to the noble cause. The foursome could within the space of a few months spot a number of probable candidates from whom, duly guided by Col. Siddiqui, they eventually selected fifteen who could be trusted not to buckle down under trying circumstances. They were invited in small groups to the sea beach not far from their flat by the four Abduls and harangued regularly to keep their motivation strong. Eventually on the advice of Col. Siddiqui they were sent in two groups to Dubai for field training. The first group was preceded by Karim and Rashid by a couple of days while Sayeed and Hamid went ahead of the second group. They received the respective groups when they arrived at Dubai and thereafter remained with them throughout their stay. Karim had to spend nearly a month, making travel arrangements for them. He received ample advice and tips from his mentor. He could thus get in touch with the kind of people who did the chores needed for foreign travel, including securing passports and visa if the right price was paid which Karim did. He did not have to hunt for an obliging travel agency though. He was asked to contact BCG Tours & Travels, and when he did so he found that the agency already knew what had to be done. He simply collected tickets from it.

When Mundkur arrived in the office in the morning he found Khot and Bhadang eagerly waiting for him. Noticing their restlessness he asked them to follow him to his cabin. As soon as he sat down Khot began fervently, "Sir, the second batch arrived last night. Our men were checking the passenger manifest of every flight arriving from Dubai; therefore, we got some advance notice. That enabled us to be at the airport in time to receive them. I was sitting next to one of the immigration officers. He found an excuse and sent me with the passport of one of them inside the room to get clearance from the supervisor. I took advantage of the opportunity to photocopy all the pages of the passport on a duplicating machine that was already kept ready there. Here are those copies, Sir."

"That's a good job done Khot," Mundkur exclaimed while picking up the copies Khot handed to him. "By the way, did you notice anything unusual when you examined these copies?"

"Yes, Sir. Something very peculiar and highly suspicious I may say," said Khot.

"What's it?"

"The passport has a departure entry from Dubai on the day following the arrival and then again arrival entry one day prior to departure for Mumbai. That shows that the passport holder spent most of his time in a different country outside UAE. But peculiarly, there is no corresponding visa endorsement in the passport nor are there any arrival and departure entries. The whole thing is very fishy," Khot surmised.

"Yes indeed, and revealing too. This shows the connivance of the immigration authorities at Dubai airport, because, as everyone very well knows, in the normal course no immigration officer will stamp departure affirmation unless the passport has a valid visa endorsement and a ticket in support. On the return journey also he would ask questions about the missing departure entry from the place of boarding. Nothing of the kind seems to have happened. If this is not blatant connivance what is it?" Mundkur asked to stress his point.

"You are absolutely right Sir, but still the question remains, where did he go? And I am sure, the rest of them including the seven whom I spotted first went the same way. The connivance or shall I say complicity at that end is far greater," Bhadang expressed his apprehension.

"Ah, that's a much bigger question and a cause for concern to us. My own hunch is, they went to Pakistan and they went for training and briefing. There is no other country in the neighbourhood that would indulge in such tricks. The connivance at the other end was of such high order that the immigration authorities there entirely dispensed with the formality of stamping their arrival and departure. Secondly, the carrier airlines also has to co-operate. All this is possible only in that wretched country."

"That indeed seems to be the case," Khot remarked.

"In short gentlemen, we are now facing an ISI-run operation of gigantic proportions that may materialise in the coming few days," Mundkur sounded his ominous warning. "And we are only scratching the surface."

"One more auspicious development I have to report, Sir, that may give us an opening," Khot said unaffected by Mundkur's despairing observation.

"What's it?" Mundkur asked impatiently.

"Sir, when this group of eight was cleared my men followed them discreetly. I was also behind them, at a safe distance. Did not want to get too close because they had seen me with the immigration officer working as his assistant."

"So?"

"When they came on to the portico where relatives and friends come to receive their guests wait, we found that only two young men received them in a restrained sort of manner. After exchanging pleasantries they also took leave of the lot as if they had completed a formality and were now free to go home. I directed two of my men to follow them. The others followed a group of four that got into a taxi but nothing of interest was picked up by them. They got dropped one by one as their homes arrived. I am mentioning this just to tie up this loose end," Khot remarked when Mundkur moved impatiently in his chair.

"Okay, carry on."

"The team that followed the two strangers had something very interesting to report. The two let go the taxi near a building named Sea Breeze, in Bandra and entered the building. It was soon obvious to our men that they live there because, lights went on in a third floor flat and after about half an hour they went off. Our guarded enquiries in the neighbourhood in the short time we got in the morning revealed that they are four of them who live in a one-bedroom flat. All of them are single, three are north Indians and one seems to be from the south though he also speaks Hindi fluently. They rented that flat eight or ten months ago. We have obtained the name of the landlord and shall contact him soon. These four are supposed to be working here as agents of a Delhi-based recruiting agency. None knows where their office is, they seem to come and go as they like," Khot concluded.

"I say that's a great find. A breakthrough, I should think. Your decision to follow them in preference to those who arrived was indeed clever," Mundkur exclaimed in jubilation. His professional instincts were aroused. "Those foursome are supervisors, to say the least. That also gives some idea of the magnitude of the operation they have launched."

"My men are making further enquiries about them. By afternoon we should get more information," Khot supplemented his earlier narration.

"I would suggest, you immediately establish a static observation post right opposite the building whatever the cost or effort required. Keep a twenty-four hour watch on the flat. Give the watchers binoculars, a camera with telescopic lens, and a cell phone. I want every one who comes to meet them snapped. Also give them photographs of all the fifteen chaps who went to Dubai. They must carefully record how many of them come to the flat, how often and how long they stay there. A good under-cover operator will never get an agent in his dwelling place but in this case there are so many of them. They can't always be met in a neutral place without fear of exposure. So I assume that at least some of them would be coming to the flat. When any of these four blokes leaves the flat he must be followed. So make arrangements for that too," Mundkur fired off his instructions.

"I should be able to organise all these things before the day sets," Khot promised him.

"Good. Also try and find out if the watchman of the building is a friendly and pliable sort. I was thinking, if we could do the Gunwanti trick here too. Of course we will have to break into the flat when all the four are away. That may not be very easy if they are trained people which I am sure, they are," Mundkur did some loud thinking.

"It is essentially a Christian building in as much as most flat owners are Christians. I suspect that the watchman is also one. In that case, it may be easier to persuade him to co-operate. I will also find out who the Chairman and Secretary of the Society are. Maybe, we will be able to enlist their help," Khot conjectured.

"That's a good idea, but be careful. We don't want premature exposure. Our aim is to net all of them and with evidence of conspiracy, not just to put a spanner in the works," Mundkur cautioned.

"I wonder why these people chose a predominantly Christian building when in fact they are collecting Muslim collaborators," Bhadang ventured to express his doubt.

"That's simple enough," Mundkur replied. "If they stayed in a Muslim building or locality many would be eager to befriend them, hang around them. Since they are young and presumably eligible several parents of grown-up daughters would keenly angle for them. All this would jeopardise operational security, hence would be unacceptable to their bosses," Mundkur clarified.

Finding a pause in conversation Khot asked, "Shall I make a move, Sir? I will put people on the job we just decided."

"Yes, please go ahead, and report to me as soon as your things are in place."

"May I also take leave Sir? I will check up if any of my watchers has anything interesting to report, and if the Gunwanti station has revealed anything," Bhadang asked.

"Yes, you too get cracking," Mundkur gestured him to leave.

When Abdul Karim and the other three Abduls went to Dubai it was not merely to identify and shepherd their proteges—the fifteen new soldiers in the cause of the faith they had enlisted. They, of course, had attended the training course run for the rookies in a secret field-training outfit near Islamabad in handling firearms and explosives, and fabricating explosive devices using RDX. It was a sort of refresher course for them. But they were required to do several other things too. First, they met their boss, Col. Siddiqui who took a detailed report from them about their activities and achievements till then in Mumbai. They were then given a meticulous briefing as to what they had to do with the help of the helpers they had recruited. The moves to be made, the activities to be undertaken were dinned into their ears repeatedly lest they commit a mistake or overlook a detail. They were also made familiar with the use of a laptop computer and cell phone for communication, because thereafter they were to exchange messages essentially through that medium, making use of the ISD facility only in exceptional situations. To their delight they were taught the use of digital camera and how to transfer images on the Internet. The second batch comprising Hamid and Rashid smuggled the equipment in their baggage when they returned to India.

During their brief stay in Dubai, Karim and Sayeed were introduced by Col. Siddiqui who had also flown to Dubai with them, to Anees Ibrahim, the brother of Daud Ibrahim and a lynchpin of the D-company. To their bewilderment Col Siddiqui took them to a princely mansion, which was obviously the property of the Ibrahim brothers to meet Anees. Thereafter Anees seemed to take charge. He introduced to them a weather-beaten middle aged man who was present.

"Meet my trusted friend Umar Haji," he said. "You will have to work in tandem with him in India in the near future, therefore, it's better that you get to know him well." On a nod from Col. Siddiqui both embraced Haji Umar who they realised was powerfully built and clumsy.

"Three weeks later you would receive a signal from Col. Siddiqui," Anees continued the briefing. "Your job then would be to immediately proceed to the coastal town of Alibagh and stay in hotel Big Splash. Umar Haji would contact you in your hotel room at night. He would take you late in the night to village Dighi or a nearby place, where in the wee hours, goods needed for carrying out the next phase of your operation would be landed by fishing trawlers. You should accompany Umar Haji and his men when they transport the consignment to a farmhouse for concealment. Umar Haji would introduce the owner of the farmhouse to you. Thereafter the consignment would be your charge. The farm owner would accommodate and help you in every manner without asking many questions. You should also not disclose anything to him. He is not an insider. We would pay him in due course for the services rendered, therefore, that should not be your concern," Anees was matter-of-fact and to the point. Both Karim and Sayeed nodded sheepishly.

Later, on returning to his hotel room along with Karim and Sayeed, Col. Siddiqui carefully went through all the steps to be taken by them when both groups returned to Mumbai after completing their training. In the end he observed with a perceptible frown, "I don't consider any of the recruits that had come in the first batch daredevil enough to launch the type of attack I had in mind, though all of them vowed to lay down their life for the cause. And I do not expect the second group to be far different either. Therefore, the job would have to be done by the two of you. I have, I may mention again, immense faith in you. I am sure, you would not betray my confidence." Both Karim and Sayeed, charged as they were by a fresh bout of fanatical indoctrination, enthusiastically proclaimed in concert, "We are prepared to die, Sir. You have only to command." Col. Siddiqui was pleased with their resolve. As far as possible he wanted to avoid sending men from his special *fidayeen* squad to carry out the assignment. "I know, I know. In you two I have trustworthy servants of Allah who would not hesitate to lay down their life while carrying out this mission. Rest assured my dear brothers, angels would be waiting to receive you at the gates of the Paradise," said Col. Siddiqui reassuringly, and patted them encouragingly on the back.

Nothing much happened for nearly a week after the second group returned from Dubai. Khot's and Bhadang's men were watching them all very carefully. Only the "Gunwanti listening-watch team" reported that Yunus had disclosed to her that he had actually been to Dubai. While this went to the credit of Gunwanti it was no news to Mundkur and his men. They felt encouraged, however, that if Gunwanti persisted she might be able to elicit something about their future plans. The next week was more rewarding. The Abduls acquired a white-coloured Maruti van from a dealer of used cars, and a couple of days later, two used scooters. Khot's men soon found out that all the three vehicles were purchased in fake names, and they took care to park the vehicles in a back lane separated from one another by considerable distance. Mundkur was very pleased when Khot informed him about this find.

"That's a good news you have given me, Khot," he said enthusiastically. "You know how we can exploit it to our purpose. It makes our job of keeping track of them much easier. Call the technical man and we will fix things right now. You realise that they are moving fast. We have to catch up with them, indeed move ahead of them."

When the technical assistant arrived, Mundkur said to him, "Murthy, we have a situation where you can render valuable assistance. I will describe the scenario: A Maruti Omni mini van parked in a lane at night. A listening device is to be installed inside it without leaving any scope for its detection. Secondly, and in my opinion more importantly, a 'beep-beep' is to be installed in the under belly of the van so that we would be able to trace its movements. Both jobs have to be done clandestinely as usual, but in a public place, and very fast. Can you do that?"

"That should be possible. At least I can try," said Murthy, with usual modesty.

"Do you have all the gadgetry needed, or would you like me to get it from the headquarters?"

"I think, I should be able to manage with what we have, Sir," Murthy said with confidence in his voice. He always prided himself on having in his repertoire the latest gadgets that could be used in clandestine operations.

"Khot, you better tie up with him and work out the modalities. You will also have to ensure that the operation does not blow up. If you can't avoid it take the local police into confidence. It's a bit premature though to let them in."

"I will take Murthy to the spot at night and show him the van. Maybe, tonight itself or tomorrow night he should be able to do the job," Khot replied.

"Incidentally Khot, did any of the watchmen respond favourably?" asked Mundkur remembering the task he had given to Khot. "You see, to get ahead of them we will have to penetrate the group. I don't suppose it shall be possible for us to win over any of those diehard fanatics in the time available to us. Therefore, the next best approach is to penetrate by technological means using tricks that Murthy has up his sleeve, where chaps like watchmen can play important roles as facilitators."

"Both the watchmen are Bihari. To me they appeared shifty and unreliable. Perhaps as a measure of security the foursome has already won them over. Appeared very well disposed towards them, therefore, I did not sound them further," Khot reported.

"I see. That's a setback. In these circumstances a co-operative watchman is a great help otherwise he can be a great obstacle also. Anyway, give it a thought, I mean our urgent requirement. In the meantime both of you, Khot and Bhadang, remember that surveillance remains our mainstay," reminded Mundkur, and dismissed them.

The next morning Khot and Murthy reported to Mundkur that the previous night they visited the spot where the van was parked. It could not be opened because it was fitted with an electronic central locking system. Murthy would have to experiment with the combination, which would take time. But they did succeed in fitting a 'Beep-Beep' to the rear axle. Later they tested it. It worked well. "So far so good," said Mundkur, encouragingly. "We will now not miss the vehicle even if it tries to dodge us in the crowd. You must however, try and open the van. If you succeed we will be able to hear their conversation, at least partly if not the whole."

"Yes, Sir. It depends upon how close the surveillance vehicle can get to them and what intervening barriers to reception they encounter," Murthy concurred, with a proviso.

The following Friday all the four left their flat around noon, Karim and Rashid in the van with Karim at the wheel and the other two on the scooters. They first went to their usual mosque for prayers and then whiled away some time on the Mohammed Ali road. Around three in the afternoon all the four headed north, finally reaching Sanjay Gandhi National Park at Borivali. At the gate of the Park they were met by two of the group of fifteen, who later guided them to a distant and fairly secluded spot in the Park where the rest of the group was already sitting. The watchers followed them but could not get very close and had to rest content observing the goings on from a distance. What they noted was rather bizarre. After a while Karim divided the group in two teams. He and Rashid joined one group while Sayeed and Hamid sat with the other group. They talked among themselves for quite some time. Later they went to a restaurant for a cup of tea finally and dispersed. Peculiarly—the watchers reported—Karim handed over the scooters to two from the group—whether they belonged to the same sub-group or different ones they could not determine. The four Abduls returned together to their apartment in the van.

The next day early in the morning, all of them set off in the van and reached the Fort area around eight-fifteen. They visited a variety of places and streets. The watchers who trailed them suspected that they had a small camera with which they took pictures. It was not clear from their movements and gestures if they had any focal point. They seemed to be taking snaps mostly of the streets around Horniman Circle and the famous Dalal Street. They then retired to an Irani restaurant near Flora Fountain and had a leisurely breakfast. Around ten-fifteen they emerged from the restaurant and again went round the same streets and places photographing them, as if to note the difference between the situations when the streets were virtually empty and when they were full and overflowing. This job done, they returned to their Bandra flat.

Khot and Bhadang had many things to report. Therefore, when Mundkur returned to the office from an engagement both of them rushed to his cabin. Mundkur patiently heard from them about the foursome's activities the previous day and that morning. Bhadang further told him that Yunus did not go straight home from the National Park rendezvous, but went to Gunwanti instead, where he disclosed to her as recorded by the listening-watch station, that he would be very busy in the coming two or three weeks as, he was engaged in an important work. Gunwanti was clever enough, however, to extract a promise from him to visit her the next week. When both finished their accounts Mundkur calmly picked up a ball point pen from the pen-stand and started scribbling with it on the paper that was lying before him. He often indulged in that past time when he was lost in thought. After a while he looked up at his two assistants and said, "Do you interpret this chain of events as I do?" None answered because he had not yet told them what his surmise was and secondly, they were confused themselves.

"You don't want to hazard a guess? Well, I will tell you how I look at these events. They have planned a two-pronged operation, that's why they divided themselves in two groups.

It should be amply clear to you by now that it is not a secret information gathering operation. You don't collect a motley crowd like that if that's your intention. It is obviously an action operation, which perhaps involves some sort of attack or assault. Their morning wanderings suggest that the targets are located in south Mumbai. Khot, ask your watchers to mark on a map the streets they visited and photographed. The outermost streets would delineate the periphery of the area within which those two targets are located. By studying the map carefully we should be able to identify with fair amount of certainty the targets they are after," Mundkur articulated his analysis.

"That sounds very plausible, Sir. We were a bit confused, I must admit," Bhadang conceded.

"Yunus has unwittingly given you the time frame within which they must act. If they are to operate in two groups that are independent of each other they must have more vehicles. So expect them to acquire at least a mini van or a jeep and a few scooters in the coming few days. I had a hunch from the beginning that they did not purchase those vehicles for easy movement. If that were their objective they would have gone in for them long ago. They could not have won over so many persons with such diverse back ground without toiling for several months. And mind you, both the scooters have been handed over to the subalterns. There's a purpose behind it. Ask your men to keep a close tab on them too," said Mundkur.

"Yes, Sir," Bhadang replied.

"I also expect them to hold more clandestine meetings. Maybe they will never again meet in such a large group now that the duties have been apportioned, but they must meet probably in small packs for briefing, for finalising details. We must come to know about these secret meetings. They must also visit the ground zero if I may borrow the American cliché, not just once but several times to get a hang of their roles. That's our opportunity to fine-tune our deductions. So, there's a job on hand that brooks no delay or complacency," Mundkur said in a tone of finality.

"Yes Sir, we now know the battlefield, the warriors and roughly what they would attack us with," Khot summarised.

"Well said," Mundkur complimented him. "Now what remains to be found out, and that's very important, is precisely how they are going to attack so that we can pre-empt them and neutralise. That's the task in hand now. Let's get going."

Karim transmitted the snaps that he and his companions had taken of the streets in the target area and the buildings that flanked them by e-mail to Col.Siddiqui as soon as they reached the flat. In two days he received detailed operational instructions which, Col Siddiqui insisted, must be carefully studied and scrupulously followed.

It had to be a Friday, the instructions said, when the charge would be made. Time would be ten-twenty in the morning. Both attacks would be simultaneous to maximise the effect. The approaches to those buildings would also be blasted, which would make the rescue operations difficult, thus causing more panic and eventually greater casualties. Karim would lead the attack on the Reserve Bank and Sayeed would do likewise for the Mumbai Stock Exchange building. Two scooters, loaded with RDX that is primed with detonator and sensor for operating remote control device would be planted on either approach road to each building at a distance of about twenty-five meters. They should be parked at the selected places not more than ten minutes before the zero hour. In addition, two nearby restaurants each would be seeded with briefcase bombs containing one kilogram of RDX. Operatives dressed as office goers should visit those restaurants for tea and leave the briefcases behind while coming out. Two tall buildings on either side of the target structures should be selected and their watchmen heavily bribed to permit men to reach the terraces before daybreak. A team of two men would be sent to each building, armed with rocket launchers and four rockets. As soon as Karim and Sayeed ran their RDX loaded vans into the porticos Hamid and Rashid who would have stationed themselves at a reasonable distance, would trigger the scooter and briefcase explosive devices. At the same time the roof top teams would fire the rockets in quick succession at the upper middle portion of the buildings and escape. Hamid who would be carrying the laptop and mobile phone in a shoulder bag would report success of the mission simply by sending the message, 'Consignment unloaded', as soon as he reached a safe place. All the surviving men would leave Mumbai at once by whatever means possible and converge at Surat in Gujarat. Hamid and Rashid would find accommodation in Hotel Kohinoor, where they would receive further instructions. Others should remain in touch with them.

In the days that followed the Bandra group acquired one more Omni mini van of light gray colour and two scooters. The first van became the preserve of Karim while Sayeed monopolised the other. Hamid and Rashid appeared contented riding the scooters when they went out on their own. There was a design behind this seemingly unjust allotment of automobiles. Karim and Sayeed who had been chosen to make the final ride in those vehicles on the D-day had to get thoroughly familiar with them. They often went for a spin in them when not busy.

The four Abduls spent the next few days after receiving operational instructions from Col. Siddiqui, selecting places for parking the vans before making the final assault, the spots where scooters would be abandoned and the restaurants where the briefcase bombs would be planted. More importantly, they identified the buildings that were most suitable for launching the rocket attack. The trickiest problem was to win over the watchmen. Since most of the watchmen were from UP and Bihar, they entrusted the job to a select group in which Yunus was included. These were the people who came from north India and were thus best suited to strike an acquaintance with and befriend the watchmen in a short time.

While the watchmen were being wooed Karim received a message from Col. Siddiqui to book a room for himself and Sayeed in Hotel Big Splash for the following Thursday. Umar Haji would meet them in their room at night. They were then to accompany him.

Karim and Sayeed met Umar Haji in Hotel Big Splash who took them to the landing site. Umar left his ramshackle jeep at the hotel and travelled with Karim in the van they had brought with them, saying that it would help them remember the way. Around three in the morning, when Karim and Sayeed were feeling extremely sleepy, two fishing trawlers arrived. There was a bustle all round. When Karim expressed his apprehension at the noise that was being created Umar Haji asked him not to worry. "The Customs officer is personally present. The local Thanedar would be meeting us halfway. They would both escort us till we touch the highway," he told Karim with an air of confidence that left the latter bewildered. The packages brought by the trawlers were loaded onto a lorry, which then proceeded in convoy, by the dirt road by which Karim had brought his van. In the lead was the Customs officer's jeep. Umar asked Karim to place his van in the rear. He would himself be travelling in the jeep to welcome the Thanedar when he join them half way. Subsequently when they reached the highway the convoy stopped for a brief while. Umar Haji embraced both the officers and took leave. He then came over to the van to join Karim and Sayeed.

After about an hour's drive, they again branched off by a makeshift road and ten minutes later entered the gate of a large farm. Umar, who had kept Karim and Sayeed away from the officers, now enthusiastically introduced them to the owner of the farm. "These are the friends I talked to you about. Please assist them in every possible way." Umar told the farm owner. He offered them tea while the packages were being unloaded and stored in a corner room of the farmhouse. Umar asked Karim to check the packages and lock the room himself. Both assured the farm owner that they would remove the cargo in a week's time, and left for the hotel.

The duo returned to Mumbai in the afternoon. On arrival, however, they got busy organising things. They were acutely aware that the ball was now in their court and they must now execute the plan without loss of time, and do it meticulously.

There was great excitement in Mundkur's cabin in the evening of the day Karim and Sayeed returned from their coastal tour. Khot's men had followed them till they checked in at Hotel Big Splash. The watchers were aware that it was a favourite meeting place of smugglers and did not venture inside. However, they followed the van it when it left late at night but had to abandon the pursuit when it branched off from the highway. It was too risky to follow it further for fear of exposure as, hardly any vehicle travelled that way at that hour of the night. If at all any vehicle moved that was of the smugglers or their protectors, the government officers entrusted with the task of guarding the coast. Both would unhesitatingly expose and harass them. So they waited for the van to return, concealing themselves in the darkness by going off the road.

The van did return after about a couple of hours, but ahead of it was a medium-sized lorry, the kind of vehicle they use for ferrying fish. They quietly followed the two vehicles till they again went off the highway. While they were wondering how to proceed further they noticed that the two vehicles had stopped. There were other lights too. Obviously it was a meeting or transaction place. Therefore, one of the watchers walked down to the spot and observed what was happening, taking cover of the darkness that prevailed all round. Thereafter it was smooth sailing.

Bhadang also had something very impressive to report. Sweta and Gayatri had been playing their part with grit and imagination. They had persuaded Gunwanti to be nice to Yunus and invite him often to her hut under one pretext or the other. Two days ago when she knew he would be visiting her she prepared a meat dish for him and also purchased a quart bottle of the local brew. That put Yunus in a generous and confiding mood. Very soon he started bragging and told

her that he was on a very important mission to destroy the
enemies of the poor. He had learnt how to fire a big gun and
would shortly be shooting it from a high building to destroy
the bloodsuckers. Even if he was later hanged he did not care.
He would go to Paradise and enjoy all that those leeches were
now enjoying here on Earth.

"The big guns have already arrived," Mundkur exclaimed.
"But let us put that aside for the moment. Now that we know
that D-day is not far away let us start in a systematic manner.
Where's the map on which I had asked the wanderings of the
Bandra team to be marked?"

"Here it is Sir," Khot laid the map before him.

"Now which are the buildings that house rich people or
their wealth, that fall within this perimeter which you have
drawn so assiduously?" asked Mundkur, and after studying
the map carefully exclaimed, "Do you see? The concentration
of their crisscross journeys is in the region of the Mint road
closer to Horniman Circle, and my God! Dalal Street. Taking
the second convergence first, it is clear that their target is the
Mumbai Stock Exchange building. There is no other building
of comparable importance in the vicinity." Mundkur looked
up and asked, "Do you agree?"

"That's a perfect deduction, in my view, Sir," Bhadang
gave his opinion.

"I too agree, Sir," said Khot, reinforcing Bhadang's remark.

"That's decided then. Now let's turn to the Mint road
cluster. We have a number of government offices, the Royal
Asiatic Library, the Town Hall and of course the Reserve
Bank building. None of them is worth all that expense and
risk except the Reserve Bank building. True, it does not

house the rich people Yunus hates so much but then what does he know of the inner motives of his masters? You destroy the Reserve Bank Building and you knock down the crown from the head of the Government of India, so to say. Add to it the destruction of the Stock Exchange building and with it the annihilation of hundreds of the blokes who play the financial game inside, and you have made a perfect mockery of the government and the people of this country," Mundkur articulated.

"That sounds very convincing Sir. In fact, we should have no doubt left in our mind, if we take note of the apparently minor observations made by our watchers in their oral reports. Their impression is that the Bandra gang if I may call them so, took the maximum number of photographs in the vicinity of these two buildings. I did not want to highlight their observations beforehand for fear of prejudicing our discussion," Khot added.

"So we there is a consensus on this issue? These two buildings are the targets of this gang, if I may also use Khot's expression," Mundkur summed up.

"Yes Sir."

"Now let us imagine the assault scenario," Mundkur resumed his argument. "They have two vans and at least four scooters. Then we have people who would be firing, I suppose rockets, from tall buildings. The work force has already been divided into two teams. Therefore it would be logical to believe that the vehicles would also be similarly divided. Karim drives one vehicle and Sayeed drives the other. Therefore, they are not only the respective team leaders, but they would also be making use of the vehicles in the assault."

"Sounds plausible. We already know that these two chaps were in different groups at their National Park jamboree," Khot supplemented Mundkur.

"Now, the watchers who followed them to Alibagh say that a number of packages and boxes were offloaded at the farm. Going by the general run of things, several of them must contain RDX or similar high explosive, in addition to 'big guns', that is, rocket launchers. Perhaps the boxes contain launchers and rockets and the packages contain the explosive. It is reasonable to assume that the vans and scooters would be loaded with the explosive and blasted inside or close to those buildings, and at the same time there would be a rocket attack from the top. This will result in total confusion and panic and of course untold destruction."

"We must prevent it, Sir, at all costs," said Bhadang.

"That goes without saying. The question is, at what stage. This is such a complicated and extensive operation that if we delay action till the end, things might as well go out of control and they succeed in causing damage, which would not be trivial. If we act now, we may prevent the catastrophe for the present but we won't be able to punish the guilty. There would be hardly any evidence against them that the courts would accept readily."

"A real dilemma Sir," Khot agreed.

"Well, we have to find a via media," Mundkur hinted. "Let's visualise what they would do hereafter. They have the teams ready. And they have the weapons ready though not at hand at the moment. And therein lies our opportunity. We know where the weapons are presumably stored. We assume that before the D-day that they might have fixed for themselves they must get the stuff here and assemble it to make it usable. The RDX must be distributed, detonators placed and timers or sensors placed so that the explosions could be precisely timed. The rocket launchers and rockets will have to be carried only in suitcases otherwise they would attract attention. All this will require time and privacy. I don't suppose they will be able to get that kind of privacy here in Mumbai, unless they have acquired a garage or some such place. If they had we would have come to know. Isn't that so Bhadang?"

"Yes Sir. Our watchers are after them. They won't miss such a conspicuous activity," Bhadang said with confidence.

"In that case the safest place for them is the farmhouse where the goods are secreted unless of course they prefer a secluded place in the jungle half way. Whatever the choice they make one thing is clear. To handle such a big consignment they must go there in strength, either all of them or a large proportion of them. Our opportunity lies in trailing them effectively and nabbing them when they are returning with the contraband. That would be smoking gun evidence against them."

"That's indeed an apt scheme Sir, but I suppose we would require help of the police to manage this sort of a thing," Khot expressed his concern.

"Of course we would. The time has come when we must take them into confidence. You keep every one on the maximum alert. I will speak to Inspector Sawant as well as to his boss and obtain reinforcements. I don't suppose we should dissipate the information to the district police, it may leak," Mundkur expressed his fear.

"Incidentally," he asked Bhadang, "Did you get the second van treated by Murthy? We cannot afford to lose track of those vehicles."

"Yes Sir. Last night we did the job. What's more, Murthy was able to unlock the doors, therefore he planted a bug under the steering wheel. I don't suppose they will be able to discover it. It cannot be normally seen, and they are not going to take the van to a garage for servicing. We are now able to hear everything that Sayeed, who drives that van, says. Unfortunately he has said precious little that is useful so far."

"I am glad to know that Murthy succeeded in this case. It's a bit late though. We have already placed most pieces correctly in this jigsaw puzzle. If Sayeed blurts out something incriminating we may be able to subsequently use it in evidence," Mundkur remarked.

The next morning the duo, Khot and Bhadang were again in Mundkur's cabin as soon as he arrived.

"Yes, what's new?" Mundkur asked while gesturing to them to take a seat.

"Sir, they have taken one more step. Last night they purchased several middle-sized suitcases, and briefcases too. You had anticipated suitcases but their purchasing brief cases is somewhat intriguing," Bhadang said.

"Yes, we had not expected that they would make use of briefcases too. Obviously they would stuff them with explosives and use them as bombs that could be planted inside a building. But I don't suppose they would like to plant them inside those two buildings. First, it would be a redundant exercise and secondly, they won't be able to effect entry, given the security arrangements at those places. They must plant them outside but in the neighbourhood. That would be killing far too many innocent people. I do not know what their objective is, but they are capable of perpetrating extremely heinous things. In any case we do not propose to let them reach that stage. As I mentioned yesterday, it is much too dangerous to take that chance, this find only reinforces that view. No, we are going to nab them on their way back when they are loaded with all that their masters have sent them through the smuggling channel. That is for sure," Mundkur declared his resolve. "Now I must get going. Must catch Inspector Sawant and his boss in their den and tie up with them."

There was no difficulty getting clearance from the head of the Crime Branch for Inspector Sawant and the commando squad to help him. In fact, the chief was so excited on learning the outline of the operation Mundkur was about to bust, that he wanted to take him to the Police Commissioner, but Mundkur persuaded him to desist from the impulse. "Time is of the essence," he told the chief, adding further, "It has always been my policy to apprise the big boss only after the job is actually carried out. He might otherwise upset the apple cart by making a suggestion that may not be feasible but cannot be ignored." The chief agreed with a big guffaw and let Mundkur have his way.

Mundkur and Sawant, old friends, decided to reconnoitre the landscape themselves before laying the trap. He called for an unmarked Padmini Premier car—a common sight in the countryside—from the car pool and dispensed with the services, of the driver, saying that he would prefer to drive the car himself. In the meantime Mundkur sent for the leader of the watcher team that had actually tailed Karim and Sayeed when they had been to collect the consignment. He was asked to hop into the rear seat and to guide them to the farmhouse where it was concealed. They were not interested in visiting the hotel or the landing site. That would be taken care of later, during the course of the police investigation. They were at the moment acutely concerned with what lay ahead.

When the watcher pointed out the farmhouse to them from a distance, they abandoned the car and on foot moved round it at a safe distance. The surrounding land was undulating and covered for the most part with thickets and bushy growth. They located a shrubbery-clad highland, which offered a clear view of the farmhouse and also provided enough cover. "This would be an ideal place to post two persons with a video camera. They would record all the happenings at the farmhouse when the occasion arrives," Mundkur told Inspector Sawant.

On their way back they fixed a particular bend in the Karnala ghat for the ambush. A truck would block their way when they are returning with the goods from the farmhouse. Policemen in plainclothes carrying automatic weapons, who would be lying on the floor of the truck, would jump out and challenge the convoy. The vehicle carrying an armed party of policemen that would be following them at a distance would close in at that juncture. Commandoes would lie in wait below the road as well as above it. They would nab those who tried to flee on foot. Mundkur and Sawant would travel in a car that would be behind the truck. Khot and Bhadang would he following the armed party in a car, accompanied by the watchers, who had first trailed Karim and Sayeed and knew the landscape. A stand-by force with spare vans would be stationed at the Karnala bird sanctuary guesthouse to be called in when needed.

Men, vehicles and weapons were on hand but what was holding them back was the inability of the people to whom the job was entrusted, to win over the fourth watchman. The Megalopolis building which had been selected for launching the rocket attack from its terrace had a very active managing committee and the watchman, to their chagrin, was from the coastal region. They found him extremely fearful of losing his job. Even mild threats did not work. On the other hand they apprehended that he might in desperation report them to his employers. When Karim apprised Col. Siddiqui of the block, he received a message from him that gave him the go-ahead without the fourth launcher being in position. Col.Siddiqui thought that the danger posed by keeping the operation in a limbo with the material stacked in a distant place, over which they had little control far outweighed the benefit of having a second rocket launching site. Therefore, Karim should ask that team of launchers also to join the first team.

This was a good compromise Karim thought and decided to go ahead. All said and done his and Sayeed's lives were at stake, which occasionally plunged them into depression. And he was not sure if the flock would remain intact if no action was forthcoming. It was Monday when he received the green signal. The next morning he dispatched Sayeed and Rashid to alert the farm owner and to request him to give leave to his servants on Thursday, when their group would be arriving in strength at his farm. He also sent a wad of hundred rupee notes to the farm owner to keep him happy though he was not expected to pay him anything. He and Hamid got busy personally alerting every member of the group. He gave rupees five thousand to every one of them as directed by Col. Siddiqui, for the sustenance of their families in case they were required be to away for some time.

Karim wanted one more car to be taken to the farm. He was not sure if the two cars they had would be able to accommodate them all and the cargo as well though he had decided that eight of them would travel on scooters. The scooters had to be taken to the farm so that the right shape and size of the explosive could be stuffed into their boots. Aziz, one of the group-of-fifteen offered to procure an old Ambassador car that his uncle plied as a private taxi. Karim was pleased at the offer and asked him to obtain the car on Thursday for the whole day. He also offered to pay twice the normal charge in advance but did not want the chauffeur to accompany the car. Aziz assured him that there would be no difficulty in managing that as his uncle would have no objection to his driving the car. Karim asked every one to arrive by ten-thirty at Persian Darbar restaurant that was situated near the junction between the Goa and Pune highways. They would proceed together from there after lunch—perhaps the last good lunch for him and Sayeed, he thought to himself.

The four Abduls left their flat early on Thursday morning, Karim and Rashid in one car and Sayeed and Hamid in the other. The suitcases and briefcases were stacked in the rear compartment. They had to collect a few other members on the way—those who would not be riding the scooters or accommodated in Aziz's car.

All the four Abduls leaving simultaneously early in the morning was unusual. The watcher on duty at the static observation post, therefore, immediately rang up Khot and Mundkur to alert them. The mobile team of watchers started after the vans wondering how long the two would remain together so that they would not have to face the dilemma whom to follow. They were in luck. The vans never parted company.

Mundkur was the first to fathom the meaning of this curious movement. His hunch was confirmed when the watchers reported that they were heading towards Vashi. He was sure now that the farm was their destination. He hurried Khot and Bhadang out of their houses and also asked Inspector Sawant to get ready with his staff for the move when he gave the next signal.

When the watchers reported to him that the whole group had assembled at the Persian Darbar restaurant, he was happy. There was a good chance of picking up all of them. He deputed the team of two that was to videotape the proceedings at the farmhouse to go ahead on their motorcycle and take position. He did not want them to miss even the entry of the group that was already on its way.

Around noon the whole group left in a sort of extended convoy with Karim's van leading. By this time Khot and Bhadang had joined the watchers. They followed the motley assemblage of vehicles at a safe distance, reporting to Mundkur the location as they progressed.

Karim and his cohorts reached the farm at one-thirty. The farmer was there to receive them. He had dutifully got rid of his servants. Asking him to go to his room and rest, Karim opened the lock of the room and like a good commander apportioned work to each one of his companions. By about five they were ready. Karim personally checked that the rocket launchers and rockets were packed together so that there was no confusion, that the RDX slabs were properly packed and their detonators and sensors kept separate. They would be implanted in the morning the following day before leaving for the final action. Having satisfied himself that everything was in order he expressed words of appreciation and patted them for the good work done. He called the farmer, thanked him for the help quietly thrusting another bundle of notes in his hands, and took leave. Karim's van was again in the lead. Sayeed's van made up the tail. The Ambassador car and the four scooters were sandwiched between the two. Karim was particular that none of the scooters lagged behind, hence this arrangement.

It was six-thirty, almost dusk when Mundkur got the signal from the static watcher he had planted about two kilometers ahead of the ambush site, conveying that the convoy was passing his position. "Lucky it is not dark yet," he muttered to Sawant. Both got into their car, alerting the driver of the truck next to whom sat a watcher who had seen Karim's van often enough to recognise it the moment he saw it. The driver of Mundkur's car gave two brief hoots of his horn to warn the commandoes who were hiding behind the bushes.

As Karim's van which was in the vanguard of the convoy came in sight—some fifty meters away—the driver of the truck started his vehicle. The truck rolled ahead. The moment the van came near him in a flash the truck swerved and blocked its passage. Before Karim could back the van to find a way out he found himself facing the muzzles of carbines that were pointed at him. The other vehicles met the same fate. They were surrounded by armed men from all sides. One or two scooter riders tried to escape by jumping down the slope only to be apprehended by the waiting commandos.

Within minutes the action was over. Karim and his companions were handcuffed, roped and herded into police vans that arrived from the nearby rest house. The vehicles and other receptacles were examined by the bomb experts who were part of the reserve force, and declared safe. Police drivers then took charge of them and a much longer convoy started vending its way to Mumbai, with a delighted Mundkur and a jubilant Inspector Sawant leading in their car.

Facilitator

NIAZ AHMED WAS A COLLEGE DROPOUT. HIS BROTHER who was an engineer employed in a construction company, helped him financially to establish a communication centre in Dongri area of Mumbai by hiring a small but strategically located shop and paying for the STD and ISD facilities that were to be installed in it. Niaz persuaded his brother to invest in a fax machine as well, for it would attract more business. His indifferent performance at college notwithstanding, Niaz was a hard-working person. That paid off. He started doing good business. As money came in he increased the facilities available at his communication centre, which he named as 'Shabnam Communication Centre' to commemorate his deceased mother. The conferencing facility that he provided became very popular with the business community in the neighbourhood.

As ambition grew Niaz decided to explore the chances of starting a business in Dubai. One of his childhood friends was doing well in Dubai. Niaz decided to pay a visit to him to study the conditions for himself. While at Dubai, his friend introduced him to a Mohammed Yakub, a frequent visitor from Karachi. Yakub invited him to visit Karachi on his return journey. Though Niaz nodded he was aware of the difficulties involved and therefore, made no effort in that direction. Niaz had incidentally travelled to Dubai by a PIA flight, which touched Karachi. He returned by the same flight.

While at the Karachi airport he rang up Yakub just to say Salaam Walekum. Yakub responded very warmly. "Why don't you break your journey for a couple of days and see the glamour of Karachi? It's no less than your Mumbai," Yakub suggested. Niaz was tempted but did not know how to go about it. "Not a bad idea Yakubbhai, but I have a through ticket for Mumbai and no visa to enter Pakistan either," he said explaining his predicament. "That's not a big problem, Niazbhai. Leave it to me. I will be there at the airport in fifteen minutes and fix everything for you. Just wait for me in the transit lounge." Yakub sounded confident. True to his word he not only arrived on the scene promptly but on arrival also arranged to get Niaz's baggage offloaded and his flight to Mumbai rescheduled. He took Niaz's passport and returned within a few minutes with transit visa stamped on a separate paper. Yakub was a model of efficiency while handling what Niaz thought was an impossible task, which thoroughly impressed him. Yakub seemed to know the right persons who also readily obliged him. "You see, I have obtained transit visa for you on a plain paper. It is not stamped on your passport. There would be no entries either in your passport to show your arrival and departure at the Karachi airport so that the Indian immigration police don't harass you," he told Yakub while handing back the passport. "So nice of you,

Yakubbhai. You need not have taken all this trouble. I had time on hand because the halt here is long, so I thought of saying hello to you. That's all." Niaz said, overwhelmed by the consideration shown to him by Yakub who was, all said and done, a comparative stranger to him. Ignoring his remark Yakub said persuasively, "Now onwards till you leave for Mumbai you will be my guest." As if to prove his point, he picked up Niaz's suitcase and said, "Let's go, my car is outside in the parking lot."

Niaz thus found himself ensconced in Yakub's house enjoying his hospitality. That night Yakub organised a small party for his new found friend from India to which he invited his other friends. One of them was Major Yasin, who was introduced to Niaz as the one who got the visa for him so promptly. Major Yasin made special effort to talk to Niaz and be affable. He courteously enquiried about his business interests in Mumbai and what his future plans were. Before leaving Major Yasin warmly shook hands with Niaz and said, "I must thank Yakubbhai for giving me the opportunity to meet you. It was a pleasure indeed talking to you. I learned so much about life in Mumbai. Until now I had only read about it." Niaz was overcome with gratitude at being treated like an important person. He profusely thanked Major Yasin for the honour given him, and out of politeness asked, "Can I do anything for you in Mumbai?"

"Why don't you come over to my office tomorrow morning and have a cup of tea with me? I shall be only too happy if you could make it. We shall have a good chat then," Major Yasin suggested persuasively, sidestepping the question. Niaz acquiesced.

Sure enough, there was a car at Yakub's door the next morning sent by Major Yasin to fetch both Niaz and Yakub for the promised tea. Yakub excused himself on the plea of a business engagement. Thus only Niaz went in the car. He was nervous and self-conscious, but Major Yasin soon put him at ease. After the tea during which pleasantries were exchanged in ample measure, Major Yasin assumed a serious stance and put up what he called a business proposition. "I am making it more to promote your business, since I have started liking you than to seek any advantage for myself," Major Yasin stressed, looking straight into Niaz's eyes.

"I quite believe that, but what is the proposal like, may I know?" Niaz asked, not sure what to expect.

"It's simple enough," Major Yasin assured him. "I would make a permanent deposit of rupees ten thousand with you, which would serve as advance to cover the charges that would be payable for using your communication facilities in Mumbai by my friends. Every month you should fax me the bill and make corresponding deduction from the advance. I would ensure that complete reimbursement is made to you within ten days. Do you find it attractive enough?"

"Looks eminently fair to me. It would ensure a steady business for me if the facility is used often enough. I do hope there would be no problems in transacting this kind of business," said Niaz, somewhat guardedly. He was relieved though that he was not required to do anything out of the way.

"Yes, one more thing," Major Yasin continued. "If our business relationship sustains for a reasonable time, I can assure you right now that I would use my numerous contacts in Dubai to secure a foothold for you in that place of wealth and opportunity." The offer made the original proposal quite tempting for Niaz, who then enthusiastically committed himself to it, without making any enquiries about the type of people in India who would be using his facility. Major Yasin effusively thanked him and gave him his telephone as well as the fax numbers. "For your and my sake please do not talk about our understanding to anyone, not even your brother. You know how your police are. They would chase you unnecessarily and make your life miserable," he warned, while bidding him goodbye.

Back in Mumbai, before Niaz could settle down to the humdrum of his business life he received a phone call from Major Yasin early one morning. "You remember our deal Niazbhai? Are you firm about it, or have had second thoughts?"

"I have given you my word, Major *Sahib*," Niaz said unwaveringly.

"I am happy to hear that. Well, the promised amount would be delivered to you before lunch by a contact of mine. You should accept it and start my account from today."

"Very well. I will do as you wish," Niaz assured him.

Two days later Major Yasin was again on the line. "Niazbhai, tomorrow a young man would come to your shop around the same time, that is, late in the evening. So please don't close your shop till he comes."

"How do I recognise him?"

"I am coming to that. He is a young man about twenty-five. Somewhat dark complexioned, thin and clean-shaven. He will be wearing brown trousers and beige coloured T-shirt. To establish his identity he would approach you and say, 'Salaam Bhai *Sahib*. I am Altaf, younger brother of Yusuf

Seth'. In response you should ask him, 'How's Yusuf Seth?' to which he would reply, 'He is bedridden. Fractured his left foot'. If the answer is right, he is my man. You should then allow him to use the telephone facility and debit the charges to my account. Is that clear?"

"Quite clear," Niaz assured him.

Sure enough the man arrived the next day which incidentally was a Sunday, and used Niaz's telephone to put a call to Karachi. Thus, Major Yasin's account with Niaz became operative from that evening.

From that day onwards Altaf became a regular visitor to Niaz's shop. When he came again after a week, instead of wanting to use the telephone facility he took out an envelope from his shirt pocket and requested Niaz to fax the contents of the paper that the envelope contained to a Karachi number. Niaz obliged and debited Major Yasin's account appropriately. Altaf took back the paper from Niaz and left the shop without a word. This became the practice thereafter. Niaz noticed that Altaf came to his shop on every Sunday late in the evening. When curiosity got the better of him he couldn't resist asking Altaf one day about it. Altaf, who was generally reticent and kept his conversation with Niaz limited to the minimum needed, said briefly, "Sunday is my off-day. The place where I work remains closed on Sundays." Before Niaz could seek further information from him, Altaf said Khuda Hafiz and left the shop.

One late evening, a month or so later Major Yasin rang up Niaz from Karachi. "A small favour from you, Niazbhai," he said sweetly.

"No problem. You have to simply command and it shall be done," Niaz expressed readiness. He was making good money from this connection which impelled him to oblige.

"The usual person who recoups you the bill amount would be delivering a packet containing twelve thousand rupees tomorrow morning. You should send two money orders, one for seven thousand rupees to Seccunderabad and another for five thousand rupees to Kanpur. You may charge me one per cent commission." Major Yasin then dictated two addresses to Niaz and hung up. As soon as he received the money the following morning, Niaz sent the two money orders and faxed the receipts to Major Yasin before destroying them.

Hardly a week had passed when Major Yasin was again on the line. "One more favour please," said Major Yasin pleadingly.

"No problem Major *Sahib*. Go ahead and tell me what you want me to do," Niaz assured him.

Major Yasin was happy to hear Niaz's ready acceptance and said so in so many words, then added, "Please get in touch with a gentleman Sikander Bukhari by name, and ask him to ring me up from your shop." He dictated Bukhari's telephone number to Niaz and further told him to let Sikander use his telephone facility in the future as well and debit the bill to his account. Sikander Bukhari thus became a regular client of his. This augured well for him because Sikander Bukhari used the telephone facility quite liberally.

Niaz was happy with the arrangement for it brought him good money every month. He was clever enough to guess that Major Yasin and his Mumbai-based contacts were involved in a deep game. He had discovered, while trying to overhear

Bukhari's telephonic talk that the latter always spoke in riddles and used words that he could not follow. As for Altaf, he sent letters to Major Yasin that concerned military matters. While faxing Altaf's letters he had noticed that Altaf often used several English words that could be related only to the military. Niaz, however, did not realize that by now he too was neck deep in the same dark, murky business.

Though he did not tell Niaz, the fact was that Altaf worked in the army canteen for *jawans* in Colaba. He had joined the canteen several years ago as a help when he was a young boy of fourteen. His mother worked as a domestic with an army Brigadier. When she realised that young Altaf could not make progress beyond the seventh standard, despite two attempts, she persuaded her employer to fix him up somewhere, and the good Brigadier obliged her by asking the canteen manager to engage him in the canteen.

Altaf took to the job instantly. It afforded him the freedom to spend money, though paltry it was, without having to account for it to his mother. Besides, a variety of snacks that the canteen prepared for its clientele also came his way albeit in bits and pieces. That was highly satisfying to his taste buds. Being an extrovert by nature and an obliging type he soon became a favourite of several of the regular customers. Therefore, when the Brigadier was transferred and his mother had to shift with him young Altaf decided to say goodbye rather than follow her. "No mother, I will not leave this job and come with you. My future is here and I mean to give it a try. You go ahead. I will remain in touch with you. When you are too old to work, come back to me," he told her bluntly. She also realised that finding a new job for him would not be easy and let him have his way.

As he became older and gained expertise he was promoted by the canteen manager to be a waiter. By now he knew every regular visitor to the canteen by name, and there were several of them. In fact, it would not be an exaggeration to say that he was quite chummy with most of them, so much so that even when some were transferred to distant places on the borders they corresponded with him describing their life albeit in a guarded sort of way.

Being in the prime of his youth and living alone Altaf often visited houses of ill-fame, which abound in Colaba, whenever he had enough money in the pocket to bestow on that pastime. During one such nocturnal visit he met a dashing young man. "My name is Hasan," he told Altaf, taking the initiative to introduce himself.

"Mine's Altaf."

"Where do you work? Are you by any chance in the army?"

"Not really, I mean I am not a soldier but I am associated with the army. I work in the army canteen," Altaf disclosed. Hasan got interested. "Why don't you join me for a booze and meal? I am going to the restaurant that's across the street. They serve good biryani. The beer is also really chilled."

For want of anything better to do and perceiving the prospects of a good meal and exchange of gossip—perhaps as a reaction to his loneliness—he accepted the invitation. They soon became friendly and often met on Sundays that were off-days for Altaf, drinking beer and eating chicken tikka, a favourite of Altaf. Hasan invariably paid the bill. That suited Altaf fine.

In reality Hasan was an undercover agent of the ISI whose allotted task was to collect intelligence about military formations stationed at Colaba. Every time they met he could collect several bits of useful information by casually questioning Altaf who, Hasan found to his delight, had a rich repertoire. He decided to give their relationship a formal base. One evening while they were draining the second bottle of beer that Hasan had ordered, he broached the subject. "Altaf, my friend, I find that you are not only an interesting person to talk to but also a talented one. Family circumstances must have landed you in the job you are now doing in the army canteen. I am sure, they don't pay you much." Before Altaf could respond to that inconvenient remark Hasan hastily added, "No, I don't want to know how much they actually pay you if that's embarrassing for you. Nor am I suggesting that you leave the job. I very well know how difficult it is to get a job these days. What I wish to propose for your consideration is that staying where you are you can add a good chunk of money to your income."

"What do you mean? You want to suggest that there is a way of earning extra money? But I don't have much time left after my duties in the canteen nor do I have any qualifications," Altaf asked, getting interested.

"You don't have to work extra hours and yet get a neat sum additionally at the end of the month."

"How is that possible?"

"I will explain to you. Listen carefully."

"You have my ears," Altaf said. He was now quite excited though unsure of what Hasan had up his sleeve.

"What you have to do is to write down whatever information about the army you can collect from your friends who visit the canteen or meet you otherwise and give me that paper at the end of the week, when we would meet like we are meeting tonight. A friend of mine would be interested in those reports. He would also pay handsomely. In our meeting that would follow I would bring the money that my friend would consider as adequate remuneration. On my part I may assure you that it would always be a generous reward for your effort." It was the opportunity of a lifetime, which Altaf accepted readily without realising or caring for the implications.

It so happened that Hasan had to beat a hasty retreat and flee the country when one of his other contacts got blown. He was lucky to have got wind of it in time, and escaped by the skin of his teeth, as it were. He could not, therefore, make any arrangement with Altaf for the dispatch of his reports, though by now he had taught him how to write them in a systematic manner discerning what was useful and what was not.

It was Major Yasin's main worry now, how to re-establish contact with Altaf whose reports he valued. Altaf was in fact for him a mole inside an important army establishment who could operate productively for years. He, therefore, took a chance and sent Rauf, an itinerant agent of experience to India clandestinely, to locate Altaf and establish a line of communication with him. Rauf succeeded in his effort without spending too many days on the hunt. Hasan had not only given a detailed description of Altaf in his report on him but also mentioned his favourite haunts including the women he visited. That enabled Rauf to spot him one late Sunday evening. "How are you Altaf Bhai? I have brought greetings for you from Hasan," Altaf heard someone whisper close to his ear as he emerged from a brothel. He looked back with a start only to see a young man smiling at him enigmatically. "Who are you? How do you know Hasan?" he asked in a low anxious voice, facing the stranger squarely.

"I am a friend of his. Could we go over to some place and talk?" Rauf suggested, and led the way to a restaurant that was not far away.

As soon as they settled down at a corner table and ordered tea, Rauf thrust a small piece of paper towards Altaf. "This is a letter for you from Hasan. Read it. It would convince you about my genuineness and what I said a little while ago." Altaf read the letter eagerly. He did not miss Hasan as much as he pined for the money that the latter regularly brought for him from an unidentified friend of his. He read the letter twice over and folding it carefully put it in his trouser pocket. The letter had briefly explained to him the reason for his sudden departure without saying good bye. His father had died of a heart attack, which now necessitated his staying on at his native place to attend to family affairs. In the letter Hasan further advised him to follow the instructions that his friend who delivered the letter would give him, so that the old mutually beneficial relationship could be resumed forthwith.

Rauf gave Altaf a Dubai 'accommodation address' and asked him to send his reports to that address. He also gave Altaf Major Yasin's telephone number and asked him to contact him on phone from a PCO on the second Sunday of every month. "Please ring up this number around nine-thirty at night and ask for Ibrahim Seth. Give your welfare in brief and answer the questions that would be put to you. Ibrahim Seth would give you instructions about the work, which you must carefully note," Rauf told him in a firm tone. Altaf agreed to follow the instructions, especially because he was promised a monthly salary of rupees six thousand that would be deposited in his bank account, or paid in cash. Tea over, the visitor said goodbye and brusquely took his leave.

A valuable source was thus revived but Major Yasin was not fully satisfied with the communication arrangement. A letter was liable to be censored or lost in transit. In any case it was a very slow and sluggish system. He was, therefore, in search of a better alternative when Niaz almost walked into his arms, as it were. He established a working relationship with Niaz and quickly handed Altaf over to him. He was thus in a position again to reap the full benefit of this operation. Inevitably, he also decided to make a monthly payment to Altaf through the same channel since both met every time the later brought a report to be faxed.

"My dear Sawant, I believe that you are as much worried as I am about the misuse that can be made of the mushrooming PCOs in the City. It has become much easier for people engaged in shady business to communicate with immunity. One may be sure that criminals and probably espionage agents are also making full use of it," said Mundkur, chief of the counter-intelligence unit of IB. He had come calling on his old friend, Inspector Sawant of Mumbai City Police Crime Branch, to express his anxiety.

"I agree, it's causing us too considerable concern. Some of them are under observation but there are so many of them and multiplying by the day!" Sawant said in exasperation.

"I am glad you feel the same way. There's no point going after every PCO. We must make a judicious selection. I feel that we must pick out some of the well-equipped PCOs that provided several communication facilities, and place them under observation in rotation," Mundkur suggested.

"That's a good idea. Let's put our resources together. We know some of them. I am sure, your people also find some of them becoming eyesores." Sawant agreed. Mundkur made full use of the contacts of his officials to identify PCOs, which usually called themselves communication centres to denote that they were providing more than mere telephone facility, and were patronised by shady characters. Before long their attention was riveted on Shabnam Communication Centre that had started in a big way and was doing good business. What was more, it was reported that it remained open for long hours and occasionally at odd hours.

First thing they noticed on scrutinising the record of Shabnam Communication Centre, maintained at the telephone exchange for billing purposes, was that several calls were made every week from that PCO to Karachi and that even fax messages were sent. They, therefore, decided to place all the telephones installed in that shop under observation and intercept even fax messages. While the telephone conversations did reveal that fishy and suspicious business transactions were going on which was also the case with several other PCOs, it was a fax message they intercepted on a Sunday that made all of them sit up in excitement and concern. It contained beyond doubt information about army deployment. Mundkur sent a copy of the fax message to the Mumbai Area Commander who promptly confirmed that several things mentioned in the message were of classified nature. This caused great alarm to Mundkur. "Bhadang, you better check their records for the past six months at least to find out if fax messages were indeed sent earlier too, or it's a recent development," he asked his assistant Bhadang, and dispatched him to the telephone exchange. Bhadang brought the information that fax messages had been sent on several occasions in the past to that particular telephone number at Karachi. "It's obvious that some ISI agent is passing on military intelligence using this channel," Mundkur observed glumly. "We must find out who he is."

Mundkur decided to mount a watch on the shop and at the same time collect all possible information on its owner. "Khot, you take charge of the surveillance and Bhadang, you make a background check on the owner," he directed his subordinates. Khot had no difficulty in establishing static watch on the shop. Close to the communication centre of Niaz was a bus top. One of his men would stand in the queue oft and on. A shopkeeper across the street was befriended. He provided sitting space for the second watcher. The third one held himself in the ready to follow any worthwhile visitor if the circumstances so warranted. Bhadang meanwhile found out that Niaz had been to Dubai once last year. There was no indication that he had ever visited Pakistan in the recent past.

On the following Sunday around eight-thirty in the evening Khot's telephone rang. The leader of the watcher team that was keeping an eye on the goings-on at the Shabnam Communication Centre was on the line. "A few minutes earlier when there was no customer in Niaz's shop a young man walked in," the watcher reported. "He went straight to Niaz who seemed to be expecting him, and quietly slipped an envelope to him. Niaz went to the fax machine, took out a notebook-sized paper from the envelope, put it into the machine and pressed some buttons. He apparently knew where to send the fax. After the job was done Niaz handed back the paper and the envelope to the visitor and went back to his seat. The visitor left a minute ago. We did not see any payment being made. There was hardly any talk between the two."

While the watcher was reporting to Khot, considerable excitement gripped the people in the monitoring room. The moment they comprehended the contents of the fax message that had been just transmitted they knew that the man Mundkur and company were in search of had visited the shop. They alerted Mundkur. "Sir, the man you are waiting for is perhaps at the shop right now. His written report has just been faxed to the Karachi number," the head of the team reported breathlessly. Right then Khot also rang him up to convey what the watcher team leader had told him. Mundkur asked Khot to direct the watchers to trail the visitor. Two watchers followed him while the third remained behind, near the shop to observe further happenings.

Soon after, Niaz closed the shop and went home. The two watchers who followed the young visitor, however, had a long journey to undertake. After eating at a restaurant he caught a bus that took him to the Gateway of India. He sauntered about a bit, ate icecream that he purchased from a wayside rendor and then strolled along the causeway eventually to enter a narrow by-lane. Two blocks away from the junction stood a decrepit two-storey building. He entered that building. For a long time the watchers waited outside at a safe distance but he never came out. Concluding that he lived there they informed Khot and withdrew. Khot's watchers picked up the young man who was in fact Altaf, early next morning from the building where they had left him the previous night, and discovered in no time that he worked at the army canteen as a waiter.

There was considerable excitement in Mundkur's cabin in the morning. As soon as he came to the office he called in his assistants to ponder over last evening's findings. "It should be obvious to us by now that the young man is a spy. He collects military secrets by talking to the Jawans who frequently visit the army canteen, unless of course he has succeeded in raising a conscious source or two, and passes on the information to his ISI masters in Karachi through the agency of the Shabnam Communication Centre. There is of course an odd chance that he is merely a conduit for someone else," Mundkur remarked, opening the discussion. "Evidently, it's an ongoing operation as the demeanour of the man and Niaz would suggest. It is worth noting that the man did not even make payment for the fax services as if he had a running account with him!"

"One very interesting thing Sir," Khot interrupted, seeking an opening for himself. "Last night I was going through the fax transmission record of this shop that was made available to us by the telephone exchange authorities. I found that this man has been visiting the shop every seven days, and when I checked up from the calendar I found that it was always a Sunday."

"That's a very interesting find, Khot. It would immensely help us plan our final move. We will fix it for the next Sunday. In the meantime an unrelenting watch must continue both on the shop as well as this elusive chap from Colaba," Mundkur directed. "I will also speak to Inspector Sawant and enlist his help for the final act."

"That should be alright, Sir. By that time we would have found out more about this man and his activities," Khot said.

"We should barge in when Niaz has just finished transmitting the letter or report whatever it is, on the fax

machine, so that we catch them both together with the report.
The report would be smoking gun evidence against them
particularly when supported with the transmission record. If
the report is not in his handwriting we would know for sure
that he is a courier and some one else is behind him. So let's
get ready for Sunday," Mundkur said, and dispersed them.

Sunday arrived. Altaf was trailed by the watchers from the
building where he lived, when he left in the evening. He had
confined himself to his room the whole day, except to go out
for lunch to a nearby restaurant. The watchers alerted Khot
who was with the raiding party that comprised Mundkur's as
well as Inspector Sawant's men as soon as they got an indication
that the quarry was out on an errand. Mundkur, Inspector
Sawant and their men took up unobtrusive positions close to
Niaz's joint so that they could at once rush inside at the right
moment and prevent anyone from fleeing.

Mundkur's hunch that he would come straight to the
Shabnam Communication Centre came true. They had waited
for hardly half an hour when Khot spotted one of his watchers
approaching the shop. The watcher was right behind Altaf.
As soon as he caught Khot's eye he indicated by subtle gesture
as to which the quarry was. Khot in turn signalled to Mundkur
and Inspector Sawant who were close by. Within a minute the
whole raiding team was on high alert ready to pounce the
moment Mundkur gave the go-ahead signal. Altaf entered the
shop unhesitatingly with the ease of a frequent customer.
From the place where Mundkur and Sawant had perched
themselves they could clearly see what was going on inside
the shop. On seeing Altaf enter, Niaz rose from his seat and
briefly welcomed him with a restrained smile. Altaf pulled out

an envelope from his shirt pocket and handed it to Niaz. He then sat down on a nearby stool and quietly observed Niaz's activities. Niaz for his part took out a paper from inside the envelope and going to the fax machine transmitted its copy. As he was picking up the original paper Mundkur gave the signal and himself rushed to the entry door of the shop. The others followed close on his heels.

Mundkur, Inspector Sawant and Khot entered the tiny room and caught both of them by hand. Inspector Sawant told them in a stern voice, "You both are under arrest, so don't make any move." He removed the paper that Niaz was still holding in his hand. Both were too overwhelmed to offer any resistance, but Niaz did manage to stutter, "What's my crime Sir? He is a customer like any other. Asked me to fax the paper which I did."

"No instructions whom to send. No payment either. Your regular customer, isn't he?" Mundkur asked scornfully. Niaz did not respond.

Inspector Sawant's assistants came forward and handcuffed both of them. "Let's search the premises. There must be something useful for us tucked in somewhere," Mundkur suggested, and himself took the initiative. A few minutes later he pulled out a register from a drawer of the tiny desk at which Niaz was seated, when Altaf entered the shop. Browsing through it Mundkur remarked, "Oh, very good. Very good indeed! Our friend has meticulously maintained the account of all the transactions made on behalf of his Karachi patrons. We could not have asked for more. Let's take them to your place, Sawant. It's time we asked them a question or two."

Fatal Entanglement

IT WAS INDEED A MOST ENTERTAINING PARTY BY ANY standards, where every guest enjoyed himself with abandon. What with liquor of every description and taste crowding the spacious bar counter, there seemed to be a competition especially among the virile lot in the gathering to down highball after highball. Wing Commander Manjeet Singh Arora, the burly Jat from Bhatinda, was no exception. In fact he had had one too many. His irrepressible fondness for the brew was not the only excuse for his inebriation. His host, Shaikh Nawaz, was all the time hovering round him, replenishing his glass the moment it was about to be empty. He had good reason for doting over his first time guest.

Shaikh Nawaz and his comely begum, Saira were known in the elite circles of south Mumbai as great party givers. People who had the good fortune of getting invited to their party enjoyed every moment of it. Drinks flowed like water, followed by mouth-watering savoury Punjabi dishes. What was equally alluring, was that Nawaz Shaikh took care of every need of his guests. The Assistant Manager of Pakistan

International Airlines was a popular figure. But there was one more reason why he was so much sought after. He was a very helpful person with a reassuring, smiling face. If you had to fly anywhere in the world and the need arose unexpectedly, you could rely upon Shaikh Nawaz to arrange a passage for you. If a PIA flight touched your destination he would straight away invite you to the airport asking you to leave all formalities to him. If, unfortunately for you it did not, he would not hesitate to use his ample goodwill with other airlines to arrange a seat for you on the right flight.

Miss Dolly D'Cruz was another person who received Nawaz's attention. It was not entirely because she was an easy on the eye, well-proportioned single woman of flirtatious disposition, who could be taken liberties with. It was also not the first time that she was attending a Nawaz party. She was the Assistant Manager in charge of reservations at a five-star hotel in the city, where the PIA flight crew normally stayed awaiting their next flight, and in that capacity often came in contact with Shaikh Nawaz. That gave him the perfectly legitimate excuse to invite her to his parties, and he did, despite Saira's dislike for her.

Saira had ample justification to disapprove her. Dolly carried a reputation that would make any married woman apprehensive if she saw her husband getting friendly with her. Nawaz had assured Saira several times that his relationship, in fact his interest in Dolly, was strictly official and related to his job. Saira could however, never be at ease when her husband flirted with Dolly, back slapping and cracking smutty jokes. Despite her preoccupation with guests she kept a wary eye on her husband's dalliance with Dolly.

Saira was very relieved when Nawaz introduced Dolly to Arora and left them together alone, steering away with him Surinder Batra, who till then had been chatting with Arora.

Wing Commander Manjeet Singh Arora was a friend and ex-colleague of Batra. Surinder Batra had recently left the Indian Air Force when he had succeeded in wangling an appointment in Air India as a pilot. Arora preferred to stay on. He was a fighter pilot and liked his assignment. A fortnight ago Nawaz happened to run into them at the airport when the two friends were sauntering towards the restaurant to have a cup of tea. Arora had dropped by to see for himself how his friend was faring in his new job. "Hello, hello. How are you Captain Batra? Long time no see," Nawaz greeted the Air India pilot effusively.

"Oh, what a coincidence! We were just talking about you, Mr. Nawaz. Let me introduce to you my dear friend and ex-colleague, Wing Commander Manjeet Singh Arora. Manjeet, this is Mr. Shaikh Nawaz, Assistant Manager of PIA, I was just now talking to you about. A gem of a person. If you ever have a problem getting a reservation on any airlines just give him a tinkle and the job would be done," Batra eulogized.

"Captain Batra is vastly exaggerating, but I do try to be helpful if I could. After all we have got to help one another," Nawaz tried to sound modest. "Where are you heading, if I am not too inquisitive?"

"Oh, just going to the restaurant to have a cup of tea," Batra replied.

"Then why not give me the honour of serving you tea in my cabin? We shall also talk about cabbages and kings. Haven't had a good chat with you, Captain Batra for a long while. Now we have the added benefit of the refreshing company of your dear friend. Please come along, don't say no," said Nawaz persuasively, and gestured them to move towards his office. Both followed readily.

A week later Arora, who had separated from his wife and was living alone in his quarters, was surprised to receive an aesthetically engraved invitation to dinner at Nawaz's residence the following Sunday. It was soon followed by a phone call from Nawaz, urging him to attend and informing him that his friend Batra was also coming. As if this was not enough his friend Batra also rang up a little later and offered to pick him up from his quarters, perhaps on the prompting of Nawaz.

Dolly and Arora hit it off well and kept each other company till dinner was announced. It was an assignment for Dolly. For Arora who had an eye for 'available' young women, it was an opportunity. Both exchanged visiting cards as dinner was announced. "I am sure I will have the pleasure of seeing you again," said Arora soulfully, while handing his card. "Oh, sure, I would love to meet you before long," cooed Dolly, gazing lingeringly into his eyes. A surreptitious brush of hands conveyed their resolve, before they separated to join the rest of the crowd who were queuing up for food.

When Dolly joined the hotel some seven years ago, on successfully completing a hotel management diploma course, she was very young and ambitious, and fondly dreamed of having a good life. Her first appointment as a receptionist exposed her to various influences that included amorous advances by guests and visitors. Before long she followed in the footsteps of some of her senior colleagues and started discreetly responding to calls. With the money that this side career brought her which was far more than what her regular job gave at the end of the month, she could indulge in luxuries she could never otherwise afford. She now lived in a small but well done-up flat on Napean Sea road. Eventually she rose to be assistant manager but did not give up her paid for nocturnal activities. It was difficult to discern whether she continued in this murky business because of the extra money it brought, or because she liked it, or because the people who were privy to her sub rosa activities did not allow her to sever ties.

It did not take Shaikh Nawaz much time, once he got to know her, to spot this aspect of Dolly's personality, and he fully utilised it, not for personal indulgence but for business aggrandisement. This is because, like Dolly, Shaikh Nawaz also had a side career. He worked for the ISI. He was not a career ISI officer though. Some twelve years ago when he joined PIA as assistant sales executive and was posted at Karachi airport, he was a 'straight' officer and continued to be so even when he was posted to Mumbai after a three-year stint at the Heathrow office of PIA. It was in Mumbai that the then Consul General of Pakistan in Mumbai who was also the Station in-charge of ISI, spotted his not inconsiderable talent of influencing people and winning friends. Therefore, when the Consulate in Mumbai had to be closed down at the behest of the Indian government, he recommended to his headquarters that Shaikh Nawaz, who had established himself well in Mumbai, be co-opted into the service and given the responsibility of keeping the Station productive. His advice was accepted.

PIA was asked to call back Shaikh Nawaz to Karachi on the pretext of giving him a reorientation course. He was then taken over by the ISI instructors and given a thorough grounding in agent running, more particularly in communication and operational security. He already had a natural flair for establishing contacts and cultivating people. He was taught how to look for the right kind of person and exploit his character weaknesses. Towards the end he was briefed by a senior officer what were the priority areas that he must focus on. Three months later Shaikh Nawaz was back in his Mumbai seat but now he was wearing one more hat. His dual role had begun.

Wing Commander Arora attracted his attention because he was a serving high-ranking IAF officer. Not many serving officers came his way. He was, therefore, in the process of cultivating Batra, who had recently left the Air Force to 'milk' him as much as possible. But he was aware that soon Batra would be of little use, as he would be flying from one end of the world to the other. At best Batra might be able to furnish him with bits and pieces of information about the current happenings that he might collect from his erstwhile colleagues when he met them by chance. Batra's utility to him was evidently limited.

When he saw a serving Wing Commander with Batra, Shaikh Nawaz seized the opportunity with both hands. It was a long shot but he was taught by his new masters never to ignore even a passing chance, when it concerned a person with access to information. Arora was such a person. Nawaz therefore, decided on the spur of the moment to play host. He found Arora quite talkative and a bit conceited. That suited him fine. Later he made it a point to meet Batra again and discreetly find out more about Arora as a person. To his delight, Batra blabbed about Arora's disrupted family life owing to his philandering disposition, which his wife resented. He was the right person to target. Nawaz had the right weapon in his armoury, Miss Dolly D'Cruz.

Shaikh Nawaz called up Batra, when he returned to Mumbai after completing the assigned flight schedule a week later. "I am throwing a party next weekend Surinder," he announced. "You must come, no excuses. I am inviting your friend Arora also, a lively person I must say. I am sending him an invitation and ringing up too, but you must also persuade him on my behalf to come. In fact I would request you to please bring him along. Will you do me that favour?" Unsuspecting, Batra agreed because he knew that Manjeet Arora liked parties more especially if they had a sprinkling of good-looking women which Nawaz's parties always had.

Having secured Batra's assistance Nawaz invited Dolly for a lunch on her day off, and briefed her on her role. "You are going to attend the party as my guest. I invite you right now. A formal invitation will reach you in a couple of days," he told Dolly. "I will introduce you to Arora—quite a playboy, I hear—and see to it that you are alone with him. You must use your charms. I want you to give him indication in no uncertain terms that you would be game if he desired to go ahead."

"That should not be a problem I suppose. You can trust old Dolly," she interposed.

"Of course I do. That's why I selected you. But I must play my part too," said Nawaz. "Please follow it up soon enough with a call and invite him to your nest."

"Take it as done. If he is really that sort as you say."

"One more thing. I am sure you wouldn't mind my fixing a few little things like a tiny video camera, a microphone etc. in your bedroom before the rendezvous. They would not be noticed. I assure you that you would be paid generously for the services rendered." Dolly did not mind going to bed with anyone if the payment was right, but she resented being photographed. When she expressed her reservation on this count Nawaz firmly told her that that's the way it was going to be done. If she insisted she might double her bill. He also assured her that the pictures would not fall in the wrong hands and that was a promise. She could not protest anymore—Nawaz could ruin her career if he meant to—and nodded her acquiescence.

On Nawaz's advice she let a day pass and then made a telephone call to Arora late in the night. He was apparently happy to receive her call. For the past forty-eight hours he was considering various strategies to get in touch with her. Now that she had taken the initiative he was not the one to let go of the opportunity. Therefore, he readily agreed to her proposal that they meet the next day over dinner. He offered to pick her up from her apartment.

He was at her place promptly at nine in the evening. She too was ready. They went to a Chinese restaurant. After a leisurely dinner it was time to return to their respective abodes. When Arora dropped her at her building she asked him with a sly smile, "Aren't you going to come up to my apartment and have a cup of coffee with me?" Taking it as an invitation he parked the car by the roadside and promptly followed her. One thing led to another. It was well past midnight when he reluctantly said goodbye to her. Nawaz was happy at the progress Dolly made at one go. The result of her labour was there for him to see when he dismounted the camera the next morning before Dolly went to work. Nawaz instructed her to continue her relationship with Arora and bill him every time he came to her flat.

Nawaz let a month pass without any move on his part. In the meantime Arora visited Dolly three times. In Dolly's judgement he was now completely hooked on to her, and would have liked to visit her more often if only she would permit. Nawaz cautioned her against getting emotionally involved with him, and jokingly added, "Don't you ever forget, Dolly that I am the sucker who's paying you for Arora's pleasures." Convinced that the big fish had taken the bait he reported the happy development to the ISI headquarters at Islamabad, and was instructed to fix up an exclusive meeting with Arora over dinner and get back to them. Headquarters would be sending Group Captain Farrukh to take the next step in the operation.

Nawaz rang up Arora that very evening and, after the usual pleasantries said amiably, "Why don't we have dinner together this coming Sunday at Hotel Ambassador? An old friend of mine from Dubai is on a visit to Mumbai. He was once upon a time in UAE Air Force. I therefore thought that since you are also from the airforce you would enjoy his company."

"I would love to come but let me see up if I can manage that evening off," Arora said tentatively.

"Ah, please do make it. I would be only too happy to renew my contact with you."

Just to allay any reservations that Arora might have, Nawaz told him that he would also invite Batra, though he knew that

Batra would be away on a flight that day. Arora agreed. "Okay, I will come. Thank you for thinking of me," he said.

"Entirely my pleasure. I will be waiting for you in the lobby of Hotel Ambassador at eight-thirty, this Sunday," Nawaz clinched the deal.

When Arora stepped into the lobby of Hotel Ambassador, Nawaz and his friend were already there. Nawaz received him effusively and introduced his friend. They then moved on to the restaurant. Drinks and dinner followed. When dessert was being served Nawaz's cellphone buzzed. He had already arranged for it. He rose from his seat and moved to a corner of the dining room to take the call. A few minutes later he returned to the table with a long face. Taking his seat hesitantly, he said glancing mostly at Arora though he meant to address both, "I am sorry, my friends, but a grave emergency has arisen in my office, therefore I must rush to the airport. I profoundly apologise to both of you for having to leave the dinner half way. I do hope you would understand." It was Nawaz's friend who responded first. "I understand your predicament, Nawaz. Such emergencies do crop up unexpectedly when you are in a job like yours. I am sure, Wing Commander Arora also appreciates your dilemma. I will attend to him in your absence," he assured Nawaz. Arora also made appropriate remarks asking him not to worry for them.

"Thank you, thank you, both very much for the consideration. I enjoyed your company thoroughly but must leave now," said Nawaz ruefully. "Please don't bother about paying the bill. I would take care of it. When you finish your dinner just leave without asking for the bill. I will instruct the manager on my way out." He then hurried away waving at both of them.

Arora and Nawaz's friend finished dessert and ordered some liquour at the latter's behest to round up the dinner. It was about eleven when they rose to leave. Arora offered to drop Nawaz's friend at his hotel that was not far, which the latter accepted gratefully. Before alighting from the car at his hotel Nawaz's friend thrust a carry bag he was carrying with him into Arora's hands. "This is a small present—a memento, you may say, of our wonderful evening together—that you may inspect at leisure at home," he said.

"Oh, no. Why a present to me? I enjoyed it as much," Arora murmured in protest, embarrassed that he had nothing to offer in return, but the latter would have nothing of it. Finally Arora acquiesced, and left for home thanking Nawaz's guest for being so good-hearted.

In the privacy of his bedroom Arora pulled out the packet that was inside the carry bag. When he opened it he found a full bottle of Chivas Regal whisky, which he relished. He was fond of the booze. To his amusement he also found two slim covers taped to two opposite sides of the bottle. Out of curiosity he unfastened the larger one and opened it. He almost shrieked in disbelief. It was a small album of photographs that vividly recorded all his activities in Dolly's flat when he had visited her for the first time. He hurriedly glanced through all the photographs, and opened the other packet with trembling hands not knowing what further disaster it concealed. It was a wad of five hundred-rupee notes wrapped in a piece of paper—twenty thousand rupees in all. The paper contained unsigned typed writing.

Full of apprehension Arora picked up the paper and read. It was a brief message that said that the bottle and money were for him. He could continue to enjoy Dolly's favours as long as he pleased but he must report on the following three points first. He must carry his report sealed in a white cover when he went to meet Dolly the next time, and leave it on her writing table. He must visit her before the end of the week. Failure would be regarded as an unfriendly act and consequences would follow. The three points pertained to the IAF capabilities in the Western Command.

Arora was in deep agony. He had not bargained for this treachery. His first impulse was to ring up Dolly and take her to task for the perfidious behaviour but on second thoughts he abandoned the idea. It would only precipitate the eventuality that he feared, he argued. He decided to give a cool thought to the predicament in which he now found himself. On the one hand there was money, ample money at that, and the pleasurable company of Dolly, and on the other there was a sure chance of getting exposed if he declined. The photographs were there to establish his physical intimacy with Dolly. Court martial and dismissal in disgrace were the most probable consequences that would follow when Dolly's connections with his present tormentors would be known. He tossed restlessly in bed tortured by these agonising thoughts. Sleep came to him only in the wee hours when the cocks in the distant slums had started crowing.

Two days had passed but still he could not come to a definite decision. Opposing considerations pulled him in different directions. He was alone in the house, still mulling over his options, when the telephone rang. Dolly was at the other end. "Don't you want to strangle me?" she asked without any preliminaries. He did not answer. "I know what you feel about the whole morbid affair, but believe me I am also a victim. If you come over tomorrow in the evening at the usual time I will explain. Let's both find a way out of this mess. So, will you come, darling?" She asked in her most inviting voice. All these torturous days, he had not been able to get over the emotions Dolly had generated in him. She was now inviting to share with her his agony, which he could not unburden before anyone. On an impulse he said, "Okay, I will come."

"That's like a good boy. And yes, for heaven's sake please do not forget to bring that silly report they want from you. If you don't, they will kill me," she said, and hung up.

Arora was at Dolly's flat on time. He had also brought a report with him. Dolly had been thoroughly tutored by Nawaz in advance, and played her part convincingly. First, she persuaded Arora to believe that both were sailing in the same boat. That rogue from Dubai had visited her a few months ago. Nawaz, poor fellow, did not know what that scoundrel was up to when he introduced him to her in good faith. He used her and started blackmailing her. He had visited her a few days earlier, cleverly found out from her that Arora was to visit her a couple of days later, and forced her to let him fix a camera. She was mortally afraid of him because he was a desperate character. She also argued with Arora that the best way to face the situation was to go along. There was money in it. And they could be together as often as they pleased. She did not understand much about the reports but surely, there should not be much risk involved in writing down those things every now and then. When Arora came to her he had already started thinking on those lines, therefore, he did not require much convincing, and they together planned the future strategy. Before Arora left her she handed him a small white envelope saying that she had been asked to pass it on to him. It contained further tasks for Arora, and a direction to deliver a report on them when he visited Dolly next.

Nawaz was extremely pleased at the outcome of Arora's visit to Dolly. He was sure that Arora was as good as collared, when Dolly told him about Arora agreeing to visit her and, therefore, had given her a list of further requirements in anticipation. A routine was thus established. Every time Arora received a questionnaire through Dolly the envelope also contained money as compensation for his previous effort. Arora had to nose around a good deal to collect the information demanded but still it was manageable. Both Arora and Dolly were now happy with their mutually beneficial relationship in terms of money and pleasure.

As time passed it became more and more difficult for Arora to meet the demands of his paymasters. He was happy till such time the queries were confined to his immediate job for, he could muster his knowledge as well as the documents he handled. They had in fact by now obtained from him photocopies of all the documents that came in his possession in the normal course of his duty. But soon they raised their demands, which made it imperative for Arora to tap his colleagues. Inevitably he started entertaining them lavishly. He had the money to throw about, and then his secret job required that he keep them in good humour. Several attributed his newly acquired generosity to his being single and in need of company, but not all thought that way. One of them was the adjutant of his Unit on whom Arora bestowed special attention as a matter of necessity, because he was the repository of all the files and documents that were processed in the Unit.

The Adjutant—Group Captain Sandeep Shenoy—who was till then intrigued by Arora's unabashed endeavours to curry favour with him, became suspicious of his motives when he tried to borrow from him the War Book on the pretext of studying it to enrich his knowledge. When he sounded some of his sober and experienced colleagues on it he realised that Arora had tried to elicit sensitive information from them too that, really speaking, was not relevant to his current assignment. Instead of alerting the Air Officer Commanding who the Adjutant knew was a bit impulsive and would react by directly confronting Arora with what he had learnt about his prying activities, he decided to tip off Mundkur, the chief of the counter-surveillance unit of the Intelligence Bureau. Mundkur never lost time when he learnt something that had sinister possibilities. He immediately made an appointment and met the Adjutant at a restaurant outside the Air Force complex. "Please do not make any move that would alert Arora. I will get back to you soon with some definite information that would confirm or set at rest your misgivings," he told the Adjutant after listening to his apprehensions about Arora.

Mundkur brought in Khot and Bhadang, his two trusted assistants. With active assistance from the Adjutant they could mount a static watch on Arora at his quarters in the Air Force colony. Within a week Mundkur discovered Arora's relationship and a couple of days later the secret of Dolly's activities on the sly. The nature of Dolly's relationship with Arora was now clear to him. His professional instincts suggested to him that this affair had to have a disquieting dimension. "Dolly was an expensive call girl. She would denude Arora of all his earnings before long. Therefore, Arora should be touching his colleagues for loans, not entertaining them lavishly," he told his lieutenants who had helped him do the spadework.

"That's true, Sir," Khot responded. "His other off-duty activities appear to be beyond reproach except for occasional drinking sprees in the Mess."

"There you are. The irresistible conclusion is that Arora makes money from this relationship rather than losing on it," said Mundkur, with a note of finality. "I suggest we continue to watch Arora's activities for some more time to ascertain if there is any other player in this game before we decide to act." He later informed the Adjutant the essentials of his findings and asked him to bear with them for some more time.

It was almost closing hours when Arora walked into the Adjutant's room. He was off duty and thought of giving a try to an idea that had struck him that afternoon. Given his reservations—in fact knowledge—about Arora, the Adjutant was not much pleased with his sudden entry into his room but the need to be tactful demanded that he extend normal courtesy to him. Taking advantage, Arora settled down on a chair apposite the Adjutant and declared, without wasting much time on the preliminaries that he had basically come to make enquiries about the short course at Hyderabad which he had been asked to attend. "What more do you want to know? We have already sent you an order in writing that also gives enough details about the course," asked the Adjutant, wondering about the true reason for Arora's unwelcome visit.

"Yes Sir. The order did mention about the objective, which gave me a feeling that I had better go well prepared for it. If I have to contribute something meaningful I would like to have a clear idea as to the line of approach we would adopt in case of a conflict with the enemy. I therefore thought that I should have a look at the ORBAT of the Maritime Air Operations. Could you lend me a copy please? If you insist I will read it here itself in your room," offered Arora.

"I don't suppose, Arora, that absence of detailed knowledge of the ORBAT would in any way become a handicap to you in contributing your bit when you attend the course," snapped the Adjutant, dismissing Arora's request.

While they were still arguing on the subject the intercom buzzed. The AOC who was at the other end, wanted the Adjutant to come to his room immediately. The Adjutant was in a fix, as Arora showed no signs of stirring. When he told Arora that he had to go to the AOC at once and almost suggested that he better leave, Arora told him nonchalantly, "It's okay with me. I am in no hurry. I don't mind waiting till you return after seeing the AOC."

"It may take quite some time. You know how it is with the AOC," the Adjutant protested.

"I understand, but as I told you, I don't mind waiting. I have a few more questions to ask you and seek your guidance," Arora said coolly. Not wanting to be very rude the Adjutant reluctantly left the room, hoping that the AOC would not detain him long.

As soon as the Adjutant left the room Arora started peering around for any useful document that might be lying about. To his utter delight he noticed that the key to the confidential cupboard that was standing in one corner was still in the keyhole. Without wasting a moment Arora darted to the cupboard and opening the shutters with care quickly glanced through the files, finally picking up one that he thought would please his paymasters.

The Adjutant had left the room very reluctantly. Halfway through to the AOC's room he remembered to his great consternation that he had not removed the key of the confidential cupboard that he had opened a little while ago. He at once turned about and rushed to his room, unmindful of the fact that the AOC was waiting for him. What he witnessed from the threshold shocked him no end. Arora had opened the cupboard and was peering inside. The adjutant stopped at the door itself to watch what Arora would do next. Arora removed a slim file and was in the process of closing the cupboard when the Adjutant decided to act. He lunged forward and grabbed the file that Arora was holding in one hand shouting at the same time, "Put back that file, you scoundrel!" Arora, however, would not give up his hold. The Adjutant therefore, gave him a shove to loosen his grip. Arora, in turn hit him hard in the belly that sent him reeling. The Adjutant was also a physically fit person, though not as well built as his opponent. He administered a kick that caught Arora on the small of the back. Arora turned back and kicked the Adjutant in return, who lost his balance and fell with a crash against the table. Taking advantage of the momentary respite Arora bolted from the room. He went straight to his car that he had parked close by, and sped away before other officers sitting in the neighbouring rooms could realise what had actually happened.

Arora cleared the main gate like a bullet. Khot's watchers, who were waiting near their car, which they had parked some distance away from the gate were taken completely by surprise. Before they realised that it was Arora who whizzed past them, he had gone out of sight. They scrambled into the car and gave a chase but in vain. Arora's car was nowhere to be seen. The team leader radioed the control room and also informed Khot. They were not aware of what had happened inside the office and therefore, did not think of alerting the City Police. Khot dispatched one more team in a car to help trace Arora but it too failed. It was well nigh impossible to locate in a short time a particular Maruti Zen car in the multitude of cars that were moving on the streets of the city.

Arora had realised that the racket that he and the Adjutant had created in the latter's room would instantly attract other officers to the room. He would then have no chance to escape. But once on the road and out of reach he grasped the gravity of his rash action. He had not only assaulted a senior officer but was also caught stealing a secret document. The consequences would be terrible for his career, and if the AOC did not relent he might even be prosecuted under the Official Secrets Act. He drove on without any specific destination in view but his mind was racing through all the possible options available to him. He had to make a choice and he made it fast.

To dodge possible chasers from the Air Force—he was still not aware of the watch that Mundkur's men had mounted on him, much less the turmoil his sudden fleeing from the office had thrown them into—he had taken a right turn at the Chowpatty to enter Munshi Marg. From Nana Chowk he turned left and eventually joined Malaviya Marg to proceed to Haji Ali. But as he reached Crossroads shopping arcade he took a left turn and passed through the entrance to the basement parking space. He parked the car in a remote corner slot and climbed up the steps to go into the shopping mall. He entered a readymade garment shop and purchased a Denim jerkin. He went back to his car but instead of taking the car out, he put on the jerkin. From the glove compartment he removed his service revolver and quickly slid it into the inside breast pocket. He locked the car and went back to the mall only to come out walking leisurely from the main exit. He waved a passing taxi to stop and hopping into the rear seat asked the driver to proceed to Juhu.

When the taxi neared Juhu he asked the driver to take him to Hotel Horizon on Juhu-Tara road. He wanted to go to a place where none would suspect that he would go, and in all probability none would recognise him. He paid off the taxi and made straight to the Bar. It was well past sundown. There was a sprinkling of early birds, mostly men occupying a few tables. He chose a corner table and ordered a large whisky and soda. When the waiter continued to look at him expectantly he said, "Okay, get me some chicken cocktail sausages and salted cashew nuts."

While sipping his drink he went over all of his none too happy life; his marital discord, his career over which he once prided that now lay in ruins. Apart from a sure guillotine from the Air Force the frightening prospect of suffering imprisonment for stealing secrets loomed large on his conscience. He thought of Dolly. She had given him some precious moments of blissful ecstasy but she had also walked him into a snare he could not extricate himself from. He brooded for a long while on his woes peering at his glass. Finally he raised his head, gazing straight ahead but at none in particular. There was glint in his eyes. He seemed to have made up his mind. It was nearing eight-thirty. He called for the bill.

When the two search teams could not track down Arora despite frantic efforts for half an hour and more, Khot decided to alert Mundkur, his boss. As soon as Mundkur put down the receiver after listening to Khot his phone rang again. It was the Adjutant, Group Captain Shenoy, on the line.

Though the racket in the Adjutant's room had attracted attention of his colleagues working in the neighbouring room none thought of immediately rushing down to investigate. It was in fact the Adjutant's orderly who was first to respond, and he was therefore the only one who had seen Arora rushing out of the room. He could have actually intercepted Arora had he been in his right place, that is, immediately outside the door but as often happens with orderlies he had been sent out on an errand by the Adjutant himself. Luckily he returned in time to see Arora flee the room. He helped the Adjutant get on to his chair and rushed out to fetch the first-aid kit for, the Adjutant was badly bruised. On the way he spread the news of the attack on his boss. Soon there was a motley crowd in the Adjutant's room. The AOC who was fuming in his chair because the Adjutant had not turned up, also walked in when he was told about the Adjutant's condition. He decided to ask the Military Police to hunt out Arora. After a while the commotion died down and every one returned to his desk. The Adjutant was now alone in his room. He rang up Mundkur and put him in the picture. He knew that only Mundkur could do something about it.

Mundkur understood the gravity of the situation. There was no knowing what Arora would do next. He called Inspector Sawant and told him in brief what had happened. "Will you please do me a favour? Could you notify all police patrols through the City control room?" he requested Sawant. When even after an hour's combing operation by the police patrol cars, Arora's car could not be traced, Mundkur called Inspector Sawant again. "I have a feeling Sawant, that Arora would in all probability visit Dolly late at night," he expressed his hunch.

"I too think so," Sawant agreed.

"In that case let's take the chance and surround Dolly's building and ambush Arora when he turns up, but only when he is inside Dolly's flat," Mundkur suggested.

"Good idea. Let's do it," echoed Inspector Sawant.

Arora arrived at Dolly's flat at half past nine. Dolly opened the door when he pressed the bell. Mundkur, Khot and Bhandang, reinforced by Inspector Sawant and two sharp shooters from the commando unit in plain clothes, had taken vantage positions around the building more than an hour earlier. Khot had actually managed to smuggle himself inside the building to keep an eye on Dolly's flat. They were all armed because Arora was unlikely to surrender meekly. It was possible that he might even be carrying a weapon and in a desperate situation like that he was likely to use it too. They did not want to be caught napping. A small posse of policemen in plain clothes was waiting at a distance.

Five minutes later they all converged on the flat without making the slightest noise. Khot was asked to ring the doorbell. For a few seconds there was no response. Then Dolly's voice was heard. She asked loudly, "Who is it?" None replied. Dolly did not open the door. They waited a couple of minutes before Khot rang the bell again. Still no response. Mundkur got into a whispered consultation with Inspector Sawant whether it was time to barge in by forcing the door open, when to their great dismay they heard the sound of a gunshot from inside the flat. It was followed by a sharp shriek. Soon there was another loud report of gunfire.

They could not hold back any longer. The younger officers in the team applied their shoulders and hit the door hard with a thud. As the door cracked open, all of them rushed inside in a systematic manner, their weapons drawn in the ready position, but holstered them almost instinctively the moment they saw the blood-curdling scene in the bed room. Dolly was lying on the bed, blood oozing from a wound in her breast. Arora was sprawled on the floor with a gaping wound near his temple. His service revolver was also lying nearby. He had apparently shot himself after shooting Dolly. Mundkur and Inspector checked their pulse. Both were dead. "Arora punished himself worse than any court would ever," remarked Mundkur, and left the room for Inspector Sawant and his men to commence the legal formalities.

All for a Daughter

"LET ME SEE HOW I CAN HELP YOU, MR. GOPAL," SAID Ramnath Gupta, Assistant Airport Director of Air India at Sahar International airport. "But as I explained to you, we don't have much discretion in this matter. We are governed by rules to which unfortunately I am not authorised to make any exception. Please get in touch with me again after a week or so. In the meantime I will consult my superiors." He neatly folded the letter of recommendation that Gopal had brought from the Director of the Armament Research and Development Establishment—a unit of Defence Research and Development Organisation—where Gopal worked, and handed it back to him. Gupta was keen to dispose of Gopal as much because he had no desire to be of help, as because his friend and colleague Shaikh Nawaz had just then made appearance in the room.

"Come in, come in," said Gupta amiably with a broad smile on his face, looking over the head of Gopal at the tall figure of Shaikh Nawaz standing behind him.

"Please carry on. I am sorry if I have interrupted something important being discussed," said Shaikh Nawaz, Assistant

Manager of PIA who also had an office at the Sahar airport. He was in more than one way the man-about-town at the airport who frequently took time off to say hello to friends and associates.

"Oh, nothing that important really. Here is Mr. Gopal, from the Armament Research and Development Establishment who wants Air India to give a special fare concession to his daughter. She has secured admission in the London School of Economics. I was explaining to him our difficulties," clarified Gupta, who then looking at Gopal said dismissively, "Okay, Mr. Gopal."

"Oh, no please. I was passing this way, thought I might as well drop in for a minute and say hello to you. I am actually on my way back to my office. I have given an appointment to someone. He will be arriving any moment. I will drop in again some other time. No problem," Shaikh Nawaz pleaded and withdrew before Gupta could say something to persuade him to stay on. Shaikh Nawaz had abruptly changed his mind. He was no longer interested in having a chat with Gupta. Gopal who, as he had just learned, worked in the defence research establishment had caught his fancy. It would be a prize catch if things worked out right, he told himself.

Outside in the corridor Shaikh Nawaz lingered on on the pretext of saying hello to an acquaintance who was passing by. He was actually waiting for Gopal, and his daughter who was accompanying him, to emerge from Gupta's room. He did not have to wait long. They almost followed him both looking very sombre and dejected. As they passed Nawaz he abruptly turned to them and said, "Mr. Gopal, can you accompany me to my office? I may be able to help you. We have some special schemes for deserving students."

Gopal and his daughter Suneeta broke into smiles. "My daughter and I shall be highly indebted to you if you could help," implored Gopal. His daughter also muttered something to that effect.

"No problem. We are here to help passengers," assured Nawaz.

Gopal and Suneeta followed Nawaz to his office, which was not far. Nawaz made them sit on the sofa and ordered coffee for them. When the coffee arrived he personally served it to his two guests, and looking up at Gopal said, "Now Mr. Gopal, tell me everything about you, your brilliant daughter and of course what precisely is your problem. Once I get a clear picture I may be able to decide how much I can help you."

Gopal put the coffee cup aside, braced himself up and began. He was so keen to appeal to Nawaz's good sense that he actually said more than what was really necessary to make out a case for travel concession to his daughter.

Ramnathan Gopal had come up the hard way. Son of a school teacher at a place near Trichy in Tamilnadu he joined the Defence Research and Development Organisation as a stenographer Grade-three, and by the dint of sheer hard work, meticulousness and dedication rose to become Personal Assistant to one of the Associate Directors in their Pune establishment. He hoped to rise to the top slot in his line of employment in not too distant a future. His eldest daughter, Suneeta had been a topper in school and college and that year had obtained a first class Honours degree in economics. Her academic performance was so good that she had no difficulty securing admission for a course at the London School of

Economics, something that she coveted most. The question now was of organising finances. Gopal had obtained a loan from the Provident Fund but that was hardly enough to purchase her air passage and to meet her daily needs for a few days in London. A South Indian charitable trust had agreed to give her a scholarship. But the amount was woefully short of her actual requirement even if she decided to live most frugally. They were hoping that Suneeta would be able to secure a part-time job somewhere to supplement the money doled out by the trust. Suneeta had put her heart and soul in it, and he as well as his wife was prepared to make any sacrifice to see that their daughter's dream came true. After all she was the first person in their family to cross the seven seas, as he put it.

"Mr. Gopal, I admire your love and concern for your talented daughter," Nawaz commented when Gopal finished his long narration and reverted to his coffee that had gone cold. "Every father wants his children to do well in life whatever the sacrifices. Look at me. I have a daughter too, almost the same age as Suneeta. I had to leave her behind at Ottawa where I was last posted, because she was keen to complete her education there. Now, really speaking I can't afford it but somehow manage to support her financially with the grace of the Almighty."

"Really! You have a daughter of my age?" Suneeta interjected excitedly.

"Yes my dear. You remind me of her. She is also good at studies though perhaps not as brilliant as you are. That's why I want to encourage her whatever sacrifices I have to make." Turning to Gopal he said, "Rest assured Mr. Gopal, I will manage fifty per cent fare concession if you decide to send Suneeta by PIA, which has thrice a week flight to London from Karachi. We will book her on a connecting flight from here."

"That would be wonderful, won't it be Daddy?" asked Suneeta excitedly.

"Yes indeed. I should be able to arrange that amount," said Gopal agreeably.

"Excellent. So, that solves your travel problem, but not the whole problem of financing her education in England. The real pinch will come when she tries to make the two ends meet after paying the fees, which are hefty. London is a very expensive place. Let me tell you that. I have lived there for three years. Getting a job is not easy either. Every student wants a job. Besides, it affects the studies," said Nawaz with a grave face. The smile on the face of Gopal and that of his daughter evaporated. Both looked morose again.

"I have a suggestion Mr. Gopal if you are prepared to give it a thought," said Nawaz after a pause. "If you accept it, it will take care of your daughter's financial worries."

"What's it Mr. Nawaz?" Gopal asked eagerly, perking up in his seat.

"I know of a London-based Foundation that is engaged in promoting higher education by granting scholarships to deserving needy students. They may agree to extend the much-needed financial assistance to Suneeta. The Foundation is not Indian, let me make it clear Mr. Gopal, but they do not differentiate among South Asian students while granting scholarships. Only merit counts and Suneeta has it in plenty. Luckily one of the trustees is coming to Mumbai next week.

If you can come over next Sunday, I may be able to introduce you to him," said Nawaz solemnly.

"I should be only too happy," said Gopal, pleased by the offer that kindled hope in his crestfallen bosom.

"Very good. Then be at this place, that is, my office at eleven-thirty in the morning, coming Sunday. I will request that gentleman to be here around the same time. As it is, he wanted to come and say hello to me."

"I will surely make it. It's a Sunday. I will take station leave and come," assured Gopal, making it sound easy. He did not want to create any impediment whatsoever fearing that his daughter would never forgive him if he missed this godsend opportunity.

"Fine. Let's then meet next Sunday. Please bring all of Suneeta's certificates and testimonials. He may like to have a look at them. Suneeta needn't accompany you. Why bother her again?" Nawaz clearly hinted that he would like Gopal to come alone. On their way back home Suneeta was agog with excitement. She repeatedly pleaded with her father to do every thing to secure a promise of scholarship for her from Shaikh Nawaz's friend.

Gopal presented himself punctually at eleven-thirty at Shaikh Nawaz's office. Abubaker, the trustee was already sitting with Nawaz. After Nawaz introduced Gopal to the visitor and offered him a seat, he made a few prefatory remarks explaining briefly why Gopal was there. Abubaker was business-like. He asked for Suneeta's testimonials and carefully perused them. When he finished scrutinising the papers he looked up at Gopal and said, "Excellent! Your daughter has a brilliant academic career. We take pleasure in encouraging such promising students so that they can build a bright future for themselves. I may, Mr. Gopal, straight away offer your daughter a scholarship that would take care of all her expenses in London while she is at the London School of Economics." Abubaker then asked Gopal to sign a few documents on behalf of his daughter as a formality, and put a seal of approval of his Foundation, of which he said he was now a senior vice-president.

Eventually to the delight and pride of everyone in Gopal's family Suneeta flew to London by a PIA flight and joined the prestigious London School of Economics. The first installment of the scholarship money reached her well in time. The second and third installments were also credited to her account on the dot. Gopal thanked God everyday for having bestowed such largesse on his daughter. "We now have no worry till Suneeta obtains her degree," he told his wife with a deep sense of fulfillment. "Thereafter she will get so much money that she can easily take care of us too."

Then one day, three months later, Gopal received a long distance telephone call from Abubaker. There was a sense of urgency in his voice. He asked Gopal to meet him the following Sunday in the lobby of Hotel Centaur that was close to Santacruz airport, where he would be staying. Wondering what the reason was Gopal left for Mumbai by an early morning train and reached Hotel Centaur in time. This was his first visit to a five star hotel, but suppressing his nervousness he enquired from the doorman where the lobby was and cautiously trudged towards it. Abubaker was already waiting for him there. "Welcome, Mr. Gopal. Nice seeing you again," he said cheerfully, on seeing Gopal approach him. As Gopal uneasily tried to sit on a chair opposite him Abubaker said, "Shall we go to the Coffee Shop? We can talk there, over a cup of coffee." Gopal meekly followed him.

After informing Gopal that his daughter was doing well and amiably nodding when Gopal expressed his gratitude for the good turn they had done to him and his daughter, Abubaker assumed a serious look and said, "Mr. Gopal, as I mentioned to you a little while ago your daughter is doing exceedingly well, and we are happy that we have had a role in building up her career but unfortunately, a snag has developed. Because of financial stringency the board of trustees has decided to terminate some scholarships. Unfortunately your daughter happens to be one to be affected, of course for no fault of hers. She just does not fit into our new criteria. I am very sorry to inform you that hereafter we shall not be able to meet our financial obligation to her."

For Gopal it was a bolt from the blue. "What will happen to my daughter?" He stuttered, his voice choked with emotion. "I can't make any arrangements that quickly. Even if she has to abandon her studies and come back I will not be able to pay for her fare." Gopal clutched his head in both hands and fell silent. He was totally flabbergasted and unnerved.

"Don't get so upset, Mr. Gopal. All is not lost," Abubaker said softly. Gopal opened his eyes as if woken up from a trance. "I understand your plight. Suneeta is a bright girl, and I would be equally unhappy if she had to give up studies for want of finances. If I were not sympathetic I would have simply intimated our Board's decision by mail or cable to you and be done with it. I have came down all the way here and called you for a personal meeting instead, because I have found out a solution if you accept it, that is."

"What is it, please?" Gopal asked, brightening up a bit.

"I have a well-to-do friend, engaged in international trade that has made him a globetrotter. When I mentioned your daughter's unfortunate case to him he showed willingness to help. He has accompanied me here; of course he has his own business to do. He is staying in a room adjoining mine. Why don't we go up to him so that you two can talk the matter over directly?" Abubaker suggested. Gopal nodded his assent.

Abubaker called for the bill and signed it. He then led Gopal to a room on the third floor and knocked on the door. A burly tall man in his early forties opened the door. His very presence overawed Gopal. Abubaker introduced him to Gopal as Mr. Mallik. The newcomer asked both of them to sit down on the two chairs that were in the room, himself moving on to the bed to find a perch, and immediately rang up room service to send three cups of coffee. "Not for me," protested Abubaker. "I have an appointment to keep. So I shall be getting along. You two talk it over, taking your own time. I have already given some idea to Mr. Gopal about your readiness to chip in."

"Are you leaving, Sir?" Gopal asked nervously.

"Yes Mr. Gopal. I must leave. Good luck to you. I am sure, you will find my friend helpful. Good bye." Abubaker extended his hand.

"I wish you could stay on," said Mallik, but that was only a formality.

When Abubaker left the room Mallik occupied the other chair and said, "Mr. Gopal, my good friend Abubaker has already told me about the excellent performance of your daughter at the London School of Economics, and his

Foundation's inability to continue to pay her the promised scholarship. It's leaving her in the lurch, but they have their own compulsions. He really feels very sorry, in fact guilty about the whole thing because he thinks, he got you in this predicament by offering a scholarship in the first instance."

"How can I blame him? He tried to help. My stars have become malevolent, that's all," Gopal said in self-pity.

"Perhaps you don't know, he pleaded your daughter's case and persuaded me to take on the responsibility because the business concern for which I work also sometimes gives financial assistance in deserving cases, though that is not our regular activity. I couldn't say no to him. He is such a good soul!" said Mallik, explaining how he got into it.

"I am very grateful to you, Sir," Gopal said humbly.

"Don't say such things, Mr. Gopal, I would consider it a privilege if I could be of help in building up a brilliant career. But I have some constraints that I can overcome only if you decide to actively co-operate," said Mallik, sounding matter-of-fact.

"What am I expected to do? Kindly tell me," Gopal asked eagerly. He was prepared to do anything for the sake of his daughter, on whom the whole family had pinned so many hopes.

"Nothing very extraordinary, or out of the way for you, Mr. Gopal. We only require your co-operation. Please remember that you are doing it for the sake of your daughter, to fulfill her dreams of a magnificent future," Mallik reminded him.

"Yes, yes. I will do anything in my power for my daughter. I can't bear the thought of her leaving her education halfway just because her father could not pay for it."

"There you are. That's the spirit. But I must be frank with you. I am not the final arbiter. I am answerable to my bosses, and they are not in the business of charity. This commitment means giving away substantial amount of money, naturally there would be some expectations. What my bosses would want from you is just some information." Mallik put his cards on the table.

"I don't quite follow," Gopal said, perplexed by the proposition.

"I will explain. You are working as PA to the Associate Director in that research establishment at Pune, right? We are also in a sort of research business of similar nature. Naturally, therefore, we are curious to know what goes on in your outfit, that's all. I don't want you to do anything unusual. You type out reports, letters and so on for your boss during the course of your routine work, don't you?"

"Yes, I do. That's my daily practice."

"There you are. Just make an extra printout, or copy what you have typed on a floppy. Secondly, several files must be coming to your boss for his perusal or consideration. I am sure, you glance through them as every good PA does, on their upward and downward journeys."

"That's true," Gopal nodded.

"Just jot down important points, or if your situation permits photocopy whatever you find too complicated for you to follow. Smuggle out of your office those papers, floppies and whatever you have in the manner you consider best. I don't have to tell you much about it. You would know your security procedures better. In short, Mr. Gopal, every important written thing that passes through your hands must reach us in one form or the other. That must be your one-point programme."

"My God! That would be breach of oath!" Gopal exclaimed in disbelief. He was stunned by the proposition.

"Yes, Mr. Gopal. That's so, but what is oath after all? How many people scrupulously observe the various oaths they take officially? Is making money on the sly while awarding contracts not a breach of oath of integrity? Does it not happen in your establishment?" asked Mallik with great vehemence. Gopal did not reply.

"It's a small quid pro quo for the immense benefit that would accrue to your daughter. My bosses will not only ensure that your daughter never falls short of money till she is on her own but you would also get substantial bonus every now and then when the material furnished by you is good. This may eventually enable you and your family to visit your daughter in England. So, think of the benefits that would come to you, not the trivialities like breach of oath or some such pretentious buffoonery which everyone throws to the wind."

Gopal kept quiet. Taking his silence as half consent Mallik continued, "You would be wondering how to reach the stuff to us. That's easy. Once you have obtained sufficient material, seal it properly in a cover and place the cover in this briefcase and lock it. We have a duplicate key." Mallik pulled out a briefcase from his suitcase and placed it on the coffee table in front of Gopal. "Then give a tinkle to this telephone number or send a brief e-mail to this address," Mallik placed on the briefcase a small piece of paper that contained both. "Just say 'Babu remembers you' and declare yourself as 'Bhayya'. Don't commit the mistake of ringing up from your personal number or sending the e-mail from your office Internet connection. Always go to a PCO or Cyber café."

Mallik then explained to him in meticulous detail how to pass on the briefcase at Mumbai to Mallik's man. Gopal was to leave by a morning train on the first Sunday of the month if it was an odd numbered month. And if he could not make it on the first Sunday then it would be the third Sunday. For even numbered months it had to be the second or the fourth Sunday. Gopal quietly collected the paper and the briefcase. His distraught daughter's face was refusing to go away from before his mind's eye.

"Lastly, Mr. Gopal. We have your address and telephone number. In case of an urgent need we will get in touch with you. If you accept our terms, which I believe you do, I will expect you to make a trip on the first Sunday of the next month. Your daughter would herself call you from London soon thereafter to confirm that she has actually received the money. I am sure, you would love to hear her happy voice. So long, Mr. Gopal. Good luck to you. God willing, we will work together till your daughter completes her education."

Gopal rose from his chair, bowed a little and trotted out as if in a daze.

But he was at Crossword bookshop near Mahalaxmi on Warden road punctually at 12:15. When he stopped near the doorkeeper, he noticed a similar looking briefcase in the jumble of handbags and briefcases that were lying there. He placed his own as close to it as possible and went inside to browse through books. This was his first occasion to enter that bookshop. He was fascinated by the rich collection of books of all varieties. He had been asked to spend at least fifteen minutes inside the shop before coming out, but he got so much absorbed in some of the books that he spent a good part of an hour before he thought of leaving the shop. He purchased a book for his son because he thought it would please him, and came to the door. Of the two briefcases only one was left in the jumble. He picked it up and straight away made for the lift not daring to look around, afraid that someone might be watching him.

Once on the ground floor, he took a chance and tried to open the lock with the key he had with him and presto, it clicked open! Cautiously he lifted the lid holding the briefcase in one hand. Inside was a copy of that day's *Times of India* and the latest issue of *India Today*. He placed the book that he had just purchased on top of the pile and closed the briefcase. At the nearby bus stop he boarded a bus for Dadar and then walked up to the Asiad bus station. He purchased a ticket for the first bus that was leaving for Pune.

The day after his fateful trip to Mumbai, Gopal received a long distance call from his daughter. She was in a jovial mood. Her stipend amount had increased. The sponsors had asked her to give the happy news to him by phone. This firmed his decision—somewhat tentative till then—to go ahead if it benefited his daughter so much.

The next month, which was even numbered, he made the trip to Mumbai on the second Sunday. This time he had good material, copies of several letters, photocopy of a project report, and small but important bits of information. The exchange briefcase contained the usual filling stuff but underneath there was a blue envelope. Gopal's curiosity was aroused but he restrained his urge till he boarded the Pune-bound Asiad bus. When the passenger sitting next to him dozed off, he took out the envelope from the brief case and carefully opened it.

To his utter surprise he found in it four five hundred rupee notes. There was, he noticed a small piece of paper too. It contained an unsigned typed message that read, '(i) Good effort. Rs.2000 enclosed as token of appreciation. If you make sincere efforts you will find the job rewarding; (ii) Please collect every possible information on the under-water weapons system that is being developed for the Navy.'

Gopal pocketed the money without much compunction. He cursed himself for not opening the envelope earlier otherwise he could have purchased some clothes for his son and wife. The demands contained in the note made him think. He realised that the task given to him was not easy. In a way, he thought, it was good that he now had a definite quest to which he could direct all his efforts. It might even bring good rewards, if the money he had just received was any cue. His determined endeavours bore fruit within a short time. In a relatively short span of three months he could send substantial information on the subject that was available in his office. His research establishment dealt with only a part of the gigantic task, a handicap that his paymasters seemed to appreciate.

Mundkur had just returned from the room of the boss, the head of the Subsidiary Intelligence Bureau, by which name the Mumbai regional office of IB was known. He had a letter in his hand that the chief had passed on to him for action. He sent for Khot and Bhadang, his two reliable assistants. When they arrived and took their seats Mundkur waved the letter at them and said, "This is a letter from the Delhi Headquarters, received by the boss this morning. It gives us a specific albeit very difficult task. It seems that the Pakistani

Naval Chief while addressing his officers on their Naval Day had disclosed that India was indigenously developing underwater weapons system for its Navy and bragged that they would get a better system even if it meant starving themselves to find the money. What has intrigued the Naval as well as our analysts at the Headquarters is, how could he describe at length the specific type of weapons we were developing, because they were at best at the drawing board stage, as they say? Their surmise is that there is possibly a leak somewhere in the DRDO that is developing the weapons system. All the regional offices to whom the job has been apportioned are suspect. For our part we have to make a discreet probe at the DRDO establishment at Pune because it is in the network."

"An outstation job after a long while," Bhadang remarked.

"Yes. I suggest that both of you Khot and Bhadang, go to Pune and meet the Director at his residence. I know, it is unusual but it's inevitable. If you go to his office it will become the talk of the whole set up. One cannot assume anything. We are touching the Director because, I have been assured that he can be trusted to be above board. But the same thing cannot be said of his PA. Therefore, we take only the Director into confidence. Please find out from him who all are working on the project, and include in your list every one from the topmost officer to the lowest assistant. The support staff like PAs, even peons should be in it. Then start the usual process of elimination to reduce the potential mischief-makers to the minimum. Once you do that, we will embark on the arduous task of systematically observing their activities and movements," Mundkur laid out the task before the duo.

Khot and Bhadang did a remarkable job after arriving at Pune. Within a space of four weeks they were able to shortlist the probable culprits to just three. One of them was Gopal. His boss was deeply involved in the project but was himself found to be beyond reproach. Gopal's record of duty showed that in the past six months he had taken station leave on Sunday at least once in a month, which was not the case earlier. They decided to make him their target number one and place him under surveillance.

Gopal's activities in Pune were routine and gave no ground for suspicion. He did not seem to be overspending nor did he have questionable company. He appeared to be a typical God-fearing middle class family man. While Khot and Bhadang were debating one Sunday early in the morning while having tea if it was advisable to continue the watch on Gopal or if they should take up the second suspect, the leader of the watcher team rang up Khot. "Sir the subject—meaning Gopal—was seen leaving his quarters early in the morning with a briefcase in hand. We followed him. He hired an autorikshaw and went straight to the main railway station. He purchased a ticket at the Mumbai counter. It is obvious that he would now board a train most probably the Deccan Queen failing which the Pragati Express that follows soon after. He is not carrying any baggage, perhaps would return by an evening train," the leader reported. "What do we do now? We too are at the railway station."

"I see, that's interesting. Please follow him, whichever train he catches and thereafter wherever he goes in Mumbai. Report again as soon as you leave," Khot instructed. Gopal boarded the Deccan Queen and so did the watchers.

Gopal got off the train at Dadar railway station and hired a taxi that took him to the Mahalaxmi temple near Haji Ali. He took *darshan* of the deity and whiled away time standing at the barricade, casually surveying the sea and the moving throng of devotees. At twelve noon he made a move and indifferently sauntered through the narrow lanes to eventually emerge on the Warden road. He turned right and picking up speed entered the Mahalaxmi Chambers. He took the lift and came to the floor where the Crossword bookshop was situated. One of the watchers who had followed him inside the building saw him keep his briefcase at the entrance where every visitor to the shop deposits his hand baggage, and go inside. The watcher followed.

Gopal went to the Fiction section, browsed through some books and later drifted to the Stationery section where he picked up some envelopes and other items of stationery. He made payment at the counter and came out with the carry bag containing the purchased articles. At the door he picked up his briefcase but instead of putting the carry bag inside the briefcase, as one would expect him to do, he carried the two separately. As he stepped out onto the road he hailed a taxi and went straight to Matunga market. When he emerged from the taxi he had only the briefcase in his hand. He had lunch at an Udupi restaurant, then strolled along the bazaar street occasionally picking up an item here and an item there. He entered a South Indian shop and made some more purchases. He then took a taxi and went directly to the Asiad bus station at Dadar. Within half an hour he was on his way back to Pune. Getting down at Pune terminus he went straight to his quarters by an autorikshaw and did not come out again.

"Nothing seemingly suspicious but intriguing nevertheless," remarked Khot to Bhadang when the watchers gave a detailed account to him after leaving Gopal at his house.

"Why should a man go all the way to Mumbai, that too to an expensive bookshop, just to purchase a few items of stationery which are readily available in Pune?" asked Bhadang.

"Yes, that's something to give thought to. Even the Crossword shop is here if he is so fond of it," Khot added. "As for the sundry articles he purchased at the South Indian bazaar, they surely would be available here too. No, there's more to his Mumbai visit than what the watchers noted."

"That's the question that needs to be pondered over," Bhadang reiterated. Both thought that a solution could probably be found by probing the Mumbai end more closely. Quite likely the watchers had missed out something subtle that held the key to Gopal's enigmatic trip to Mumbai. There was no way but to patiently wait till Gopal travelled to Mumbai again. But in the meantime Mundkur, their chief had to be apprised.

Khot and Bhadang consulted their watches. It was about ten in the night. Mundkur would be at home but not asleep yet, they thought. "No harm ringing him up," said Bhadang. Khot nodded and was about to pick up the phone to dial Mundkur's number when the telephone bell rang. Khot answered. Mundkur himself was on the line. He asked about the outcome of the surveillance on Gopal during the day. Khot briefly narrated the sequence of Gopal's movements and activities on his Mumbai errand. He also mentioned to Mundkur the question that this seemingly innocuous journey had raised in his mind.

"Can you describe the briefcase in detail?" Mundkur asked. Khot gave the description as given to him by the watcher. While talking to Mundkur he beckoned the watcher who had followed Gopal inside the shop and supplemented his own narration with prompting from him. In the end he asked Mundkur, "Why to you want so many details Sir? Anything you find peculiar in it?"

"Look, something very sensational has happened here in Mumbai. Around one in the afternoon a young man riding a motorcycle met with a serious accident near the RTI building, on the sloping portion of Pedder road that emerges from the Kemp's corner flyover, I should say. He was apparently riding fast and rammed head on into the car in front when the driver of the car applied brakes suddenly perhaps because the traffic light turned red. But that's not very relevant to us. Such accidents do take place in Mumbai frequently. What's relevant, in fact important to us, is the briefcase he was carrying with him. He lost consciousness the moment his bare head hit the asphalt road. He was removed by the traffic police to GT Hospital. Someone picked up the briefcase that had been thrown off and was lying at a distance, and luckily he thought of handing it over to the police. The police forced open the lock of the briefcase because they wanted to know the name and address of the injured man and thought that the briefcase might give them the clue. To their amazement they found several secret papers. Even a floppy was there. You may be interested to know, those papers are from the DRDO establishment at Pune, which you are presently investigating."

"My God!" exclaimed Khot in dismay.

"Don't get worried. There is a bright silver lining to it. You are bang on course. The description of the briefcase that our friend Gopal was going about with tallies remarkably with the briefcase the motorcycle rider was carrying," Mundkur disclosed.

"But Sir, Gopal brought his briefcase back," Khot expressed his doubt.

"My hunch is that Gopal and the accident victim exchanged similar looking briefcases at the Crossword bookshop. Your watcher missed to note the swap. It is obvious to me that Gopal and his accomplice were not physically meeting at the bookshop but switching the briefcases at the place where all customers are supposed to deposit their handbags. You get it?"

"Yes, Sir. It's now clear to me, a very clever ruse indeed!" acknowledged Khot.

"So, Gopal is the man, in fact your quarry who passes the DRDO secrets about development of underwater weapons."

"Should we nab him immediately, Sir?" Khot asked.

"No, no, not yet. That will spoil the game. It will be difficult to prove a charge against him as things stand at the moment. Besides, we have not yet found out to whom precisely he was passing those secret papers. Let him start collecting secret material again for his next delivery. You should nab him when he is making unaccounted for extra copies or better still, when he is smuggling them out. And this should be done before his masters warn him, which would be in a day or two. In the meantime we have ensured that the press does not get wind of what the briefcase contained. I only hope to God that that fellow regains consciousness and we are able to interrogate him at length about his masters. He is obviously only a courier. The police are also trying to trace the owner of the motorcycle but there is no guarantee that their quest would be very successful."

"We haunt Gopal from tomorrow itself, Sir. Now that we know that he is the culprit it should not be difficult to catch him red-handed."

"Yes, do that. And search his house the moment you catch him. You may find the duplicate briefcase there. That's important," advised Mundkur.

"Unluckily he became unconscious the moment he hit the road, otherwise I am sure, he would have bluffed his way out. He is a smart lad, though a bit rash. I know him well. The police would have treated it as an accident, at worst a case of rash driving. We would have seen to it." This was Shaikh Nawaz, Assistant Manager of PIA and under cover station in-charge at Mumbai, talking to Colonel Shamsuddin Siddiqui, the Operations Desk officer in ISI headquarters at Islamabad, on a long distance call.

"Hmm, a tricky situation indeed," observed Col. Siddiqui stoically, which unsettled Shaikh Nawaz.

"The briefcase is in police hands. I am sure they have opened it by now, if only to establish the identity of the goofy. And what do they find? Top secret papers! When that son of a bitch gains consciousness they are sure to make him spill the beans. That would be the end of me. I would be finished, kaput! No, I must leave this country at once, Colonel. You owe it to me, Colonel" Nawaz pleaded fervently.

"Don't panic so much, Nawaz. We will attend to that. If we find that there is no way out we will ask you to fly out. Till then simply wait and watch. We are asking Shakeel to do the needful," assured the Colonel and hung up.

It was visiting time at the hospital. Friends and relatives of patients were coming in hordes, some making straight for the room where their patient was lying; others were rushing from room to room looking for the right person. Suddenly there was the deafening sound of rapid gunfire from the general ward. Every one ran helter-skelter, women shrieked, children howled, men shouted. Every one was in deadly hurry to clear out. Five minutes later everything was quiet. There was stunned silence all round. No one knew for certain what had happened, who had fired, who died.

The motorcyclist lay dead. Blood was oozing profusely from the several gunshot wounds he had received on his chest and abdomen. The constable in uniform who was standing guard on him lay nearby sprawled in a pool of blood on the floor, gasping for breath. He too had several gaping wounds that were spurting blood. In the melee, no one had the sense to take note of the two men in jackets who hurried out from the general ward and mingled in the scurrying crowd.

Around the same time Khot and Bhadang nabbed Gopal while he was leaving office. They found copies of a number of classified documents neatly concealed in his lunch box. A search in his house revealed the briefcase that had so puzzled Khot.